GIRLS JUST WANT TO HAVE SUN

JO LYONS

B

Boldwood

First published in 2022 as *Benidorm, actually*. This edition published in Great Britain in 2025 by Boldwood Books Ltd.

Copyright © Jo Lyons, 2022

Cover Design by Alexandra Allden

Cover Images: Shutterstock

A CIP catalogue record for this book is available from the British Library.

Paperback ISBN 978-1-80557-213-8

Large Print ISBN 978-1-80557-214-5

Hardback ISBN 978-1-80557-212-1

Ebook ISBN 978-1-80557-215-2

Kindle ISBN 978-1-80557-216-9

Audio CD ISBN 978-1-80557-207-7

MP3 CD ISBN 978-1-80557-208-4

Digital audio download ISBN 978-1-80557-209-1

This book is printed on certified sustainable paper. Boldwood Books is dedicated to putting sustainability at the heart of our business. For more information please visit https://www.boldwoodbooks.com/about-us/sustainability/

Boldwood Books Ltd, 23 Bowerdean Street, London, SW6 3TN

www.boldwoodbooks.com

To Mam and Dad
(If only we'd had more time)

1

Less than two years after my mother's death, my father has taken to wearing a shirt and tie with his jeans, dyeing his grey hair the colour of hummus and, rather awkwardly, 'dipping his toe', as he calls it, into a lady called Madge. They met at the local hiking club where they bonded over a shared love of walking across lumpy fields with a biting wind scraping across their faces like sandpaper. And even though they have only been going out for five minutes, with my poor mother still warm in her grave, Madge has invited him to spend a few days exploring what the Lake District has to offer by way of a romantic minibreak.

He has stopped by my house to inform me of this latest development in their relationship. 'Connie, loneliness and grief can eat away at your mind,' my father says hesitantly as he flicks a shy look over to Madge waiting for him in the car. 'Madge thinks we both need to move on, love. Meet new people. Try new things.'

It would certainly explain the goatee. She'll have him manscaping next and growing a hipster topknot, but seeing his face all lit up with nervous excitement makes me feel he might have a point. My last boyfriend ran screaming for the hills as soon as my mother became sick, and the nearest I've come to having a romantic relationship since is watching the *Bridgerton* buttocks scene on a continuous loop.

'I'm fine, Dad,' I say. 'I have my career to focus on. I don't need to "try new things".'

He leans in to hug me. He must be nervous because he has pickled himself in Eau Sauvage.

'Go and have a lovely time,' I say, trying not to be tearful at seeing him open the car door ready to drive off with a companion who isn't my mother.

I stand in the doorway staring sadly after them until my phone bursts to life.

'Just in time,' I say to Nancy, my agent at We've Got Talent. I'm desperate for extra singing work now that my temporary day job as a data input cleaner – could anything sound more glamorous? – recently came to an abrupt and unexpected end. Nancy has been my agent for the last six years. I'm not sure where to start. With my disappointing part-time singing career? With my father hurtling his way to the Lakes to do the deed with his new girlfriend? With my two newly engaged BFFs about to tie the knot and set up home together? Or with my poor mother dead and buried instead of living her life with me at her side?

'I'll just stop you there, Connie, pet,' she says in her husky, twenty-cigs-a-day voice. 'It's about the gig for tonight. Wait...'

While she pauses to take a few puffs of her ciggie, I take the opportunity to blink away the tears. I've just remembered something very important. Nancy is not a huge fan of her artists sobbing down the phone about things that go wrong in their personal lives. As if to prove the point, she lets out an exasperated sigh.

'I hope you're not crying? Jesus, it's not even wine o'clock.' Nancy tuts loudly. 'Well, it is if you're me.'

She cackles. It's never too early for a pint of wine in her world.

'No,' I croak, taking a deep, calming breath. 'No, I'm fine.'

'Connie, love, you better not make a mess of this gig tonight. You know Sheila is a personal friend of mine. It's her wedding anniversary and I have promised her a magical, uplifting, happy evening... not some depressing Billie Eilish-fest,' she says. 'Speaking of which, please do not wear those cheerless black robes of yours. It's a party, not a witches' coven. You're the singer so I expect you to bring some sparkle. Can you do that?' Nancy carries on before I can try to deny that I have indeed been using my repertoire of tear-inducing songs to encourage audiences to share in my ongoing grief. 'You sound upset to me. If you're not up to it, just say. We can't have a repeat of—'

'I won't let you down! I'll be fine. I promise.'

* * *

The following morning, I'm practising my singing scales in the kitchen with a wooden spoon and trying to forget the whole strenuous evening before when my phone pings with a notification that I'm tagged in a photo. I make the mistake of looking at the latest We've Got Talent social media post. As I scroll through hideous photos of myself on stage, my two live-in flatmates-cum-therapists, Liam and Ged, are absolutely no help whatsoever. They have heard me whining and have come to my immediate aid, because as well as being very caring friends, they are also experienced musicians. After we all graduated with our music degrees, Liam began working as a music teacher while Ged became a music producer, which makes them an excellent sounding board because they are very talented but also incredibly nosy.

They're newly returned from their dreamy getaway to a spa hotel in Northumberland that had a rose petal and jasmine-scented hot tub with disco lights and a built-in glitter cannon. They have been full of tales of Ged's elaborate wedding proposal involving strawberries dipped in chocolate, couples' vision boarding, and bubbles squirted in places they probably shouldn't be. It is bad enough trying to be happy for my dad without my two best friends gearing up to leave me behind too. I am twenty-seven years old, my commitment to fast fashion and bottomless brunches is almost impossible to underestimate and I spend my weekends singing covers in old men's social clubs. I am very clearly not living my best life.

Ged looks at one of the photos I'm tagged in and gasps. 'When did you get punched in the face?' He flicks his finger back and forth across the screen. 'Sorry, false alarm. Stage lights can be so unforgiving.'

'You look divine, darling,' says Liam hurriedly. 'Very...'

I watch him struggling to find the right word as he points to the photo of me with one eye half shut, mouth wide open and a chin that has disappeared into my neck.

'...invested. Yes, that's it. Invested.'

'Were you singing Adele again?' asks Ged.

I nod.

It has been viewed thousands of times and received 420 likes. *Huge, huge embarrassment.* I could do without these off-putting images of me floating around on the internet. I'll never get hired again at this rate.

'I'll ring Nancy,' I say, jabbing at my phone, 'and ask her to take the photos down.'

'Oh, Connie, it's you,' says Nancy, sounding disappointed.

'Hi, Nancy. Just a quick call to see if you can take those awful photos of me down, please. Especially the ones where I have a face like a melted welly. And, on a more positive note, I'm available for work next weekend. I did my new set at the party last night,' I say, choosing my words carefully. Nancy is very astute. I will stick to the facts. 'Sheila said she'd never seen or heard anything like it.'

A silence hangs in the air as I hear Nancy taking a long drag on her cigarette.

Pah, pah, pah.

'You did the dreary songs again, didn't you?' She exhales loudly into the phone.

Christ.

'Yes, but they loved them. Even the men were bawling their eyes out at my "Pie Jesu".' I can hear myself flapping. 'That's what good singers do. They move people. It's an art form.' I'm on rocky ground here. Very rocky.

'Yes, love. You were being paid to move people,' Nancy says stiffly, 'to move them onto the dance floor, not have half the guests wailing into their drinks. Sheila's refusing to pay up, and you've put me in a very difficult position, Connie.'

My mind flicks back to Sheila yelling at the DJ to hurry me off the stage and him blasting out dance tracks before I'd even finished the final notes of 'All Out of Love'.

'I'm sorry, sweetheart, but I'll have to let you go.' Nancy's gravelly voice sounds flat.

I take a beat to understand what she's saying. She's known me for years. I sang my way through university for her. She found singers to cover for me when my mother was ill, and in turn I dropped everything to cover for her whenever she needed me to.

'You just haven't got what it takes any more, pet. Recently I've had nothing but complaints that you look and sound like a wounded animal. But good luck with your Royal Northern Sinfonia audition. Is it today? You'd be a perfect fit for that sort of hoity-toity singing. Lord knows you've tried hard enough to get in.'

And while I'm sure she has a point to a certain degree – I may have lost my passion for singing and getting crowds going – singing the *lead* in an orchestra choir and following in my mother's classical singing footsteps is the only link to her that I have. I will never stop trying.

* * *

'Connie, your phone's ringing!' yells Ged that evening. He and Liam have retired to the safe confines of the kitchen while I howl the place down in the living room. My audition for the Royal Northern Sinfonia could only have been worse if I'd shat myself on stage and thrown it at them.

It's Nancy.

'Good Lord, you're not crying again, are you? Honestly, I'm amazed you're not in some permanent state of chronic dehydration. It's very ageing, you know.'

'No. Hi. No. I'm not crying. I'm just—'

'Well, whatever, listen to me carefully. I've had a cancellation. Total nightmare. Our most popular tribute act, Ted Sheeran, has broken his chin on one of those electric scooters and you're the only singer I know who is available and desperate. I'm going to give you one last chance to redeem yourself.'

I am desperate. Everyone in my life is moving on except me. I wipe the tears from my cheeks.

'I'll do it,' I shriek. 'Whatever it is, I'll do it.'

'Okay. Ring Jezebel Music. Ask to speak to the boss. Say I gave you her deets and you're the replacement talent.'

Nancy texts me the details and I ring the number. A woman picks up.

'Hello? Is that Jezebel Music? Nancy asked me to call. I'm the replacement for Ted Sheeran.'

'What sort of act are you?'

This simple and very reasonable question throws me. I should know what sort of act I am.

Not very good.

'Well, erm, I guess you could describe me as taking my audience on a deep dive into the very essence of—'

'Can you sing?' she asks abruptly.

'Yes, I can definitely sing. I'm classically trained in all forms of—'

'We need someone to entertain a lively crowd. Can you do that?'

'I'm from Newcastle,' I say by way of explanation. 'All crowds are lively.'

Well, that's how they start off, anyway.

'We need someone with great stage presence. Someone who can get the crowd singing along.'

Ah. Nancy's words echo in my mind. *Wounded animal. Reducing grown men to tears.*

'Erm, I'd definitely say I'm more of a musical experience.'

'Oh?'

Please refrain from talking.

'I mean, I take my audience on a journey. Of enlightenment.'

Jesus Christ.

'We just need a singer to do covers. Is that you or not?' She's beginning to sound annoyed. I confirm that singing is what I do best, and she proceeds to give me all the necessary information before hanging up.

* * *

A short while later, Ged and Liam wander through, dressed in their outlandishly skimpy jogging gear, to see why I've suddenly gone so quiet. I can't move. My mouth is gaping open.

'I'm going to Spain. To perform in clubs. I'll be on stage in Benidorm for a whole week,' I say dazedly, barely able to take it in.

'Benidorm as in the party capital of the Costa Blanca?' asks Ged.

'Benidorm as in where all the drunks go to holiday hard?' supplies Liam.

My voice is barely a whisper. 'I have to meet my support band at Newcastle Airport to fly over to Alicante together. I'm replacing Ted Sheeran.' I crumple to the floor while the boys leap about excitedly. There's a huge knot of anxiety twisting around in my stomach. 'Oh God. Talk about a fish out of water.' I bury my face in my hands. *I'm a moronic fool. An imposter. An impulsive charlatan.* 'The flight leaves first thing tomorrow morning. What have I done?'

You've oversold yourself. That's what you've done.

Moments later, we're flicking through images of my new support band on Ged's phone. 'I love them,' Ged says. 'I mean, "The Dollz", can you believe it? Love the name, love the outfits, love the tribute vibe. It's so Benidorm.'

'Look at them singing and doing upside-down splits at the

same time. They have a lot of complex choreography going on,' Liam says, browsing through the video clips of the lead singer exuberantly twerking her huge thigh gap an inch from an audience member's nose. 'Christ, they're amazing. Absolutely stunning.'

'How do I follow that?' I wail, panicking. I could never imagine an occasion where I'd need to wave my thigh gap in anyone's face. 'I'll be booed off stage if that's what they're expecting. I mean, I'm classically trained, for fuck's sake.' I hear an ugly hint of indignation creeping into my voice. 'I take my audience on a musical voyage. I give them a feeling of deep connection, human depth, tortured souls. I prefer my audience to leave having learnt something. Surely that's got to count for more than flashing my knickers and singing cheap covers at them?'

'They have Instagram down to a fine art,' says Ged admiringly, ignoring me and my incredible moment of musical integrity. 'It takes real skill to seem like you either have something terribly important on your mind or like you're greatly surprised to find, once again, you've woken in full make-up wearing only a thong and some oversized earrings. Real skill.'

This is so not helping.

'The lead singer looks like she's just walked naked through a silvery mist,' says Liam.

Neither is that.

'I hope they don't expect me to wear costumes like that.'

Liam peers at me over the top of the phone. 'We keep telling you to dress up and make an effort on stage, but will you listen? No, you won't. You have award-winning legs, Connie. You can't turn up in Benidorm dressed for an archaeological dig.'

'I'm a pitch-perfect classical singer. I don't belong somewhere like that,' I say, trying to keep the terror from my voice.

'Singing cheesy covers to a sea of bald heads. It's like scraping the professional barrel. Maybe I should ring Nancy back and explain I made a mistake?'

'What other options do you have? I don't hear the London Philharmonic knocking and you have no money coming in,' says Ged bluntly. 'Connie, you need a bit of a reality check. Life doesn't always turn out the way you expect.'

'I know that,' I say tightly. 'I know that more than anyone.'

Ged puts a comforting arm around me. 'Sorry, hun. I just mean that perhaps it's time to let go of this perfect life you had planned and embrace the one that might be waiting for you instead.'

'There is nothing waiting for me in Benidorm. Have you seen the state of the place? Besides, I only know one Ed Sheeran song.' I let out a worried groan. 'Everyone will hate me, won't they?'

Ged and Liam exchange sympathetic noises before completely backtracking. 'No, of course they won't hate you. All you need to do is style it out. Just tweak a few things.'

I blink at them and feel relief flooding through me as Ged pushes a glass of wine into my hand. No matter how difficult I can be, they always have my back.

'Just change the way you dress, the way you sing, the way you dance... Oh, and smile at the audience more,' Liam says. 'Your nerves can come across as a bit stand-offish at times.'

Shitting hell.

I can feel a panic attack coming on. This is so far out of my comfort zone. Nancy may as well have asked me to charter a private jet and fly it to Taiwan blindfolded with one arm tied behind my back while singing 'I Will Survive' in Welsh.

'It's no good. I can't do it.' We all take a beat to stare at each other while I flounder for words, my mind awash with dread at the thought of going. 'I can't be that type of bubbly, joyful person they need me to be.'

And just like that, their faces collapse.

'We know how difficult things have been since you lost your mum,' Liam says, stepping in close. I hear the break in his voice as he continues softly. 'But, honey, sometimes it feels like we lost you too.'

'You've become this numb husk muddling through life. Moping from day to day,' says Ged, suddenly sounding like David Attenborough describing an endangered species, 'without a shred of desire to make new friends or to fall in love.' He pauses to sigh elaborately. 'We just want to see you happy, Connie. Living your best life. Having the odd shag from time to time. You know, dust off some cobwebs once in a while instead of watching the *Bridgerton* buttocks scene every night.'

'He's right, babes.'

FFS. I'll just add that to my growing pile of emotional and professional wounds, shall I? I mean, no one likes to hear the actual truth about themselves, and this is very close to the bone.

'I'm pretty sure I'm not the only one of us watching horny aristocrats having sex in manicured gardens and on ornate staircases.' I throw an accusing stare in Liam's direction.

Liam shakes his head at me.

He's right, I'm being petty.

'And,' Ged tells me firmly, 'just because Benidorm has been voted the cheapest place in Europe for watered-down beer, blow jobs and designer knock-offs, and just because you've seen The Dollz on TikTok, dry-humping each other while wearing less than you'd wear to the beach, does not mean you should fall to pieces.'

'You're right. I'm sure I'll be fine.' *I must remain positive.*

'Hopefully, the crowds will be small, the standards really low, and they'll be too drunk to notice what I'm singing or what I'm wearing.'

Ged looks up from swiping with wide eyes.

'Your stage costumes won't be the biggest problem anyway,' he announces. 'It says here Ted Sheeran has over eight hundred thousand followers. He sells out every night of the week in Benidorm. It says he's... the best tribute act since Adam Lambert joined Queen.'

Fuuuuuuuuuuuuck!

2

'You'll be fine,' Liam says as we screech to a halt at Newcastle Airport drop-off at four thirty the next morning. He shoves me towards the terminal with my carry-on case as though he's terrified I might change my mind. I may have kept them both awake with my loud and frequent panicking. The Dollz are standing at the entrance looking as though they've come straight from a burlesque nightclub in Paris. Liam flicks a worried glance at my Converse, my boring denim shorts and T-shirt, my long hair hanging in no particular style and my make-up-free face.

'Don't worry. A nice smile can go a long way,' he says, patting me on the arm. 'Just remember to give the audience what *they* want, not what *you* want them to want, and try to put on a bit of a show.'

'I'll try my best.' I hug him tightly. 'I wish you were coming with me.'

His eyes fill as he peels me off him. 'Just go and have a great time. That's all we want for you.' I watch him race off before our emotions get the better of us, tyres squealing. All I can do is hope for the best as I walk hesitantly towards my new support band. My heart is thumping triple time.

'Hi, I'm Connie,' I say cheerily to hide my nerves. All five Dollz swivel round. 'Connie Cooper. I'm the new Jezebel Music headline act for next week.'

I am met with blank stares until a woman with fabulous over-here-look-at-me, pillar-box-red hair gasps.

'Headline? *You're* the new headline act? You mean you're going to replace Ted Sheeran? On The Strip?'

I nod. They all stare back, aghast.

'Poor you. No one's as good as him.'

'Not even the real Ed Sheeran.'

'Christ, his regulars will be so disappointed, won't they, Tash?'

Tash, the Dollz' lead singer, nods gravely. 'Yes, they'll be fucking furious. And they'll hate it if you don't do *all* of his hits.'

Shitting hell.

* * *

While we make our way up the escalator to departures, the girls bicker over whose idea it was to save money by only bringing carry-on luggage. Apparently, it was Cherry's idea, so she is keen to divert attention.

She flicks her bright red hair over her shoulder and links her arm through mine. 'Connie, so this your first time away on tour, yeah? Who do you do?' she says, trying to place who I look like for my tribute act.

I sweep my eyes around the group. 'It's hard to describe. I kind of take the audience on an emotional journey. I start off a cappella, all melancholic and ethereal, and then segue into more dramatic, contemporary ballads, you know?'

I hesitate at the lack of reaction. I should refrain from talking, but nerves have got the better of me.

'I thought I'd mix a few classical numbers with Latino seeing as we're in Spain. I could do *Phantom* in French and "Nessun Dorma" in Italian, bel canto obviously.' I emit a nervous, nasally yipping sound, quite the opposite of endearing. 'Oh, and I did once sing a Gregorian plainchant in the original Greek, but I'm not sure how that would go down in Benidorm.'

For the love of God, abort. Abort.

They frown at one another, confused.

'Yeah, they'll hate all of that,' Tash says quickly, rolling her eyes at the girls. 'Just stick to pop tunes or maybe songs from *The Greatest Showman* if you must show off, but don't cover anything that we're doing.'

'Okay,' I say, dread swirling up from my stomach. 'At least I don't know any Pussycat Dolls hits, so there'll be no chance of that.'

'Neither do we,' says Tash, flicking her mane of jet-black hair extensions over her shoulder. 'We channel their vibe, but we do Beyoncé, Taytay, RiRi and a bit of Little Mix. Which is why they love us over there.'

Tash and her band are quick to reveal they have wiped everything I've just said about my stuck-up, horrific-sounding singing completely from their minds and proceed to tell me how Benidorm has got everything you can possibly need for a girls' trip abroad.

'Don't worry. There's plenty of English-speaking natives, so you don't even have to speak Spanish at all. Not. One. Word!' Tash reassures me.

'I have an A level in Spanish, actually,' I say, keen to make amends. 'So that might come in handy.'

They do not look the slightest bit impressed and carry on as though I'd not even mentioned it.

'Don't worry about having to eat any Spanish food either,' says one of them, wrinkling her nose at me. 'You can get all sorts of English food over there. You know, like pizza, kebabs, McDonald's.'

'Big Mand is right. And absolutely everything's dripping in garlic sauce,' Cherry tells me enthusiastically.

Simply delightful. Cannot wait. Wonder why this was not given top billing on Tripadvisor.

'And it's swarming with English men,' Tash explains gleefully. 'Absolutely heaving. All totally, *totally* pissed.'

Lovely. Also wonder why Expedia not leading with this.

'I like my men how I like my fruit,' a girl called Liberty boasts, twirling a long strand of hair.

Ripe?

My eyes balloon as the Dollz automatically chorus, 'FIVE A DAY!'

I blink, unsure of how seriously to take this startling revelation. As we make our way through the airport, they also tell me that it is simply impossible to get any of these things, decent men and suchlike, in England, and it is much better to go abroad for them. It is especially easy to ensnare the good-looking ones at festivals, I'm told.

'They're all on so many drugs, and they have no idea what they're doing! They can barely speak! Last year I handcuffed a guy to myself for two days,' says Liberty, giggling. A prickle of alarm creeps through me as I imagine getting arrested for something *they've* done.

I've got a whole week of this.

Seven days.

Seven days of witnessing men being kidnapped and falsely imprisoned. I told Ged that forcing me out of my comfort zone before I'm good and ready would be a mistake, but would he listen?

No, he would not.

As we stand in the queue to go through security, I'm told all five of the girls' names, what they do for a living when not on tour singing or breaking several laws and what their views are on pubic hair. It's all very mixed.

'Nancy must think very highly of you if she's put you as our headline act,' Big Sue, the tallest woman I've ever seen, says. 'You must have a similar style to us. Raunchy, is it?'

'No,' I say. 'Unfortunately not, no. I'm not the, erm, sexy type.'

'Don't worry, hun. We'll soon have you looking and acting like one of us,' Tash says confidently, eyeing me up and down. 'If you want to fit in over there in Benidorm just copy everything we do.'

'Yes. Being sexy is all about spontaneity,' Cherry says, flinging her leg over Liberty's shoulder and dipping into a backwards crab shape as though to demonstrate.

'And the way you look,' adds Liberty, pouting at me.

'And being completely in sync with one another,' adds Big Mand, posing alongside them.

I scan the group and quickly run through a mental list: Tash is the lead singer and is very single at the moment, Cherry with the flaming-red hair is in charge of choreography and is very scary, Liberty with the inflatable lips is the very image of a Kardashian and is inexplicably drawn to married men, Big Sue is a sensible giantess, and Mandeep, or Big Mand as she has introduced herself, seems to adore Big Sue because she keeps looking up at her with obvious cow eyes. I'm just thinking what a cute couple they make when Cherry suddenly roars, 'SLUT DROP!'

Oh Christ.

The Dollz draw the eye of everyone in the near vicinity, especially the already irritated security control officers whose heads whip around to witness the Beyoncé-style move with distaste. The armed police guards instinctively reach for their guns. Tash, looking thrilled, flicks her hair in their direction and switches her lashes to bat on their most powerful setting. As an outraged security control officer marches towards us in the queue, I am equally unnerved to feel several pairs of hands pushing me forward with whispers of, 'Go on, Connie, you're the headline act. You deal with them.'

I'm appalled, but I suppose technically, according to Nancy, I am in charge. The officer rapidly asks me several questions to which he greets each answer with a disdainful tut. I tell him yes, I appear to be suddenly in charge of the group, while thinking to myself I am certainly *not* in charge of the group for any longer than the length of this conversation, and *no*, of course we should not be dancing like prats while we go through the baggage check area, and *yes*, their outfits are little more than denim G-strings and bra tops and finally, that *yes*, I will absolutely do my best to persuade them to cover up around families with children.

Next, under the watchful glare of several officers, we are instructed to get our toiletries out of our cases. This proves to be very unpopular and causes a ripple of lady-panic.

'Should super-quick spray tan foam be classed as a liquid though? Because it definitely isn't,' Tash says sharply with some authority.

'Liquid!' snaps the officer, snatching the can from her and

throwing it in the bin. There's an almighty gasp from the girls as though he's just thrown away a newborn kitten.

'Is hairspray allowed?' Tash asks.

The officer points to a massive sign that says: *No aerosols. No liquids. No gels over 100ml.*

'Is hair mousse allowed, though?'

The officer sighs, pointing to the *100ml* bit of the sign.

'Is conditioner a liquid, cos it's more of a cream really, isn't it? And body mist? It's mostly air. Jesus Christ. Air's not even on the friggin' list!' Tash screeches at him.

She gawps at the rest of us for backup before returning to face the accusing officer, who delights in explaining the basic chemistry behind an aerosol. The atmosphere is super tense and thick with outrage, as though the security officers have taken everything off the Dollz out of pure spite. Cherry finds herself once again in the firing line for wanting to save money with carry-on luggage and forgetting to warn the girls about the dire consequences.

'Connie, follow me. Let's get those pasty legs sorted,' she says, grabbing my hand. We all scuttle through to the duty-free where a well-groomed sales assistant makes a timid enquiry to the group to ask if they need any help, only to be met with an unfriendly glare as they swiftly crowd her out.

In less than five minutes, everyone is encrusted in fake tan that costs more than our accommodation and travel put together. ('Excuse me, ladies, those brand-new St. Tropez bottles you're opening and spraying all over your legs are not testers. They're thirty-nine pounds each! They're not faulty, just empty because you've used it all!')

For the sake of bonding purposes, my legs now have a strange yellow glow, my palms are a solid brown colour, and I have allowed Tash to draw some ludicrous eyebrows on me which extend a fraction above the natural eyebrow line.

'They need to stand out on stage,' she is explaining as I take in her own terrifying jet-black eyebrows. 'You really should have them tattooed on for a much stronger look. Like mine.'

I peer anxiously at my reflection in the mirror. I will now arrive in Spain looking very surprised. As if I had expected to arrive in Finland or Japan or somewhere.

In the middle of the aisle, Cherry bellows, 'SHOPPING CART!' which rocks me to my core. Everyone stops to stare, taking photos of the girls putting imaginary toiletries into their imaginary shopping carts while gyrating their hips. We all inhale sharply as Tash, in a pair of vertiginous strappy sandals with heels like chopsticks, falls noisily to the ground, taking thousands of pounds' worth of beauty products with her. Her shoes might look spectacular but, to be fair, it was only going to be a matter of time before someone twisted an ankle. There's much slipping and sliding as bottles and creams are strewn everywhere, with Tash screaming at the top of her lungs about being in 'complete aggs'. 'Get help!' she yells forcefully in my direction. 'But make sure it's from a man. A big, strong one. With a neat beard.'

Seven days!

* * *

Even though it is now only 5.30 a.m., we're at the departure lounge bar as Tash, in her newly acquired wheelchair and bandaged ankle, is greeted like a returning war hero. She immediately downs a bottle of fizz, saying she'll be up and twerking in no time.

'Remember, girls, chicks before dicks! Sisters before misters! Hoes before bros!'

A glass is quickly thrust into my hand for the toast. I stare at the bubbling liquid dubiously, already exhausted from the effort of keeping up with them. Tash spins her wheelchair round with an alarmed expression.

'Connie! Why aren't you drinking? You're not...' She squints up at me and then down to my drink. 'You're not one of *them*, are you?'

One of them?

'You know, someone who refuses to enjoy alcohol?'

I take a beat to consider how badly I want to fit in with these girls and, against my better judgement, drain the glass good and proper. There is a collective sigh of relief, and the glass is immediately topped up. And to prove a point, though I absolutely should not be trying to prove anything this early in the morning, I order three more bottles from the bar, just as we hear our flight being called.

'Just ignore it,' says Liberty, gleefully taking the bottles from me. 'They always do that.'

'Yeah,' says Cherry. 'Last call never means last call.'

Nancy will be furious if I miss this flight. She'll never trust me again, and my singing career will definitely be over.

'We've got loads of time,' agrees Big Mand. 'Enough to do you a proper nose, lip and cheek contour, babes. Come here.'

'How can you even leave the house without your face on?' enquires Big Sue.

They dig into their bags and pull out what look like finger paints and fat crayons and crowd round me. I am beginning to regret making a vague, Prosecco-based promise earlier to become an honorary Doll for bonding purposes. Minutes later and they have pulled, rubbed, blended and smudged me into looking 'like a woman who cares'.

'Perfect. Now you look just like one of us,' Tash says, topping up my drink.

BING BONG.

'Attention, please, boarding for flight 4079 to Alicante is now closed.'

Shite!

3

The upside to being part of a group of drunk women wearing obscene, butt-cheek-revealing thongs, dancing inappropriately in the terminal and having a wheelchair user with us, is that the ground crew become immediately intimidated at screams to reopen the frigging gate and see fit to prioritise our very late boarding of the plane as they whisk us straight through the empty departure lounge. As we clamber on board, we collect resentful stares from the other passengers. The stern-looking pilot comes out of the cockpit to inform us that because we'd failed to hear that we were last-called many, many times, we have now missed the take-off slot and could we hurry up.

'That would be her fault. She got the round in late,' Tash explains, pointing to me while undressing him with her heavily made-up smoky eyes.

Unbelievable. What happened to 'hoes before bros'?

Before I can react, the girls get busy wiping the smiles off the cabin crew's faces by taking an age to bash passengers left and right as they all struggle with their too-heavy luggage, their too-high sandals and their too-tipsy-to-care attitudes. Next, the girls have a period of swapping seats as they need to sit next to their drinking partners. Stuck in the aisle behind them, I glance at my seat number and realise I will be sitting on my own.

Nobody asked but it's fine. It's fine.

'Mind, I'm glad to see that we're sitting according to breast size. I'm a 28F,' Tash boasts, laughing hysterically before telling all the passengers around her that she's very recently become more of a double G.

'And Big Sue is only a 30A!' shrieks Liberty. 'Big Mand! Over here, yer daft cow.'

Oh yes, I forgot, Liberty also has the yeast infection, a PhD and a tendency to overshare.

Big Mand has to retrace her steps.

'I'll swap with Liberty!' yells Cherry. 'Because me and Tash are reading *Heat* magazine.'

Cherry, she has two children and the vagina in tatters, that's right. It looks like a butchered chicken. Her doctor had never seen a mess quite like it.

'So where am I now then?' Big Mand asks, confused.

'Back down to where you were, next to Liberty.'

Big Mand twists herself back round, clipping someone's head with her case as she goes. 'Big Sue!' she yells, ignoring the yelp of pain and subsequent complaints from the passenger. 'Can you lift this up for us? Ta, love.'

Big Mand. Midwife. Caring disposition and excellent bedside manner.

Big Sue is six feet of muscular Amazonian-like woman. She strides up the aisle to swing the case easily up into the overhead bin, giving the nearby passengers a glimpse of her all-encompassing back tattoo.

Cherry suddenly roars, 'BUGALOO!' which frightens half the passengers to death. The Dollz immediately stop what they're doing to shake their arms out wide and shimmy, a bit like Turkish dancing, while they belt out an a cappella version of the famous Cyndi Lauper hit, changing the words to 'Girls just wanna have suu-uuun'. Cherry cranes her neck to make sure I'm joining in.

I am absolutely not going to join in. No way. I will not be making a spectacle of myself. The plane is full, and the cabin crew are already making stern eye contact with me. I scurry up the aisle to my seat until I'm shaken to the core by Cherry bellowing down the plane, 'Connie! Do the friggin' dance!'

I spin around, immediately copying their moves as though I simply had no choice. I'm sure she doesn't mean to sound so menacing. She stands with her hands on her sharp hips, watching my panicked attempt to dance before there's a huge, exasperated sigh from the captain over the tannoy for us to stop messing about and to sit down so that he can give the weary crew the instruction to close the doors and get ready for take-off.

Luckily, I'm right by my row so I leap into my seat in the middle, climbing easily over the old lady in the aisle seat thanks to my long, yellow-streaked legs, my many years of jogging and my recent consumption of alcohol. I notice the man in the window seat is shaking his head at me and realise instantly that he is incredibly good-looking with his Mediterranean features and overgrown, dark glossy hair. This is embarrassing enough without being judged by someone of such superior genetics. His eyes pop at the full force of my heavily made-up face and freakishly surprised eyebrows before he turns quickly towards the window.

The girls are asked several times to be quiet during the safety instruction demo. The cabin crew team leader eventually announces over the tannoy that while, yes, she agrees that the make-or-break relationships of celebrities and their many baby daddies are terribly important, and yes indeed, they should not be giving their poor children such ridiculous names as Bear and Nest, could we please save our empty speculation until after the demo, and also keep that discussion between ourselves if we wouldn't mind, and not assume that the entire plane-full of passengers holds celebrities in the same regard, thank you kindly.

I quickly buckle myself in, but as the plane lurches forward, building up speed, I grab the armrest for support, only to find the man in the window seat got there first. We both glance down at my hand clamped round his forearm, then when I take my bronzed palm away, we gawp at the perfect fake-tan hand-print I leave on his pristine long-sleeved white T-shirt. I'm immediately even more embarrassed because that 'Ultra Dark Tan' stain is the sort to never, ever come out. I'd be so annoyed if I were him.

'Typical,' he says, rolling his eyes at me before I can apologise.

He's understandably patronising as well as judgemental.

Trust me to sit next to a total smokeshow while I look like such a clown with all this make-up on and Prosecco swilling inside me. I give him a sympathetic shrug.

'Why do you look so surprised?' he shouts above the rever-beration of the engine as we hurtle off the safe, solid ground into thin, flimsy air.

Why do you look so handsome and well-groomed? I inwardly panic. I seem to have lost the ability to use words to express myself.

'I'm not surprised,' I eventually yell back. 'It's my eyebrows.'

'Your what?' he bellows over the deafening rattle of the wings and engine combined.

'My eyebrows! They're supposed to be strong, not surprised!' I holler, just as the pilot takes the opportunity to switch off the ear-splitting roar.

My words hang in the air as I smile at him awkwardly. Maybe it's the Prosecco, but he's the first attractive man I've noticed in years. I surreptitiously glance down to see his fingers are ring-free as he drums them impatiently against the armrest before swiping up his bottle of designer water from the tray table. He's got incredibly attractive hands. Perhaps Ged and Liam were right about me deliberately not giving anyone a chance. Maybe some light chit-chat about stain removers might ease me back into being sociable. Who knows, he might see past the hideous make-up and be interested in my opinions on the big questions of the day. While I build up the courage to talk to him, the seat-belt sign is switched off, and like lightning, the Dollz scramble to the toilets. Two go marching to the back and the other three to the front in perfect formation when Cherry suddenly shouts, 'HAIR WHIP!' and points immediately to me.

Sweet baby Jesus.

I leap up obediently and hurl my head around in all directions until, what seems like an age later, Cherry finally breaks eye contact with me. I thump back into my seat as though recovering from an exhausting spin class or a five-mile reverse run. This is all very tense.

Mr Window Seat is agog. He is also covered in water. It is dripping down his face, and his top is soaked. My eye is drawn to his magazine on the tray table. That, too, is drenched. I notice his iPhone on the table is also dripping wet. He sits there, unable to speak, as water droplets hang off his chin and drip onto his already saturated lap. My eyes travel slowly down to his crotch. It looks like he's wet himself. He glares angrily at me before the penny drops.

'Oh, my goodness,' I say, full of apology. 'Did I by any chance have anything to do with you throwing water over yourself?'

We are so close, our arms and legs are touching. I glance back down at his crotch again. It really is soaked. In a panic, I do the only thing that springs to mind. I grab the magazine and hold it up to the air con. After years of dealing with my mother's illness, I'm nothing if not reasonably adequate in an emergency situation.

'I'll dry it!' I shout, flustered, twisting all the little white knobs on the panel above our heads. The icy air comes out at full blast. 'And rice! I'll ask the cabin crew for some rice. For your phone,' I explain, flapping. 'Although they've probably only got microwavable Mexican-style rice... with vegetable bits in... but it might still work.'

He exhales loudly in response, gripping his phone tightly. This is why I should not be interacting with members of the opposite sex. I'm too out of practice and they are all too difficult and moody. An almighty roar vibrates through the cabin.

'Connie! Stop talking and do the mop!'

I peer nervously over the seats to see the entire group energetically swishing imaginary cleaning implements with much gusto down the aisle, dusting people's faces and ruffling their hair.

I reluctantly leap up again. This is humiliating. I have my bum in Mr Window Seat's wet face. As if he isn't angry enough. I'm literally waving my thigh gap an inch from his nose. My only hope now is that we are over international waters, and he can't sue me for some sort of human rights breach in a European court of law.

'Connie!' Cherry booms, drawing attention to me. 'Why are you so stiff? Bend from the hips. Like this, babes.'

At last, the twerking comes to a natural end and I am left with but a teaspoon of dignity. I put his magazine back down on the table. It's ruined. I forgot I had it in my hand while I was panic twerking and I'd rolled it up without thinking, so the soaked pages are now twisted and ripped. The poor man. Now he has nothing to read for the whole flight.

When the cabin crew eventually reach our row with their trolley, I order a croissant and a black coffee and, when he orders the same, I insist on paying. He objects very loudly, and we end up in a bit of a tussle with me thrusting my card at the cabin crew.

As we drink our coffees, I apologise once again for twerking in his face, spilling his drink, ruining his magazine, possibly breaking his phone *and* wetting his crotch. There is no way that will dry before we land. He is craning his body away from me, doing his level best to make sure our arms and legs do not touch. I dare to peek down at his wet patch. I'd be annoyed too, if that was me.

'Stop looking at my crotch!' he barks, making me jump with fright, which sends the remains of my coffee leaping from my cup. We both watch in horror as the coffee arcs through the air to land with precision... on his crotch.

I gasp, instinctively lunging towards him with my serviette.

'Jesus Christ!' he yells, swiping my hand away from his groin. 'What's wrong with you?'

Yes. Good question.

'I didn't mean to touch your...' I frantically search for a non-sexual word to describe his wet bulge. 'Your privates. I just wanted to help dab them dry.'

He gives me an outraged look.

Dab them dry? DAB THEM DRY? We have crossed the
Channel and thanks to Brexit I have no safety buffer. This is
most definitely harassment, no matter how sexually free and
easy we may believe the French to be.

He stands up, and Mrs Aisle Seat huffs and puffs as we both
get up to let him through. There's an uncomfortable moment
where we are squashed together in the aisle, and I appreciate
just how tall he is. He's very tanned with an attractive amount of
stubble. He shakes his dark glossy hair out of his eyes and pulls
his wet, tight-fitting top down over his taut stomach, which I am
going to ignore completely because I'm not one of those preda-
tory types, although I do catch his woody, soapy, fresh-man
scent before he barges roughly past me towards the toilet.

When he eventually returns, my eyes are drawn back to the
patch. It is dry now, but where there was once a huge dark wet
patch surrounding his crotch, there is now a dry yellow stain. I
don't know how but this seems even worse. He is so apoplectic
with rage, he can barely look at me. I lower my gaze and move
to let him through. We still have an hour to go before we land
in Alicante so, to avoid any further upset, I slump down in my
seat and close my eyes. I am shattered. The last thing I hear is
the cabin crew murmuring something about turning the heat
up to make us fall asleep.

* * *

A loud tannoy announcement startles me. Something about
scratch cards before we land and sunshine and glorious
temperatures. My still-heavy eyes refuse to open. Instead, I
snuggle back into my comfy warm pillow and throw my arm
across it. I twist sideways, crossing my legs for comfort, and nod

straight off again. Moments later, a second rude announcement penetrates my sleepy brain.

Ping.

'Ladies and gentlemen, we will shortly be arriving in Alicante. The crew will now pass through the cabin, so please ensure your big lips and heavy eyebrows are securely fastened, your eyelashes are stowed in the upright position, and your leg tattoos are clearly visible for landing.'

This is swiftly followed by the ping of the seat-belt sign reminding us to fasten them up again. There's simply too much pinging going on. I reluctantly open my eyes and adjust to the harsh bright light pouring in. I see a heavenly blue sky and feathery clouds. For a moment I forget I'm on my way to Benidorm and professional humiliation. I gaze out of the window, my head still lying in its warm resting place.

Wait, warm what now?

Suddenly I jerk fully awake, realising with dismay the position I am currently in. My head is snuggled into Mr Window Seat's taut chest. I've never in my life felt a pec like it. It's rock solid against my cheek. My arm is resting across his firm tummy area. This too feels like some kind of body armour. My leg is casually slung over one of his.

Fucking hell. I'm all but dry-humping him. And no more international waters!

I carefully peel myself away from his body. I have left a near-perfect imprint of eyebrows, red lipstick and a suspicious brown streak across his white shirt.

Where to begin with the apologising?

I sneak a glance at his face. It is a stony, rigid mask. We are so close I can see an angry tic in his cheekbone, suggesting that I have maybe prevented him from sleeping or moving or working for the remainder of the flight. He is staring hard at the headrest in front of him.

How embarrassing.

'I'm so, so sorry.'

He rudely holds up his hand to block my apology. I should remind him that manners maketh the man but, to be fair, he has been through quite a lot.

As Alicante comes into view, the plane hits an air pocket and unexpectedly sends everyone bouncing up from their seats. Then we hit another, this time much stronger, and we are all shaken about for a good minute or so before it calms down and the pilot comes over the tannoy to explain that it is going to be a bumpy landing due to our *late* departure, which he reminds us, was due to the *late* passengers boarding and refusing to be quiet during the safety demonstration.

The aircraft properly sounds like it is falling apart. The rattling is deafening and, as if on cue, a baby starts wailing. The atmosphere changes dramatically as panic sweeps through the cabin. The captain announces in a cheery voice that although it does indeed sound like the plane is falling apart, he would like to take this opportunity to reassure all the passengers that this is indeed highly unlikely, that the plane is indeed built to withstand air pressure like this and on behalf of himself, his co-pilot, the cabin crew and the airline he would indeed like to wish us a pleasant onward journey and indeed thank us very much for flying with them today, *bing bong*.

We hit another massive bump of turbulence that sends everyone, despite the seat belts, crashing into the people next to them. Try as I might, there's no hope of me not touching my neighbour as he's gripping the armrest between us like a vice, his eyes wide and unblinking. My first hope is that he's simply meditating very, very deeply and hasn't had the heart attack that he appears to have had. He's definitely *not* okay. He's gone very pale. Instinctively, I grab his wrist and feel for a pulse.

Nothing!

I jab at the call button above me and quickly lay the palm of my hand on his pec to feel his heart. His skin is cold. We're going to need a defibrillator and the ground crew on standby.

'Leave me alone!' he bellows, peering sideways at me, scaring me half to death, as if the pilot wasn't already doing a good enough job of it. 'You are making this flight much worse than it needs to be!'

'I thought you'd had a cardiac arrest. I was doing advanced first-aid checks on you!' I shout back defensively over the roar of the engines and the flap of the wings being adjusted.

'By groping me?'

Oh God, he's going to have me arrested, and I'll spend the rest of the week in jail. Nancy will kill me. And I have only myself to blame. Well, actually, Liam and Ged can share some of the blame for encouraging me to come on this trip in the first place. I knew it would end in disaster.

'I'd hate to know which medical school you graduated from,' he adds sarcastically as the plane hits another bump, throwing us all forward. He puts his arm up to protect himself and his elbow whacks my eye. 'Sorry,' he yells at me while I'm doubled over in pain.

In-fucking-credible. I try to save his life and this is the thanks I get?

His knuckles are white as he grips the armrest. His chest is billowing out increasingly quickly. He's obviously having a panic attack. I open my mouth to speak but he hand-blocks me again. *Fine.* I grab the sick bag from the seat pocket in front of me. With one hand nursing my poor throbbing eye, I hand him the bag with the other.

'I'm not going to be sick,' he states bluntly.

'It's not for that,' I say. 'Breathe slowly in and out of it. You're hyperventilating.'

He turns his wild eyes on me, sweat pouring down his forehead. I demo it for him, but he shakes his head.

'You're having a panic attack. You need to close your eyes and blow into this paper bag.' The pilot throws us around a bit more and the plane dips onto its side and back up straight again. My stomach lurches, and I can hear retching noises from further down the aisle.

'Okay,' he says, studying me for a brief second before warily taking the bag and closing his eyes.

'It's so your brain can send signals back to the amygdala to say that you're calming down and that everything's okay,' I urge gently as he puts the bag to his mouth. He has perfectly generous lips, I'll give him that.

The cabin lurches about again, causing several passengers to start praying loudly and voicing regrets. It's very off-putting. I should take his mind off our possible imminent death. I peer out of the window to see towering hotel and apartment blocks glistening in the distance.

'Did you know that Benidorm has over three hundred skyscrapers?' I yell at him.

The bag billows in and out.

'And a thousand bars. In fact, it's cheaper to drink beer there than water.'

What else did Google tell me?

'It has the highest pickpocket rate in Europe, so I'll need to be careful,' I say, sounding rather like I'm in charge of government foreign travel advice. 'Oh yes, and it has a nudist beach and a restaurant especially for the Germans, dedicated entirely to sausage.'

He opens one eye, sliding it my way.

Christ, he'll think I have sex on the brain.

'And yet millions of people still want to go there.'

Well, that's the Benidorm chat out of the way, and Mr Window Seat is showing no visible signs of interest.

We finally drop below the air pocket and the aircraft flies smoothly downwards, touches down on the runway and brakes to a stop.

As the whole plane erupts in relieved applause, Mr Window Seat and I sit in silence. I keep eye contact with him the entire time. While everyone is jumping up and grabbing their bags, desperate to get off the plane, we stay where we are, and I count with him. Soon his breathing becomes normal again and he takes the bag away. He looks like shit. Suddenly, I'm exhausted and wilt back against my seat. I hear, 'Harlem Shuffle!' but I am literally too drained to care. He raises a tiny smile, and his face instantly softens, which transforms him, causing me to become self-conscious. I'm drawn to his eyes, which are incredibly dark and striking, just like the rest of him.

'Let me see your eye,' he says as I gingerly take my hand away. It is stinging like mad. His face drops instantly. 'Sorry about that,' he says. 'But in fairness, you were a little too close to me for the entire flight.'

Rise above it. Be civil.

Tash yells up the plane to me that we have to wait until last because they'll bring a wheelchair to carry her off. I quickly scoop up my belongings off the floor, which is littered with stuff that has been hurled around, and get up to let him out.

'Is this yours?' he asks, squeezing into the aisle with me. He tugs my case free from the overhead locker, the sleeves of his T-shirt clinging gently to his bulging biceps as he puts it down with a heavy thump.

'It's the standard 10-kg allowance and the rest is all emotional baggage,' I joke nervously. 'It's the fear of what's waiting for me in Benidorm.'

He doesn't seem to find this funny and reaches above me to get his bag. We are stuck waiting for the cabin crew to open the doors. The seconds tick by like hours. Our eyes wander the cabin awkwardly until they connect for the fourth time.

He still seems incredibly tense and, because the sheer relief of landing safely and the gust of fresh air from the doors finally opening has suddenly turned me into Mary Poppins, I say, 'Well, it was jolly nice to meet you.'

Why? Why am I like this?

I feel the heat rushing to my cheeks at his borderline-hostile stare. 'Where are you headed?' I ask to defuse the tension. 'Somewhere nice?'

'Home,' he says in an unimpressed tone. 'To Benidorm, actually.'

Oh.

4

Mr Window Seat speaks Spanish to the cabin crew and disappears down the steps. I have clearly lost the ability to talk to men. Especially tall, ripped, attractive men on the receiving end of my clumsiness. When Cherry clocks my swollen eye, she recommends I sue the pilot, just as the pilot himself emerges from the cockpit.

'I'm a paralegal, love. I know about these things. You'll need to press charges against the airline. I mean, you can't go on stage looking like that, can you? You'll need compensation from someone.'

The pilot's face becomes thunderous, and I quickly tell him no one is suing anyone. As we hurriedly pass by the cabin crew with their plastered-on professional smiles, something is said in rapid Spanish and the ground crew can't get us out of there fast enough.

Again, the upside to being a group of drunk women wearing denim G-strings and having a wheelchair user with us is that we are whizzed through passport control at the Spanish end with no fuss. The guards take one disappointed look at the riff-raff entering their beautiful country and barely check our passports. I hear disgruntled comments from the rest of the passengers joining the huge queue. The girls invite the crowd to hear them singing in Benidorm as they click-clack past. Trailing behind the rest of the group, I nurse my sore eye as I doggedly drag my case along. I catch a glimpse of Mr Window Seat on my way to the exit. His face gives nothing away.

There's a lot for him to process, I guess. After all, I did practically save his life. And the truth of the matter is, it's not every day that two people share such an intense connection. For the first time in a long time, I feel like I should write a song or maybe a short haiku about the experience. That way, the memory of our deeply profound shared encounter will linger on in written form for the rest of time. I'd like to think I've made him a tiny bit better, more humble, more compassionate. I give him a half smile and a wave, but he doesn't return it.

Horrible man.

We are wheeled straight through to the exit, stopping briefly at the Alicante arrivals duty-free shop to purchase a few bottles of tequila from the rows upon rows of colourful bottles of booze.

For the love of God, why? Why do we need more drink?

'For the journey,' Tash says, as if reading my mind. 'It could take up to forty minutes.'

We all crowd through the sliding doors to meet our minibus driver, who we immediately spot waiting for us at the far end. He is holding up a huge sign with 'The Dollz and Ted Sheeran' on it. As we make our way over, his eyes look about to burst from their sockets right out of his face and across the tarmac. It takes Jorge, or Hoargghhhay as he pronounces it, a few minutes to remember who he is and what he does for a living while we wait for Big Mand who thinks she has lost her passport and has retraced her steps to the duty-free.

Cherry and Big Sue take the opportunity to smoke three back-to-back cigarettes each and, finally, Tash hobbles on to the minibus with an ankle the size of Gibraltar to sit next to Liberty, who is in a dead sleep next to her, having taken her travel sickness tablets too late. Her huge lips are vibrating softly like a pair of pink inflatable lilos. We all look battered. It is barely ten in the morning and instead of feeling fresh and wholesome with the whole trip yet ahead of us, we could be returning from a year volunteering in a war zone.

Jorge takes the opportunity to smoke a cigarette himself and admire the girls' boobs. He lets us know he is available for hire if we need him during our stay. He says if we need him for *anything* at all, just call. He gives us a lascivious wink. His meaning is very clear. We choose to strategically ignore him until he puts out his cigarette and sheepishly climbs on to the bus.

'We get that a lot,' explains Cherry, tutting.

'Except me,' laughs Big Sue.

'Are you a couple?' I ask her and Big Mand politely, noticing how close they are standing to each other. They both instantly flame red, and I am met with a torrent of denials. 'Sorry,' I say, 'I didn't mean anything by it. You just seem very close, that's all.'

Cherry reminds me not to be so judgemental and sexist. 'Or homophobic or whatever it is you're being,' she adds.

If anything, I have nothing but respect for same-sex couples and their struggles for equality and what have you, but I'm denied the chance to defend myself as Big Mand and Big Sue turn huffily away from me.

Eventually, Jorge drives us up the coast, where we are rewarded with a beautiful, twinkling Mediterranean Sea, bright sunshine, and picturesque mountains dotted with white villas and bright blue swimming pools. My thoughts drift back to the flight and Mr Window Seat, his wet crotch and furious face and those dark moody eyes. After half an hour, the natural landscape gives way to the infamous tower blocks that mark our arrival into Benidorm.

As we pass a quaint pedestrianised avenue lined with colourful flags, criss-crossing from rooftop to rooftop across the cobbled boulevard, home to one bar after another all the way down to the beach and its palm-tree-lined promenade, Tash shouts to Jorge, 'It's The Strip! *The Strip!* Stop the bus!'

I imagine the girls will want to take selfies at such an iconic tourist landmark.

'Stop the bus right now!'

Jorge turns to the girls. 'No stop here. Villa just two more minoots.'

'Hoargghhhay! Stop the friggin' bus! I've just seen a "four cocktails for the price of one" offer!'

'Laydeez, is only two minoots to villa. I have important job to do after,' he says, admirably sticking to his guns.

'Five friggin' minutes. Jesus Christ, what is wrong with you, Hoargghhhay?'

The bus screeches to an immediate halt and the moment I step off, I question my life choices. I try to keep up with the Dollz as they march down The Strip. The street that appeared quaint and colourful from the bus has turned out to be home to several bars featuring live sex shows, a baffling variety of tribute acts and topless, pole-dancing bar staff. This is my home for the next week.

'Here it is,' yells Tash. 'The Knee Trembler. It's our favourite bar. Free tequila shots with every drink.'

We pile into the bar, which has only just opened up for

cleaning purposes, following what I presume was a night of throwing drinks and wet napkins around. It stinks of ripe cheese and vinegar. This feels like a new professional low.

The girls order the poor beanpole teenage cleaner, now barman, to get them four Skanky Lady cocktails each, as per the special offer on the sign outside.

'They're named after us,' Tash tells me, insisting I have at least one.

My drink comes in a hollowed-out pineapple with a sorry-looking cocktail stick full of limp bits of fruit jutting out of the top. It tastes of melted ice lolly mixed with Haribo and a dash of diabetes. I drink it very warily, unsure if now is the right time to reveal that, for the sake of not losing a leg, I would very much like to go teetotal.

'I can't bear these people who are afraid of a bit of sugar,' Tash is saying to the other Dollz, which makes up my mind to keep quiet, although none of the toxic drinks appear sanitary as the barman pours them into an assortment of jam jars, coconuts and obscure medical bric-a-brac to give the impression that, here in Benidorm, a simple clean glass will not do. I watch Cherry sucking hard on her colostomy bag while Liberty's has come in a roller skate.

Even Jorge resigns himself to a few small beers, about forty cigarettes and a plate of something long and fried that could well have been a bicycle tyre the way he's chewing on it.

As the second round of cocktails are being whizzed up in blenders, a group of nuns stagger past the bar. I can't help but notice they are all wearing trainers and have unusually large feet. The tallest of the nuns turns abruptly towards us, stroking his beard.

'Holy shit! Mother of God Almighty! Lads, would you just look at these stunners,' he says, sweeping his bulging gaze over us. As they stop in their tracks, Tash bats her lashes and casually asks the beefy, bearded nuns where they are off to.

'Church,' one of them, with an elaborate head tattoo and a huge murderer's moustache, is quick to say. 'But first, would you mind if we, women of the cloth, join you ladies for a drink?'

Tash nods her head, giggling.

'I'm the Mother Superior. This is Sister Kevin and Sister Hugh Huge Ones,' he says, holding his hand against his heart while he introduces us to the rest. I take in their wrecked faces and wonder how many days they've been here. Too many, by the looks of things. Sister Kevin has red eyes and a bewildered look about him. I can't help but worry if we'll end up in the same sorry state after our own tequila-soaked visit.

'Been here long?' Tash asks.

'Flew in last night.'

Dear God.

'Shame you're leaving,' he says, nodding towards our driver. 'Looks like you've had a messy one though. You can tell us where best to go.'

'Literally just arrived,' Tash says defensively.

'Fuck me,' Sister Kevin says in surprise. I try to take great offence, but I am simply too pissed to care.

'Now, have you gorgeous beauties anything to confess?' the Mother Superior asks cheekily.

'Not yet, but hopefully we will later,' promises Liberty with a suggestive cackle.

'Ah' – the nun nods thoughtfully – 'but are we not *all* martyrs to the sins of the flesh?'

'You what, love?' asks Cherry, confused.

'He's asking if we are all up for a good shagging later,' barks Tash, and everyone bursts out laughing.

I bristle with alarm as these cross-dressing clergywomen sit down amongst us and much flirting and making of plans to meet up later in the day 'for confession' takes place. Liberty asks them to keep us in their prayers as the Mother Superior lifts his habit, rummages round in his undergarments and pulls out his phone to put in her number.

I'm relieved to head back on to the bus. I gaze tipsily out of the window as Jorge navigates the one-way system with what he probably thinks is expertise and panache by the way he keeps turning around and nodding expectantly at the Dollz. He narrowly misses a family of four, clips the mirror of a moped parked up at right angles to the road and laughs as he upends a rubbish bin. The narrow streets are littered with people absent-mindedly crossing roads whenever the mood takes. To my untrained eye, every man, woman and child in this town seems totally shit-faced. I see the bar and kebab-shop-lined streets whizz past as though in a hypnotic daze.

Why am I here? When did my life take such a catastrophic wrong turn?

Moments later, we pull up outside our new home for the next week. It is a spectacular villa with terracotta tiles, palm trees peeping over the huge white walls surrounding it and, I do a double take here, an extremely hot guy standing by the gate.

'Why is Enreeky Iglesias waiting to let us in?' Cherry asks, eyes wide with disbelief.

'No, babes, it's Justin Bieber. He must own this friggin' villa,' Liberty says, bursting with excitement.

There's a mad scramble to get off the bus while Jorge is left to unload all the bags, gutted that his departure goes totally unnoticed. Tash is the first to try and communicate with the heart-throb. He welcomes us in his sexy accent, and she responds with a shriek. I'm instantly amused to see her go beetroot red and flustered, keen but quite unable to articulate a sentence in this beautiful man's language.

'Has anyone else got fanny flutters?' asks Cherry as he takes us all in.

We are all transfixed. It's one of those moments where language barriers must be overcome through tone and facial expressions. A respectful silence falls despite the deafening clang of eggs exploding from ovaries. Finally, he introduces himself as Nacho.

'Nacho?'

'As in the dips?'

'Not dips. He means the triangle-shaped crisps, babes.'

'Doritos?'

After much bickering, Nacho concedes that the ladies can call him Enreeky if they want to. There's a definite whiff of pheromones in the air to accompany the stronger whiff of stale tequila, and although they barely know him, I suspect he could sleep with any one of them he wants.

'You're gorgeous. Totally fucking unbelievably fit. *Too* fit if anything,' Tash tells him.

'I will definitely do you, Enreeky, pet. Just say which,' says Liberty boldly.

'Don't you mean *when*, love?' says Big Mand.

'No.'

'Cherry, you're married so that's you out,' says Tash, swiftly eliminating the competition.

'Cheeky cow. Don't listen to her, Enreeky, pet. I am definitely *in*.'

'I am heartbroken, remember?' says Liberty. 'I should have first go on him. To get over Mehmet. Then the rest of you can have him.'

Ah yes. Liberty's harrowing account of her two-week affair with a married barman comes back to me.

'Pointless. He'll be ruined after that,' Cherry declares.

Nacho seems, understandably in my view, a little apprehensive. We make brief eye contact as I hastily introduce us in crude Spanish.

'Ask him if he's gorra massive cock. You know, with your A level Spanish and that,' asks Tash.

There's no bloody way I'm asking him that. It would demean the both of us and make him feel like a piece of meat. If I'm anything at all, I'm about respect and equality between the sexes.

'Connie, for eff's sake! Just ask him!'

I swallow anxiously. Five pairs of eyes bore into me. 'Erm... *perdona, Señor Nacho, tienes un gran... erm... zanahoria?*'

I've had to ask if he has a big carrot because we didn't cover the word for cock or fanny flutters in the A level syllabus. To my relief, he laughs and ignores the question, which seems to keep the girls happy.

For now, that is.

Even I can feel the sexual tension building. Everyone is unreasonably assuming that he has a huge one, or 'a clit destroyer' as Liberty is calling it, and he'll be putting it proudly on display after he has shown us the villa. The group surges forward, keen to get the tour over with.

5

Nacho opens the big white entrance gate, and we follow too closely behind him into a glorious courtyard, paved in terracotta tiles and dotted with enormous palm trees. It is stunning. We all coo as we trot through the double-width front door, which opens on to a large entrance hall and a sweeping staircase, bathed in colourful light from the huge stained-glass window at the top. There are two large archways either side of the hall, one leading to an American-style kitchen-diner and the other to a spacious all-white lounge, with a glossy white grand piano at the centre.

'The acoustics in here will be perfect for practising scales and vocal warm-ups,' I say.

I am met with blank stares. Nacho quickly ushers us out to a twinkling, kidney-shaped swimming pool surrounded by expensive wooden sunbeds with thick white mattresses, matching parasols and even a brick BBQ and pizza oven over in the corner. It resembles something out of a magazine. I'm amazed that Nancy has sprung for this, until I remember it was meant for Ted Sheeran. The most popular tribute act on the whole Costa Blanca.

'Good job this place is so private because I'll have to sunbathe nude.' Liberty gives Nacho a hefty pantomime wink. 'My stage costumes are very demanding. I can't risk any tan lines.'

'We are going to have *such* a great time!' Tash screams.

For the first time, helped by a belated rush to the head of whatever was in that last cocktail (two kilos of raw sugar cane and fourteen shots of vodka, I suspect), I think she might be right.

Nacho explains that there are three exceptionally large and luxurious double rooms upstairs, two with en suites. I hesitate. It'll seem a bit weird sharing a room. I'll feel self-conscious doing my tongue trills and lip bubble routine in front of anyone, and I'm not sure I could take their constant bursting into dance routines every five minutes. I need a moment of calm to meditate too, and I like to do a full humming chant. I quickly try to convince myself that perhaps the Dollz will be able to learn from me as much as I will from them.

Nacho leads the way as Big Sue effortlessly sweeps Tash up into her muscular arms to carry her up the marble staircase.

'I'll need a room to myself because of my ankle,' Tash says firmly.

'And because you bite in your sleep,' Cherry reminds her.

'Yes.' Tash slips down from Big Sue's arms and hobbles into a bedroom, leaving the rest of us on the landing. A huge quarrel ensues over who doesn't want to share communal facilities because of certain medical conditions.

'You always have to get your own way and I am *sick* of it!' bellows Big Sue to Liberty.

'You can talk, with your thrush! Yes, we all saw you trying to hide those tubes of Canesten in your case,' Cherry says accusingly.

'It's supposed to be good for tired eyes! It was in *Heat* magazine!' Big Mand shoots back.

A massive row breaks out over who does and who doesn't currently have thrush.

'I need a sea view. The air is good for my thrush *and* my asthma.'

'Piss off, Mandeep. You've not got asthma. That's your twenty cigs a day, that is.'

We are treated to Big Mand's gravelly smoker's cough. 'I should still get the sea view, though.'

Cherry yells, 'SLUT DROP!' and is told to fuck right off as this is *clearly* not a good time. This causes outrage.

It's exhausting. I feel the tiredness of the last eight hours sting my eyes. Nacho raises his eyebrows and asks me if he can leave the keys with me. I find out that Nancy has not only paid for the entire villa, but she has also prepaid the two-thousand-euro deposit and that Nacho will come next Sunday morning, before checkout, to make sure everything is how we found it.

Oh dear.

'There is a small room at the back of the property,' he tells me quietly in Spanish. He obviously feels sorry for me.

I follow him downstairs and outside and sweep my gaze around the pool area but can't spot anything that immediately strikes me as an extra room. Nacho leads me round the pool, past a Jacuzzi bubbling away, to a break in the wall which is so brilliantly white that the gap is almost invisible from any angle. It's an optical illusion. The gap opens to reveal a white wooden gate opening to a short path, lined with pink cherry and almond blossoms. It leads directly to a white cottage that is entirely hidden from view. It's totally gorgeous. I waste no time seeing what the place has to offer. The lounge area is flooded with light from the patio doors leading out the back to a private area with its own manicured garden and its own Jacuzzi. Nacho briefly explains how to use it before I follow him back into the cottage. Off the lounge is a glorious double bedroom with the biggest four-poster bed I've ever seen, covered in crisp white cotton sheets and huge swathes of white toile draped over it. The en suite is stocked with fluffy towels and toiletries with posh-sounding names. It resembles a honeymoon suite.

I think of Ged and Liam and feel a sudden pang of longing. What must it be like to feel in love? Consumed with desire? To be on honeymoon with the love of your life?

A jangling of keys pulls me back from the moment. Nacho shows me a remote that controls the lights, the air con, the music system and even a massage function on the sunloungers. It's all amazing. So, no matter how badly this week goes, at least I will have the calming sanctuary of this lovely place.

Before he leaves, we swap numbers. He says to me in English with a grin, 'In case you want to see me and... in case I want to see you.'

Oh my.

There might be a flirty subtext going on and, if I'm not mistaken, a lusty glint in Nacho's eyes. Suddenly, the sweltering heat, the heady mix of cocktails, his exposed skin and rippling muscles cause a lapse of judgement.

'Well, erm, we're doing a warm-up gig tomorrow at The Jolly Roger if you're around?' I say, trying to sound poised and cool. It's been a very long time since I noticed anyone flirting with me. 'We're on from nine.' A ripple of panic at the lack of rehearsal time rips through me.

'You and the other girls are in a band?'

'No,' I say. 'I'm not with them. The Dollz are my support

band. I do... a different sort of act. More thought-provoking, you know... classy, sort of avant-garde.'

Please stop talking.

Nacho smirks. 'Maybe, yes. I'd like that. I imagine you are all very loud, very dancing.'

'Yes. Yes, we are. Very dancing. Yes.'

I have no idea why I included myself in that statement. I was once described as a singing statue.

It's the sun, the heat.

I have heatstroke.

'*Hasta pronto*,' he says, kissing me lightly on both cheeks in that very Spanish way.

After I see him out, I accidentally catch sight of myself in the patio door reflection. My right eye has swollen up and is all but closed. My hair has frizzed in the heat but only on one side and my face is glistening with sweat. All I'd need are a few smears of blood on my face and some rubble in my hair and I could easily pass for the victim of a major earthquake. I should totally get a grip of myself. There was no lusty glint in Nacho's eye. It was pity. Or worse, he's simply a polite landlord with a clear and procedural check-in routine.

What was I even thinking?

* * *

After I have unpacked and located an ice pack for my eye, I go through to the pool. Big Mand and Big Sue emerge from the patio doors into the bright sun. I am relieved to hear the bickering has stopped and they have huge smiles on their faces and seem super relaxed.

'We've just downed four tequila shots each,' Big Mand says, offering me a swig from the bottle they are carrying.

'Maybe later,' I say hesitantly. 'I still need to run through my set list, decide on my costumes, do my vocal chanting exercises, you know, that sort of thing. At least swimming is good for the lungs.'

When they don't respond, I put down my melted ice pack and slip into the cool water. I notice Big Mand gazing wistfully after Big Sue, watching as she dives into the pool and executes a perfect Olympic-style turn before swimming underwater back towards us. Big Sue's legs are even longer than mine and she has a rose-vine-type thing climbing all the way from her toes right up her left leg to her crotch.

'I love your tattoo,' I say as she emerges for air, to get her back on side.

'Mandeep has a great one,' Big Sue says. 'Show her.'

I try not to look prudish as Big Mand pulls her bikini down below her bottom.

'It's the entire cast of *The Greatest Showman*,' Big Sue says proudly.

'And I've got Sanskrit writing down my arms,' says Big Mand, showing a tramline of writing down the inside of each arm to her wrists. 'It's out of respect for my Indian heritage.'

'What does it say?'

'"If the doors of perception were cleansed"' – Big Mand pauses for dramatic effect – '"everything would appear to woman as it is: infinite."'

There's a small silence as they absorb the enormity of this wisdom.

'So beautiful,' says Big Sue, her eyes glistening with wonder.

What did I miss? What am I not getting?

I'm too embarrassed to admit to being baffled, so when I

make the mistake of admitting that I don't have any tattoos, you'd think I'd let down women everywhere.

'What? Not even a little back tattoo?' Big Mand says, appalled.

I shake my head.

'Not even some stars under your hairline at the back of your neck? Surely everyone has some of those?' They both lift up their hair to show a trail of stars.

'No.'

'Not even some ankle flowers?' Big Mand lifts her foot to display daisies sprinkled around the outside.

'No.'

'Nothing on your vagina?'

'Definitely not. No,' I say before either one of them can show me an example.

'Honestly, Connie, what is wrong with you?' Big Sue says in a tone that assumes laziness is at the root. I've blown it with them again.

Tash emerges to let us know how blessed the whole villa is and how blessed she is with her beautiful room and how blessed this Jacuzzi is and how blessed Spain is to have us all there and that she's thinking of suing Newcastle Airport over her throbbing ankle. Alcoholic fumes billow from her glossy pink lips.

'Are we doing "Tash or Gash" tonight?' Cherry yells over from the patio doors.

Sweet baby Jesus, what on earth does that even mean?

'Does a bear shit in the woods?' Tash brays with laughter. 'We're meeting the nuns tonight at 9 p.m. so if we go out at 8 p.m. that'll give us time to see what other fellas are out beforehand and we can play "Tash or Gash" then.'

I'm not even going to ask.

'It's about volume when it comes to men,' she adds. 'And keeping them distracted.'

It's as though she has forgotten our real purpose here. 'Should we rehearse the handover and compare set lists, before we go out? To make sure we don't duplicate. Or maybe we could discuss it over dinner?' I say assertively. 'Pizza or pasta is good for me. And then I'll probably have an early night, so I feel refreshed for tomorrow's performance.'

They all look at me as if I've just suggested we eat raw sewage.

'Who wants to eat in this heat?' Tash says, horrified. 'And what do you mean have an early night? We're in the city that never sleeps.'

I'm pretty sure that would be New York but I'm not going to correct her. 'Fine, no problem. I'll eat here before we go out,' I say. 'I'll do a shop for some bits.'

'I'm quite food-shy when I'm on holiday,' Big Mand says. 'So if you could just pick me up some cheeses, maybe a watermelon and some Pringles and some Diet Fantas, oh and a large jar of mayonnaise, make sure it's Hellmann's, mind, and maybe a few baguettes... and lemons. Lots of lemons. I'm detoxing.'

'Yes, we need lots of lemons for the tequila,' agrees Tash. 'Thanks, Connie. You're an angel.'

'I'll probably need help carrying the bags if I have to get so many... lemons.' I wait for someone to volunteer to come with me. Everyone smiles mutely at me.

'I'll use some lemons for my hair. I'm thinking of going beach babe, so I'll need to squirt it all over my extensions.' Big Sue runs her fingers through her hair. 'And I'll need some coconut oil for a deep tan. Or is it olive oil? Connie, get me a couple of litres of each, just in case.'

'How about some factor 50 instead?' I ask but the look of

horror on their faces is all the answer I'm going to get. 'Well, why don't you come with me to choose the oil yourself?' *Because you can all see I'm not a bloody weightlifter.*

'I'd love to, but I can't. None of us can.' Big Sue raises her eyebrows at the girls. 'We have a strict Cyndi Lauper policy, don't we, lasses?'

Policy?

All becomes clear when they start screeching, 'Girls just wanna have suu-uuuuu-n!' at me, nodding their heads from side to side in perfect sync.

Bob, bob, bob.

'Thas-all we really waaaaaaa-aaaant. Some suuu-uuun.'

Bob, bob, bob.

It's exasperating. A simple yes or no would have done. And so, after the tenth time, I give up. 'Fine, I'll go on my own.'

It will take more than common decency to prise this lot from their sunloungers. They seem welded to them.

'We should really start getting ready for tonight if we want to be out by eight,' shouts Liberty from an upstairs window. 'We've only got six hours.' After some gasping, there's a stampede back into the villa.

'Don't forget the lemons!' they cry as they disappear.

So much for the Cyndi Lauper policy!

I head off back to my cottage to shower and scrub off the streaky tan from my legs. I put some cover-up foundation on my face and a lot more over my eye and cheekbone. The swelling is going down a lot already thanks to the ice, but it still looks dreadful. I put some mascara and black liquid liner on my good eye but when I try to put some on the swollen one it stings too much. It's all a bit *Clockwork Orange*, but I can hide it behind sunglasses. I might have to sing with shades on tomorrow which, if you're not a massive rock icon or registered as blind, is a big no-no for singers in my league.

I throw on my denim shorts, some flip-flops and a T-shirt and slip quietly out of the house, keen to get the food shopping over with so that I can rehearse my set. I feel panicked at the lack of preparation the Dollz seem to require. I, on the other hand, will need a lot of lead-up time to psych myself up. The nerves are already getting the better of me.

Once outside, I have no clue which direction to go in, so I look up a supermarket on Google Maps and find one about a mile away. It all seems downhill from the villa. God knows how I'll get back up these hills with heavy bags, in this heat. Twenty minutes later, and I'm sweating like a ripe cheese, but I've found a supermarket of sorts. Half the shop is given over to the sale of crisps and lemons (hoorah!). The other half seems to be for cans of pop and booze. So much for the healthy Mediterranean diet you hear about. It doesn't take long for me to pick up almost every heavy, insanely overpriced item on the list and heave the basket over to the lady behind the till. Of course, none of the girls thought to leave any money with their huge list of demands, did they?

It takes me a lot longer to go up the hill in my flip-flops in this heat, so I keep stopping every few minutes to put the bags down and give myself a rest. I feel my eyes stinging as sweat drips into them. I reach a junction and, just as I step out to cross, I dither as to which direction I came from. I take off the glasses, wipe my eyes and juggle the bags so that I can take my phone out of my pocket to check my location.

As the bags slip down my arms, I wrestle with my phone when suddenly, out of nowhere, a moped comes hurtling towards me. I panic, try to step backwards, trip over the kerb and I'm knocked right off my feet. My shopping bags connect with the driver's helmet and split, sending the contents crashing to the ground. I land with a thwack on the pavement, banging my back, barely managing to keep my shoulders up to stop my head from smashing against the stone. The wind is knocked right out of my lungs. As if in slow motion, the Fanta cans explode all over the place, spraying me in fizzy rain. Lemons are bouncing about everywhere.

Oh dear, everything is whirling around, the sun is beating down, and I feel faint with the heat. I can't quite catch my breath. My lungs refuse to let in any air. My eyelids feel heavy as they close, blocking out the glaring harsh light and replacing it with soothing, cool darkness. I hear the screech of tyres, followed by running footsteps.

A panicky voice full of concern yells, 'Hey! Are you okay?'

I feel a body thump heavily down next to me.

'You have got to be kidding,' I hear him say.

6

I risk opening the one good eye I have left and stare at the face looming over mine. It's blurry – probably because my good eye is full of Fanta – but I could swear moody Mr Window Seat from the plane is hovering over me. I must have sustained one of those severe head injuries where my most recent embarrassing accomplishment seems like reality. I feel my cheeks being squeezed like a lemon and a pair of warm lips covers mine. Just as everything goes black, I feel a sharp slap to my face.

'Stay with me, Connie! Stay with me!'

Apart from anything, at best it's an appallingly amateurish attempt at first aid; at worst, it's bordering on assault. I gingerly rub the Fanta from my good eye so I can see who this Good Samaritan really is. My vision clears slightly as I squint in the sunlight.

Christ Almighty, it is him.

'What the hell are you doing?' I croak.

'I'm checking you're alive!' he yells at me in a panic, his nostrils flaring like a spooked horse.

'By kissing me, then slapping me?' I say as sarcastically as I can manage, which isn't much as I'm very injured and can barely speak, but at least my short-term memory has not been affected. 'I'd hate to know' – I pause as a wave of exhaustion and dizziness hits me – 'which medical school you...' I'm losing momentum as the world begins to spin slowly around me. *What was I saying? Oh yeah.* '...graduated from.'

He politely waits for me to finish the world's slowest sentence before we continue to stare at each other. I fear the sarcasm has petered out to nothing.

It's as though time is standing still around us. I open my mouth to give him a thorough lecture on the grave repercussions of flouting the three P safety rules of first aid: preserve, prevent, promote. He hasn't even checked to see if a bus or a lorry full of bananas is hurtling down the road towards us, but it's simply too tiring. I ask to see his driver's licence instead because he obviously has no idea how to drive properly but instead of producing the required paperwork, he suddenly bursts out laughing and his whole face softens.

'You're funny.'

I take a moment to continue scowling.

The cheeky, cheeky bastard.

He's so close I can feel his minty breath tickle my cheek. I'm incensed at his cavalier attitude towards my life, but because his laughter is surprisingly infectious, and even though I'm quite appalled at myself, I giggle along. Soon it builds into a gut-wrenching belly laugh. The more I think of how ridiculous this day has been, how much pain I'm in, how battered I am and how most of it is this handsome fucker's fault, I start crying with laughter.

'How are you even here?' I ask.

Maybe fate is throwing us together.

'You have my phone. I've been following the tracker on my iPad.' He points his thumb to his backpack.

'Your phone? I haven't got your phone,' I say.

'You must have picked it up on the plane by mistake.'

After a few bizarre moments, he helps me to sit up while I rummage in my little fanny pack. I take out his phone. 'Shit. I have no idea how it got there.'

'That flight was... well, it was... things were thrown all over. Don't worry about it. I'm just glad it's not broken. I run most of my business from it so I kind of really need it back.'

We glance over at his once pristine moped lying on its side, dripping in non-fat Greek yoghurt. It has half a watermelon sticking out of the front wheel and a baguette firmly wedged under the mudguard. There's a can spraying Fanta over the seat and handles.

'Shame. It looks brand new.'

'It is.'

We are completely drenched in Fanta, which seems unbelievably funny in my woozy state. I think we might both be in a bit of shock. I try to lift a hand to my head. It feels broken inside.

'Any minute now I'll probably start speaking fluent Chinese. You hear about that kind of thing happening with head injuries, don't you?'

His eyebrows shoot up.

He is very, very attractive.

We are distracted by the wheel of Brie that is rolling casually down the hill being chased by a herd of zigzagging lemons. He gets up to salvage what is left of the groceries. The crisps, the melon and the bread are completely flat and covered in dirt and the rest is covered in mayonnaise. He picks up my arnica gel and ibuprofen and brings them to me with an expression that is almost an apology. His face is sticky. Fanta is drying his hair into weird horns. I smile at him, and he smiles reluctantly back.

'Seriously though,' he says, 'you wandered out into the road looking at your phone instead of where you were going. It could have been much worse. You should be more careful in future.'

This brings my smiling to an abrupt halt. I squint up at him. 'Just hold on there, pal,' I say. Just to be clear, I have never called anyone 'pal' in my life. It must be the concussion. 'I clearly had right of way as a pedestrian. *You* hit *me* with your' – I glance over to his bike – 'your old-lady scooter.'

'It's a moped,' he says moodily. 'A GTS300. Limited edition.'

Like I would care!

'Whatever,' I sigh, struggling to get up. He immediately hoists me gently to my feet. I yelp as pain shoots up my back.

'You're injured,' he says, his voice suddenly full of concern. 'We need to get you to a hospital.'

'No, honestly, I'll be fine,' I say. A trip to the hospital is the last thing I need right now. If I have to cancel the gig tomorrow and Nancy finds out, then my career is over. 'I'd rather get back to the villa, take some painkillers and lie down for a bit.'

A wave of dizziness swoops over me. I give him my full weight and feel him tense.

'Where are you staying?' he asks. I groggily show him through my cracked phone screen where the villa is. His face falls. 'Ah,' he says, 'you're one of Nancy's tribute acts? I should have guessed.'

'No,' I say. 'I mean, yes, but not with the Dollz. They're just my support act. I'm the headline. Standing in for Ted Sheeran.'

Like that makes me sound important!

'I'm more of an upmarket type of act.'

Now I just sound desperate.

'No, I mean I'm more avant-garde. More ethereal. I take my audience on an emotional journey.'

Now I just sound shit.

'Right. Of course,' he says, avoiding eye contact. 'Right. Let's get you back to the villa.'

* * *

Two minutes later, we pull up outside. I climb unsteadily off the lady scooter. 'Well, thank you for bringing me back,' I manage, stumbling slightly as I walk away from him.

He insists on seeing me properly into the house but as we let ourselves in through the gate, we hear the sound of arguing sailing out through the open windows. He flinches as we catch a torrent of squabbles.

'Who used all the Vagisan? It's for making my hair sleek, not for your vaginal dryness, Liberty. Get your own!'

'Who had a bath? You've used up all the bloody hot water.'

'Who left the straighteners on? You've burnt the fucking rug!'

We slide past the house, I nod towards the BBQ, and we tiptoe to the gate, quietly shutting it behind us.

'They've been like that since five o'clock this morning.' I yawn, suddenly very tired.

'You have such weird taste in friends.'

'Oh,' I say, 'they're not my friends.' Another pain shoots up my back, stopping me in my tracks. 'We only just met. Like I said, they're a tribute act, whereas I'm more avant—'

'I'll get you some water for the painkillers,' he says, helping me over to a sunbed. The mattress is soft, and the light breeze is lovely on my hot skin. 'Try this.' He turns the control to a gentle massage, which instantly soothes my aching back. He goes off and comes back with an ice pack for my eye. 'I'm worried you might be concussed so is it okay...?'

He's asking me something, but I can't focus... I fight to stay awake, but my eyes are so heavy... I feel so soothed and relaxed... My stinging eye feels so much better... He's asking me to... No, he's asking if he can go... He's leaving... My good eye is sticky with Fanta and, once it closes, I can't unstick it. It feels so heavy. Both eyes are clamped shut.

A fog of exhaustion takes me as I drift in and out of sleep, waking briefly to hear strange male voices. One of them is saying he is a doctor of cheese... No, he's asking for some cheese... He's checking my pulse and feeling my head because he thinks I'm lying on top of the cheese.

'*Queso*,' I say, pointing to the kitchenette. '*Mucho queso grande.*'

I'm in awe at how fluently I can now speak the lingo because of my lovely head injury. My hand feels like a ton weight as I attempt to indicate the whereabouts of the cheese. I hear mumbled talking again and... *plenty of rest... keep an eye... acute whiplash.*

* * *

I wake feeling like I've been hit by a truck. Ah, yes, a cheese truck. For a moment, I forget where I am until my eye stings to remind me, and my back aches. I feel cold. My good eye snaps open. I am still outside on the sunlounger, but the sky is dark. I try to sit up and feel a stiffness go through me. My ice pack has slipped off and is somewhere near my neck.

'Here, take some more painkillers.'

Alarmed, I discover Mr Window Seat is sitting right next to me. He's holding out the tablets and some water.

'Sorry to startle you. It's just me, Matt, from the plane. From the accident, you know, whatever...' He trails off.

I feel so groggy. Even lifting my arm is a huge effort. He leans in to help me sit up and puts the water to my lips so that I can swallow the tablets. It feels a bit too intimate, but he smells incredible, and he's got very strong arms. I tear my eyes away from his muscular forearms that look like they should have boxing gloves at the end of them.

'Wait, you're not drugging me to get at my kidneys, are you?' I half-joke croakily. 'Was there a doctor here? And did I eat some cheese?'

'Doctor Sanchez is an old family friend. He says you'll be fine. You told him your Spanish was very tall, that he was a lovely man and then you kindly offered to eat his entire family.'

So much for Spanish A level preparing me for real life.

'Doctor Sancheese,' I say dazedly. 'Thanks for getting him to come over. That was really kind of you, Matt, erm... Matthew.'

Best not to get too familiar. In case one of us ends up in court suing the other for damages or some such.

'No problem. And it's Matteo,' he says, watching me check him out. 'My mother is English. I lived there for a while before I moved here. That's why I have no Spanish accent.'

I should make enquiries about this interesting dual-heritage upbringing but I find myself staring at his bare legs.

'Is that my robe?'

'I took a quick shower. I hope you don't mind. I thought you'd be out for longer, so I borrowed one of the robes.'

Instead of being outraged at all the liberty-taking, my immediate thought is that he was naked in my shower.

'You were in my shower? Naked?' I blurt without thinking, and I turn hurriedly away in case he can sense me sexually objectifying him in my dazed state.

Too late.

'Doesn't everyone undress to take a shower?'

Good point, well made. Now I'm picturing him naked and soaping himself extravagantly instead of answering him.

'But I, erm, cleaned the shower afterwards.'

Now I've made him feel awkward.

I'm picturing him naked and bending to clean the shower doors. I'm definitely concussed.

He hurries to explain himself.

'Don't worry,' he says anxiously. 'I know this looks bad but I'm not trying to make a move on you.'

Charming.

'I have no interest in you whatsoever, I promise.'

All I can do is stare at him with my one eye. There is now a huge uncomfortable silence between us. He peers down at his naked chest peeking from the robe that is swinging halfway up his bare thigh.

'Sexually, I mean. I have no interest in you sexually,' he says, pulling the robe together and clinching it shut as though I might lunge at him any second. 'Not at all. I'm just trying to help. You're quite safe,' he says, hands splayed, eyes unsettled.

Oh well, I'm glad he's cleared that up so... clearly.

I glare at him for a few seconds. I need to make it clear that I have not just been fantasising about him. 'Well, I have no interest in you either.' I sound very tit for tat. 'Sexually or otherwise.'

He clamps his lips shut. 'Good to know. Good to know. Anyway, my clothes should be dry now,' he says, pointing over to the patio furniture draped in shorts and a top.

'What time is it?' I suddenly ask, alarmed that I'll be late for the 'Tash or Gash' night out. I need to transform into a skanky lady for the sake of performance purposes. I can't afford to let the audience or Nancy down.

'Eight o'clock.'

'The Dollz are expecting me to be dressed up like a prostitute,' I say, 'so that I can play a game where we have to guess whose fanny belongs to who or something like that.'

Matteo raises his eyebrows at this. Maybe he thinks the bash on the head has affected my grammar.

'I mean whose fanny belongs to whom.'

He seems a little worried.

'Ah. I mean sex worker, not prostitute.'

I need to get a grip. These pills are very strong. They appear to have affected my filter. 'In no way am I being offensive because if I'm about anything, it's equality in the workplace.'

I'm not sure how this is relevant, but Matteo agrees.

'It's just the "girls" have invited me out to bond with them, so we'll have some on-stage chemistry.' I use my fingers to make quotation marks and, when he furrows his brow, I realise that, again, that was irrelevant, and now I have made him think that some of the girls may not actually be girls. 'No, I mean that if I'm about anything then surely it must be gender equality in the workplace equality.'

I think I might definitely be a bit concussed.

'So,' I blurt out, rather exhausted from it all, 'could you please leave now so I can get dressed to go out?'

'Are you sure?'

I leave his simple question hanging in the air. For some inexplicable reason, probably the concussion, my brain wants to interpret this as, *Are you sure you wouldn't like to stay here with me instead?*

'Yes. Yes, I'm sure,' I say in a voice that suggests I'm not in the slightest bit sure. I think I've accidentally created an air of sexual tension, even though he explicitly told me a moment ago that he is not in the least bit attracted to me.

'Bye then,' he says, swiftly disappearing into the villa with his clothes. He can't get away from me quickly enough.

Message received loud and clear.

'Bye,' I shout feebly after him. I shuffle over to the en suite, look in the mirror and let out a chilling scream, which sends Matteo racing back through the cottage to find me. As he charges into the bathroom, he sees me staring at myself in the mirror.

'Oh, yes. Right. Of course,' he says.

Jesus Christ, what a mess. Even if we just forget for a second that my hair – which has dried in the sunshine in a truly remarkable, gravity-defying manner, helped by a can of fizzing Fanta and being slept on awkwardly – isn't the main problem. My face, whilst it has a sticky orange sheen, also has black streaks from the liquid liner that I put on my good eye. The streaks are right down to my chin. The swollen eye, while it has gone down a lot, has also turned black. The overall effect is somewhat horrific.

'You might feel better after a shower. Also,' he says, sounding embarrassed, 'I'm very sorry, but I think that the girls have already left to go into Benidorm.'

'They've left? Without me?' I feel a tightness in my throat. 'But did they at least come to check on me while I was unconscious?'

His silence tells me that not one of them had even noticed I wasn't there or that I hadn't returned from the supermarket.

Pathetic. That's how important I am. Nobody cares. Literally nobody cares.

I let this information sink in.

'Well, thanks again for helping me,' I say self-consciously while keeping my eyes glued to the ground.

'It's the least I could do,' he replies rather formally, doing the same. The atmosphere is suddenly uncomfortable between us. I'm still totally fucking stunned at how on earth I could have imagined there'd be any sexual tension between us while I look like a two-year-old child has painted a portrait of me and left it out in the rain. I am beyond embarrassed.

'Good luck,' he says, edging away from me and closing the bathroom door on his way out. I lean against it, my heart pounding, until I hear the front door shut and the distant roar of his moped driving off.

7

I peel off my grungy clothes and step into the mosaic-tiled shower, and as the hot water washes the sticky Fanta from my body, I treat myself to a little pity sob. As always, my thoughts drift to my mother. Apart from when she'd go on glamorous tours with the world's leading orchestras, we were inseparable. She used to say I was born singing. Our passion for music bonded us together like no other relationship I've ever known. She taught me everything she knew. And when she reached the pinnacle of her career, she happily sacrificed opportunities to stay closer to me. She was my champion when I failed my first few auditions for the Sinfonia. She used to tell me my time would come, and I believed her. Even after all this time, it still makes me unbelievably sad that she died and isn't here to watch me blossom into a proper nobody. Failing at life. Her hope for me died with her. My breathing halts for a brief moment as I feel the grief wash through my soul, squeezing the very life from my veins. My sniffle turns into a good, noisy, no-holding-back weep as I let the shower wash away my heartache.

Within moments, the tears are replaced with a succession of some of my favourite heart-wrenching ballads. It's been the only way to deal with the tidal waves of grief since my mother passed. As I'm belting out the desolate lyrics, I take in a huge lungful of air and hold the note like a pro. At least this counts as practice, and I don't care if I can be heard over in Morocco.

Afterwards, I massage the complimentary oils and creamy shampoo into my hair, which envelop me in delicious calming scents. I condition my hair from straw-based back to silky and soon I feel clean and refreshed. I put a bit of concealer on my bad eye to cover the black. It almost works so I try adding some powder. Miraculously, I feel almost normal again. Even though it is only for my benefit, I dry my hair and straighten it so that it's soft and shiny and swishes gently round my face. The wild expression from earlier has gone and the nicely drugged-up, painkiller eyes are wide and relaxed. I spray some more spa aromatherapy oils over myself and breathe in the fragrant bergamot and jasmine.

Even the stiffness in my back is easing. I put on the fluffy white robe that is hanging on the back of the door and momentarily stop to notice the spare peg next to it. An image pops into my mind of Matteo showering here. It causes a momentary fluttering in my stomach before I head into the lounge.

You're concussed, I remind myself, *and hungry.* Also, he went to great lengths to make sure I knew he wasn't attracted to me. My phone pings, and through the cracked screen, I see a notification from the Dollz' Facebook page. It's a new post of what I hope is a gentleman's moustache dyed pink, until a message pops up underneath, announcing Tash has won the designer vagina competition, accompanied by lots of photos of them having fun. They seem to be about my age and yet manage to balance professional careers with singing while maintaining a deranged and enviably carefree zest for life. And here I am, alone. Again.

I wander through to the kitchen to make some snacks. I'm just about to open the fridge when I hear a noise outside. I stop to listen and immediately let out a high-pitched scream as the distinct sound of the patio doors sliding open in the other room is followed by footsteps crossing the lounge. I dart round, attempting to grab something off the bench for protection.

'It's okay! It's just me,' Matteo yells as I brandish a pair of salad tongs at him.

'You gave me such a fright,' I say, clutching a hand to my chest as I lower the weapon.

Matteo looks at the salad tongs. 'Were you planning to toss me to death?'

We both frown awkwardly at each other, leaving the unintended sexual innuendo hanging between us. There's a high possibility it's only in my head.

After a beat, he says, 'I wasn't sure if you'd be hungry after your accident. I hope you don't mind, but I ordered pizza for you.'

What a cheek.

'*My* accident?' I say to him. 'You knocked me over. If it was anyone's accident it was *yours*!'

'You weren't even looking where you were going,' he says, eyes wide with disbelief. 'You just stepped out in front of me. And if we're going to split hairs, I'd say you tripped over the kerb.'

We stare crossly at each other before he rolls his eyes away from mine. 'You're right, I should have the intuition to know that at any given moment, a pedestrian, busy checking their Snapchat, will walk out in front of me, and next time, I'll be more prepared!'

I find his derision unnecessary and, at the risk of sounding like a stuffy English professor, it shows a real lack of vocabulary and syntactical prowess, which I explicitly share with him.

'Sarcasm is the lowest form of wit.'

Yes, I'm aware that I used it earlier but that was different.

'Yeah. Whatever,' he snaps. He clearly doesn't care about syntax or sarcasm. 'The pizza's getting cold.'

He stomps away, and I stomp after him, but when I reach the patio, the table is laid with snacks. There are two glasses full of water sitting next to the plates and cutlery and an unopened bottle of wine. The air is thick with the delicious aroma of pizza. The lights are twinkling, and music is playing softly in the background. Matteo looks as if he wishes he hadn't bothered. I immediately feel ungrateful. I stare at the beautiful surroundings and begin to appreciate the effort he has gone to.

'Thank you. It's lovely.'

'I just wanted to make up for your support band letting you down,' he says, sounding hacked off. 'They shouldn't have gone off and left you like that.'

Oh. That's unexpectedly sweet of him.

'How about we drink all of that wine instead, and start the evening over?' I say. 'I'm sorry if I've been a bit... whatever. I think I'm a little concussed. And hungry.'

He thinks about it for a few seconds before holding a chair out for me. I dive straight for a slice of pizza and groan with delight as the cheese melts against my tongue and slides down my throat.

'This is so delicious,' I say, licking my fingers and wiping them on the napkin. Matteo seems relieved to see me tucking in and reaches for a slice. We eat in comfortable silence for a few minutes before I become acutely aware that I am naked underneath my dressing gown and we are totally isolated here, yet I make no move to get dressed. Matteo says nothing as he watches me knock back two more painkillers and gulp at the crisp, cold wine like it's water.

After we've had plenty to drink and are stuffed with pizza, he asks, 'How come you know so much about panic attacks?'

I drain my glass and hold it out for a refill. As he pours, I study his face. He has kind eyes. I may as well open with the truth.

'My mother died.'

It still feels unreal. Somehow untrue. I still feel wobbly when I hear myself say the words out loud. He gives me a moment to let it sink in. I will never be able to say it without feeling devastated. It's as though it happened only yesterday.

'From the moment we heard the news that she had cancer, and the doctors wouldn't be able to cure it, I started suffering panic attacks.'

I check to make sure he is comfortable with this reveal because my experience is that generally people are not. They often make an excuse to leave or tell me about lots of other people who have died of cancer and isn't it such a shame, but it's just part of life and don't we all just have to learn to get on with it and make the best of every day because it's a gift and you owe it to everyone, especially yourself, to live your best life. Matteo does neither. He sits, listening.

'At first, I would have them at the hospital worrying about my mother while we watched her waste away,' I say quietly, fiddling with my napkin. 'Then I'd have them at home worrying that my father would die too. I know it sounds silly.'

Matteo still doesn't move or say anything.

'But now I'm fine. I'm absolutely fine,' I say, taking another gulp of wine. It really is helping to loosen my tongue. 'And my father is moving on with Madge. Ged and Liam are engaged too,' I continue. 'They're my lovely friends. We moved in together after uni, but I suppose I'll need to move out now.'

Matteo tilts his head, encouraging me to go on. Just like my lovely live-in therapists. I feel a wave of calm come over me. Maybe it's the tablets or maybe it's him. His eyes really are the deepest pools of kindness I've ever seen. I top his glass up before continuing with this detailed chapter-by-chapter account of my autobiography.

'And then I lost my job. I ruined Nancy's friend's wedding anniversary because I'm so weighed down with sadness. And finally, I fluffed my audition for the Royal Northern Sinfonia. Again. I think they expect me to live up to my mother, who was the best soprano they've ever had. But I just had them all in tears. They practically shooed me out of the place. Not that I can blame them. I've spent the last five years in chronic free fall, especially after I helped nurse my mother through cancer... only to lose her. I've been devastated ever since.'

I lean over to top my own glass up. I'm acutely aware my life is no page-turner, but I'm having difficulty stemming the tide.

'And now Nancy has given me this one last chance to stop boring my audiences with sad songs, but the thing is, I'm not even sure if I'm capable of singing happy songs any more. How could I when I'm not even capable of being happy?'

Matteo leans across to me and gently strokes his thumbs across my cheeks to wipe away the tears. I hadn't even realised my face was wet. I'm immediately embarrassed and apologise. I feel like I've been crying non-stop for years.

'That's quite a voice you've got,' he says, changing the subject. He must have heard me singing in the shower. And the song choices, could I have sounded more tragic?

'Oh, erm, I was practising my two-octave pitch. For tomorrow. I'm not the manic depressive you probably think I am. Despite what you've heard me sing. And say. And do.'

Sweet baby Jesus.

Our eye contact suddenly feels a bit intense, so I clear my throat and reach for my wine glass. I've demolished the bottle, and there's only a thimbleful left.

'Finish it,' he says, smiling.

'You've not roofied it to sex-traffic me off, have you?' I ask, trying to lighten the mood.

Sex again? Honestly, what is wrong with me?

'Anyway. I shouldn't really drink so much the night before a performance,' I say, slightly embarrassed at the irony. 'Not when I am under strict instructions to impress the "music guys" Nancy is working with. Though, from what I've seen, the place is full of drunks who'd be happy with any old shite.' I'm babbling. 'No offence, but there's no culture here. How can I put it without sounding too...'

'Judgemental?'

'Yes. But you must know what I mean.'

Matteo tilts his head. 'It's a wonder you came all this way.'

'Well, I wouldn't have if I wasn't so desperate. For a classically trained singer with a wide vocal range like mine, this is so beneath me, but I'll never set foot in the place again after this week. No offence.'

Please shut up now.

'Sorry. That came out wrong. It's the alcohol. I just mean someone like me doesn't belong somewhere like this. I'm not that sort of entertainer.'

'And what sort of entertainer are you?'

The wounded animal type.

'Oh, I guess you could say I'm...' A full minute goes by as I stare wildly around for inspiration. In the end, I look Matteo square in the eye. I might as well be honest about this too. 'I don't know. I really don't know. I can sing, but I have no voice. Does that make sense?'

Part of me is now relieved that I'm not out binge-drinking with the Dollz if this is the way I behave, and just as I wonder what they are up to, I hear an almighty commotion going on. A thunderous clacking of heels against ceramic tiles is accompanied by much hooting and cackling.

'I should go,' he says quickly.

I blink slowly, realising how much I've enjoyed his company. He's as good as any therapist I've seen. And a million times better-looking. Something in the way he stands up and shakes the hair from his eyes draws me in like a magnet. He's magnificent. He rakes a hand casually through his hair. Of course he does. He checks his phone before putting it back in his shorts pocket. He's about to leave.

'Hey, I was wondering... If you're not doing anything tomorrow night,' I say, emboldened by the wine as I put my hand out to stop him from clearing away the plates, 'perhaps you might want to pop by The Jolly Roger if you want to hear me sing something more upbeat than shower ballads?'

I allow him approximately one nanosecond to respond before my deep-rooted insecurity takes over.

'Only if you're not doing something better. Of course you'll be doing something better. In fact, absolutely don't come. It'll be shit.' I roll my eyes theatrically. 'Total waste of time. A musical black hole. Not even real music, really. Forget I mentioned it.'

For the love of God, girl, stop talking.

Matteo sounds confused. 'Okay.'

That hardly helps. Is that a yes or a no?

We are distracted by a thunderous roar. The Dollz are

yelling for Enreeky as though he comes with the place and is just standing around waiting like a human Alexa. I quickly turn off the music and dim the lights.

'They've been boozing all day,' I explain. I am such a hypocrite, but all that wine has made me incredibly nosy, so I beckon Matteo to follow me, and we creep down the path and open the gate just wide enough to peek through. The girls are staggering around by the pool until Cherry suddenly remembers something. They instantly forget all about Enreeky because they simply must dance. Immediately. Like their lives depend on it.

'Enreeky?' Matteo whispers. Our cheeks are almost touching as we crouch down.

'Nacho,' I murmur. 'The guy we are renting the villa from. He's insanely hot.'

'So I've heard.'

Our lips are hovering ridiculously close. For a magical second, I think he's going to lean in and kiss me before I realise something very important. It's me who is doing the leaning. Me. My lips are pursing, plumping themselves up, ready to make first contact. I feel like a giddy teen.

It's the wine. Far too much wine.

His eyes widen when he sees what my lips are doing. I should tell him they are acting independently of the main body, but I don't get the chance.

'You filthy shower of bastarding whores!' shouts Tash above the music now blasting out from the main house. With the magical spell broken, my lips make a hasty retreat. I don't even have time to feel suitably mortified because something must have gone terribly wrong in the last two seconds while we were, let's say *whispering*, because the truth of what just happened and him looking slightly horrified must never be acknowledged. I will erase it from my brain and get on with my life as though the moment simply never occurred.

'I fucking *love* the lot of you!' Tash screams, and suddenly there's lots of hugging. 'Best friends *forever*!'

'Listen!' Liberty shushes them all. I hope they haven't heard us. 'Even though I'm full of drink right now, I want you all to know... that we are...' Liberty is hanging by a thread. Emotions are getting the better of her. 'We are best friends *forever*!'

'I literally just said that,' Tash says, sounding annoyed.

'Did you?'

Next thing, all the girls are parading round the pool just like a fashion show. Matteo and I exchange a dubious look as the girls strut dangerously close to the pool edge, left hands on hips, right arms swinging in perfect formation. As drunk as they are, I have to admit it is pretty impressive. Until, that is, Big Mand catches the back of Cherry's sandal mid-clomp and sends her crashing into the pool with a loud thwack. Some hair extensions float to the surface of the water without the owner attached, followed by a cigarette butt and what looks like a couple of round bread buns. Matteo stares at them, baffled.

'Chicken fillets,' I whisper, wondering when Cherry is going to emerge. A sandal floats to the surface while the girls carry on with their dance moves, quite oblivious.

Matteo slides his eyes towards me, muttering, 'Jesus Christ, I'll have to jump in and get her.' But at that moment, Cherry splutters to the surface and doggy-paddles over to the steps.

'Good job I didn't drown. My poor kids. Their baby daddy is fucking useless.' She climbs out and slaps her soaking wet handbag onto the side. 'But I love being a mother. It's a real privilege. I hope they're okay without me.' Cherry wrings out some water from her hair and kicks off the remaining sandal. 'Wherever they are.'

Above the music blasting across the pool area, we hear an unpleasant choking sort of sound. Big Mand says she's going to be sick and could someone quickly hold her hair back for her as she'd had it imported from China. Chinese virgins, to be exact, and she can't afford to replace it.

We watch the scene unfold with a mix of morbid fascination. No one fancies the job of holding back such precious and expensive, bum-grazing hair, and Big Mand is understandably upset. 'I've held everyone's hair tonight when you've all been hurling chunks, and now that it's my turn, how *dare* no one do it for me.'

'I'll do it,' says Big Sue reluctantly as a row breaks out about the communal bathroom and how Big Mand isn't allowed to be sick in there as it's a shared area. In the end, Big Mand emits a quease-inducing, strangled sound and throws up on the patio in front of everyone, before Big Sue can lunge across to get her hair to safety.

'It must have been a dodgy cocktail.' Big Mand wipes her mouth on her arm.

'Or maybe it was that kebab you bought from the man on the bike?' Big Sue suggests.

'Kebab?' This is news to Big Mand. She removes her soiled hairpiece and holds it up.

'There's lumps in it!' Cherry and Liberty shriek, instantly throwing up in unison.

'You ate food, Big Mand?' roars Tash incredulously. 'While out drinking?' Tash's face is twisted into an ugly scowl. 'Can everyone just stop throwing up, please? You selfish fuckers!' She is hobbling around unsteadily. I notice her ankle is ballooning out over the tight strap of her high-heeled platform stilettos. It has gone an angry purple colour.

'Twerk!' screams Cherry, and everyone suddenly starts

twerking, instantly forgetting how outraged they were mere moments ago. I sense Matteo trying not to snigger next to me. He rolls his eyes, and I feel a faint gust of butterflies in my stomach. It appears that he too is happy to draw a veil over the incident with my lips.

The twerking is interrupted by Big Mand slipping in a pool of vomit and landing heavily onto the tiles. Big Sue runs to see if she is okay, slips too and lands on top of her.

'My arm! It's broken!' shouts Big Mand, sounding in real agony but still managing to hold her burning ciggie aloft and out of harm's way.

'I'll get you something for the pain,' volunteers Tash, making her way to the kitchen. She waves a bottle of tequila at her. 'Ice and lemon, Big Mand?'

'Yes, but ring an ambulance. Call 123 or whatever it is in Spain,' she wheezes.

Tash nods, taking charge. 'Good idea. I'll get the shot glasses and the salt first though, hun. And I'll do a quick wee in case the paramedics are quite fit. I imagine they will be, in those uniforms. In fact, I might get changed.'

This is not her finest hour.

Matteo shakes his head in disbelief. Suddenly it seems that the girls can no longer hear or see Big Mand lying by the pool or remember quite what happened as they stampede into the house, easily leaving her behind. Then all hell breaks loose in the kitchen when the discovery is made that there are no lemons. Suddenly, I hear my name, and Matteo and I both freeze.

'Where the fuck is Connie with the lemons?'

'Connie? Connie who?' asks Liberty, sounding genuinely mystified. And literally, two minutes later, they've all stampeded off to bed. Even Big Mand manages to haul herself up using only one arm to trail drunkenly behind them yelling that she's okay, she just needs to sleep it off.

'Sleep what off?' Tash yells back.

'I can't remember,' replies Big Mand, stubbing her cigarette out on the patio before she goes inside. She must also have forgotten that she needs an ambulance.

The whole house falls silent. Matteo and I wait a few minutes to make sure no one is lurking around downstairs. Just as we make a move to go, a burning smell drifts over to us, accompanied by a sizzling sound.

'Jesus Christ, the hair. It's on fire!' Like a whippet, Matteo darts over and kicks the burning hairpiece into the pool, quickly checking nothing else is going to go up in flames. I dread to think what Big Mand will make of that in the morning.

With his hands on his hips, he looks over to where I'm hovering by the gap in the wall. He lets out a huge, bewildered sigh.

'Goodnight, Connie.'

I wait to see if he asks me for my number, but he doesn't. Of course he won't ask for my number. Why would he? He's completely not attracted to me sexually or otherwise. I pull my dressing gown tightly round me.

'Well, goodnight then, Matteo.'

He gives me a lingering look that fills me full of flutters before he disappears off round the far side of the pool to avoid all the patches of sick. I hear the click of the front gate shutting and the quiet rumble of his old-lady scooter as he drives off.

8

The next morning, I awake feeling a bit tender, despite having had the best sleep of my life thanks to all the wine and those painkillers. I ease out of my four-poster bed like a gazelle (a slightly injured one, perhaps from a run-in with a moody-but-handsome lion with a great mane of glossy hair and eyes you could get hopelessly lost in) and head out into the sunshine on my private patio to enjoy a coffee.

Flashbacks of Matteo being all gallant, calling the doctor, fetching me pizza and saving us all from the villa burning down put me in the mood for being creative. I'm surprised to feel a slight thrill in the pit of my stomach at not knowing if he'll come and see me perform later.

After an hour of writing lyrics and rehearsing melodies, I'm pleased to discover it's just like riding a bike. Next, I consider going over my set list, but there's still no sound from the main house, and I will definitely wake them up if I start singing, even from this distance. The mere thought of Matteo coming to see me sing on stage brings on a heady sensation and for the first time I feel excited about it. Checking the time, I decide to go for a run before I start panicking about the gig tonight. I'll jog past the venue so I know where it is, and I'll also jog past some shops to see if there's an outfit that might be better than the ones I've packed. Ged and Liam are right. Maybe it is time to add a little sparkle to my act.

I set off from the villa, in the opposite direction to the supermarket, and discover that we are not far from the beachfront. I run the complete length of Benidorm promenade from end to end. My body is soaking up the sun, the heat penetrating right to my bones, healing my back and making me feel strong and healthy as I weave in and out of the early walkers dotting the wide pedestrianised path. The bustling cafés, British bars with their Union Jack flags and towering hotels overlooking the sandy beach become a blur until I reach the cobbled lanes of the Old Town, and I discover that the narrow lanes lead through to another crescent-shaped beach. It has a quaint marina lined with palm trees and is virtually deserted.

I take in a deep lungful of fresh salty air and set off at a much faster pace to really push myself. I feel my pulse racing and adrenaline flowing through my veins. My thoughts turn back to my performance tonight. I must channel this positive energy and rethink my song list. Nancy was adamant about the happy songs. I must try and make a good first impression on the patrons of Benidorm. And one patron in particular.

Just as I reach the end of the beach, I notice a jogger running towards me. He is extremely athletic and, as he comes closer into view, he seems familiar. For a split second, I panic. I recognise the dark hair, the perfectly tanned, lean torso and those biceps pumping up and down like pistons. It's Matteo, and he's about to see me all sweaty and dishevelled instead of poised and elegant on stage this evening. I become immediately flustered.

What should I say? What should I do?

I am suddenly reminded of our non-kiss moment and the startled look in his eyes. I make a snap decision to play it cool. After all, he did make it very clear that he is not, I repeat *not*, sexually attracted to me. Not in the slightest. Nor did he ask for my number, which I'm pretty sure, along with spelling it out verbally, is also very much a sign of non-attraction. So why, in the name of all that is holy, do I find myself waving and shouting to get his attention?

'*Buenos dias, señor!*'

Why? Why am I yelling in Spanish? I may as well be bellowing, 'Over here! Come and get it, big boy!'

As what little confidence I have deserts me, I'm about to turn around and run as fast as I can in the opposite direction out of sheer mortification when I recognise the jogger is Nacho and not Matteo. They are so very similar, except Nacho is a good few inches shorter and in no way as alluring. It's the moodiness of a man's eyes that can draw you hopelessly in. I find, anyway. I try to clear my mind of last night and that lingering look.

Clearly still concussed.

I'm all of a kerfuffle, so I try hard not to stare at Nacho's tanned arms and legs pounding along the sand, nor to pay any attention to his tight-fitting shorts that hug his thighs in such a perfect way, and I'm certainly not going to get all het up just because he's not wearing a top and reminds me terribly of Matteo. When we finally reach each other, Nacho asks how I am.

In a state of raging hormonal collapse would be putting it mildly.

'How are you enjoying the villa?'

As I double over, panting, I decide not to tell him that his pool area is covered in vomit, scorch marks, fag ends and stray bits of Chinese virgin hair or that Cherry's sandal has sunk to the bottom of the pool or that there's a new burn in his rug. To be honest, my linguistic skills are simply not up to it.

'Lovely. It's really lovely.'

'Coffee?' Nacho points to a sweet little café at the side of the beach.

'Sure, why not?'

I'm sure the song lists and the costumes can wait a few minutes longer. As we walk, I ask Nacho all about his life and what he does. He answers in a mix of both English and Spanish and, nodding in all the right places, I listen, enthralled, to how well travelled he is, how many adventures he has been on and his plans for the property-developing business he owns with his brother. It is so impressive compared to me, even though we are about the same age. Thankfully, he doesn't ask any questions about me at all, so I am spared the embarrassment of admitting that I have done very little with my life. Nothing at all, actually. Nothing.

'My brother is the good-looking, clever one.' He tuts. 'He has many businesses.'

I stare at him in disbelief.

'It's true.' He laughs, clocking my expression. 'I have achieved nothing compared to him. He is very about the work, you know? All work and no play? Very serious.'

If Nacho is a walking detonator that makes all the ovaries in the near vicinity explode as soon as he ambles through the café door, I'd hate to imagine the effect his brother would have. Even as we chat, he's attracting glances from literally everyone. And every female seems to know him, so every few words he has to stop and kiss people on the cheek and take selfies with them. He proudly tells me about his many, many followers on Instagram and encourages me to check out his stories.

By the time we reach the point in the conversation about how many hours a day he works out, how many days he fasts per week to maintain zero body fat and his love of dangerous-sounding water sports, I really must go. He insists that we take a selfie with our coffees for his Instagram.

'I'll see you later,' he shouts as I race away from the café. 'For the big show and the dancing!'

Oh no. I forgot I told him about The Jolly Roger. I need to stop inviting every dreamboat I come across to the show tonight.

I pick up speed as I run back along the beach, imagining both Nacho and Matteo watching me sing from the front row while I belt out soulful anthems at them, drawing them in with my ability to go from soprano to baritone in a blink. They will be enthralled by my vocal range and then fight like gentlemen to take me out on a date. I haven't been on a date in years. Back through the bustling, narrow, cobbled, restaurant-crammed lanes of the Old Town, I remind myself that this trip is a spiritual journey to connect with my inner voice, not a spiritual journey to connect my pelvis to every hot guy I come across. But by the time I reach our villa, covered in sweat from head to toe, I am *buzzing*.

* * *

The main house is still completely silent as I walk quietly round the pool, taking in the clinging smell of vomit now the sun is rising high in the sky and the heat has begun to build. If they don't clean it up, it will become unbearable and so caked on we will probably have to pay for it to be cleaned out of Nancy's deposit. I pick up all of the abandoned bags, shoes, bras and hairpieces that were left behind last night and put them on the table near the patio. As the door suddenly slides open, Tash appears, squinting at me. I take in her crumpled face. She has a fake eyelash stuck to her forehead, mascara down her cheeks and hair all over the place.

'What have you been up to?' she asks suspiciously.

'Jogging,' I say. 'It's good for my breathing. You know, holding the notes?'

Tash stares blankly at me.

'Anyway, I bumped into Nacho,' I say, trying to hide my flushed cheeks. 'And he's coming to see us tonight.'

'Who?'

'Enreeky.'

Tash bristles. 'You've been out with Enreeky? Without telling us?'

'No. Well, yes. I mean not out out. Just a coffee. I've also been picking up all of your stuff from the pool area,' I say, steering away from the subject. 'Although, I think Cherry might have to dive down to the bottom of the pool to get her sandal back.'

She stops, confused, and for a moment I wonder if she remembers my alarming disappearance from the previous day. She has yet to enquire.

'Great night though, wasn't it?'

'Great night?' I echo in disbelief.

'Yeah,' she says simply, giving me a vacant, questioning stare.

Really?

'Remember when I started dry-humping Sister Kevin while he was trying to eat his curry and chips? They went everywhere,' she recalls happily. Poor fella. It sounds more like assault to me.

Her face changes to a frown as her short-term memory

returns in full and she goes on to say that Liberty was fingered at the bar and asks me if I thought that was bang out of order. I genuinely think it is, so I act all outraged. I wonder if the police were called. I'm pretty sure they'd take an unsolicited fingering very seriously.

Tash purses her lips. 'I know! She'd already been with the Mother Superior. She's just greedy. I mean, Liberty by name and liberty by friggin' nature. Mind, we did have a very loud falling-out over it.' She screws her eyes at me. 'I think, anyway.'

I'm not sure how to react to that. 'It's been an intense twenty-four hours, what with your swollen ankle, Big Mand's arm, Cherry almost drowning, the fire, the constant fingering and those photos of your gash all over Facebook,' I say.

I could go on. In fact, I think I will.

'And we haven't even started rehearsing for tonight's show. I mean, we should at least go down to The Jolly Roger to do a soundcheck this morning. Make sure they have all the equipment set up where we want it. We don't want to show up at the last minute to find nothing works.'

Bit rich coming from the girl who set off this morning to do just that and forgot all about it the instant a six-pack was put in front of her.

'Good idea.' Tash stops halfway to a sunbed, glances up from her phone and sighs dramatically. 'Oh no. Oh no, no, no.'

Christ almighty, what now?

'It's my phone. I forgot to plug it in last night. It's only on 2 per cent. I'll have to go back to bed and wait for it to charge up. We'll do the run-through at the bar later. I promise.'

Who forgets to charge their phone? I experience a pang of pre-stage nerves and pat my pocket. All of my backing tracks are stored on my phone. Forgetting to charge it would be like a surgeon forgetting to clamp a main artery or a bomb-disposal expert forgetting to take his clippers.

It takes the girls another hour to get up and lounge by the pool. I am already swimming lengths, powering up and down with Big Sue, who has also promised that we will rehearse later, once the whole band is together.

Cherry wanders over. 'This place stinks. Look at all that sick.'

'It's a disgrace. That's what it is,' says Liberty, plonking herself down onto the sunbed. 'Someone needs to clean it up.'

Big Mand approaches with a frown on her face. I expect she will volunteer to clean it up. After all, she did start it.

'I've just remembered,' she says to Big Sue. 'Who I was trying to think of last night. It's Aquaman. You remind me of Aquaman,' she says. 'You've got incredible definition.'

Big Sue blushes.

And the pools of your vomit? Any thoughts about them?

Big Mand grabs a lilo and slips into the pool, playfully splashing Big Sue every time she tries to climb on. They seem oblivious to the unbearable stench.

'It will take ages to clean the vomit off the patio now you've let it dry like that,' I point out uneasily. 'And it smells awful. You really should clean it up as soon as possible.'

I am met with an eerie silence, but I think I have made my point. Big Mand raises her sunglasses in an accusatory manner. Liberty does the same, her lips billowing out from her face. I wish I hadn't bothered. A massive row breaks out between them all as to who had actually thrown up, ending with everyone denying it and glaring at me as if I had been the culprit.

I give up.

I spot a hose nearby and think I may as well hose the tiled

pool area down and try to get the worst of it up. It is mostly a collection of blue, green and yellow puddles. After half an hour's back-breaking work, I have finally managed to sloosh all of the sick into the drains away from the pool. Not one of them offers to help. I ask if we can talk about the song choices for the show so that we have no clashes, but the girls are so hungover that they can't be bothered. Tash has emerged from her bedchamber with a bottle of Prosecco in each hand, announcing she needs to hydrate to get rid of her hangover.

'But you could go to the shop and get more lemons,' she adds. 'You obviously didn't get enough yesterday. Be a love and bring some glasses out, will you?'

I am baffled to find myself trotting to the kitchen to fetch them. *Why?*

'Yeah, get me a pack of Fantas as well while you're there, Connie, love!' shouts Liberty from her sunlounger.

'All that fingering must have brought on quite the thirst, has it?' snipes Tash.

'I'll need some painkillers, so can you pop to the chemist too? Gerrem extra strong, hun. Me yarm smarts a bit.' Big Mand shows us her swollen arm, which is black and blue. It looks horrendous. Like a giant inflated sausage with a lump in it. I've no degree in medicine, but that is definitely broken.

'How did that happen?' Liberty asks as I hand the glasses around.

'Dunno,' Big Mand replies in a baffled tone. 'But I'll just self-medicate through it until we get back home. At least it's not me pulling arm. I've got to deliver a set of triplets when I get back. I hope it's not a forceps, or I'm buggered.' Her glass is quickly filled with Prosecco to soothing murmurs of appreciation. No one can be bothered with a medical drama this morning.

'Big Mand? What did the magazine say we should use as a dark tan accelerator? Was it butter?'

'No, I think it was base-coat olive oil for a sun glow or coconut oil for a deep mahogany. Or the other way round. I've done both just in case. Found some in the kitchen.'

'Connie, can you get more oil too, please?'

I swim to the edge, ignoring Liberty, who is clearly mistaking me for the hired help. 'Doesn't anyone want to come with me to The Jolly Roger to do a soundcheck?'

I am met with complete silence as they lie on the loungers, eyes closed, pretending they haven't heard me. Not one of them moves a muscle. As the silence grows, I get a pitiful look from Big Sue before she disappears underwater to do her Olympic-type flip turn, swims back to the other end and heads for the last sunlounger. I'm still amazed that no one has even asked where my room is. As I get out of the pool ten minutes later, I realise that the girls, awake and out of bed for less than thirty minutes, are flat-out asleep and snoring on their loungers. There is no bloody way I am going to the shop again after what happened yesterday.

My mind drifts to Matteo. I find myself absent-mindedly wondering what would have happened if we'd kissed. He has very kissable lips and dark, longish hair that would be great to tangle my fingers in, if only it was on someone not quite so unattracted to me. He was very quick to leave last night without so much as an attempt to keep in touch. That's the second deeply meaningful experience we have shared and, once again, it has passed him completely by.

I shake the thought of him from my mind. Now is not the time to get distracted. There are only nine hours left until the gig and I must sort out the playlist, find something nice to wear and think of some way of connecting with the audience so that they find me bearable to watch. I'll head to The Jolly Roger and do the soundcheck first. Nancy is probably expecting me, as the headline act, to take the reins and lead by example.

My phone pings. It's a message from Nacho asking me if I fancy going cliff diving this afternoon.

I really shouldn't. But I'd hate to offend our host. And politeness costs nothing. But the gig is the important thing here. I must prioritise. Although, time management is one of my superpowers, I suppose. And I probably do need to experience something thrilling if I am to bring a bit of sparkle to my act. And show Matteo a different side to me.

Cliff diving sounds so adventurous and sexy and totally in keeping with my new image... as long as it doesn't involve actual cliffs or diving.

9

I quickly text Nacho back, agreeing to meet him at the beach in an hour. I throw some concealer over my eye bruise and water-proof mascara on my lashes and finish with a slick of pink gloss on my lips. I change into my sensible bikini, throw on some denim shorts, a vest top and flip-flops and make my way stealthily out of the house. I edge round the pool area so as not to disturb the girls. They are still asleep on their sunbeds and look boiled. Like lobsters. As in blisters will follow if they don't wake up soon. They have fully committed to their *girls just wanna have sun* policy. I sneak past and contemplate waking them.

But then I remember earlier, when I cleared up their sick without so much as a thank you and yesterday when I went to the supermarket for them and none of them questioned why I never returned, and, oh, they forgot to take me out with them last night for the big game of 'Tash or Gash'. And so I decide it might be best to just leave them where they are rather than invite them cliff diving. At the gate, my conscience gets the better of me. Glancing back at the girls baking in the sun, I nip into the kitchen and put the cooker timer on to wake them up in ten minutes. I slide out of the gate and close it quietly behind me.

On the pavement outside the villa, I casually pile my hair up on my head and put on my sunglasses, feeling lean and athletic. Just as I head down to the beach, I hear the familiar rumble of a lady scooter pull up behind me. Goosebumps immediately prickle my arms. Matteo is astride the moped, long, lean legs akimbo, helmet slung casually under his arm as though he's posing for a magazine shoot. I immediately go to pieces as though he knows I've been thinking about him all morning. Imagining what might have happened had I leaned in a bit further and kissed him last night.

'Hi,' he says, his face giving nothing away. 'Thought I'd come check on the patient. Make sure you are okay.'

Something about him rattles me and sets me immediately on edge. I'm not sure if it's his overpowering masculinity or what, but he simply oozes whatever it is. He runs a hand through his hair, which I find utterly mesmerising, and when he drops his eyes from the loose bun in my hair slowly to the bright coral nail varnish on my toes, I feel shivers down my body as though he's run his hand lightly over me.

I gulp, dumbstruck.

Try to be normal. Stop gawping. Do not, I repeat, do not look at his legs, his strong arms or his crotch.

'Off anywhere nice?' he asks, sounding as awkward as I feel. I take in his strong jawline and sultry full-lipped mouth. He's stunning. He has lashes to die for, curling up towards perfectly shaped eyebrows, which are currently forming a frown. He repeats the question to snap me out of my staring at him like an obsessive stalker.

'Oh, no,' I say. 'Not really. I'm...'

Yes, what am I *doing?*

'Going to practise for your gig tonight?'

I lick my lips, which have gone dry all of a sudden. 'Yes. I mean, no. No, I'm actually going to go cliff diving with, erm, the guy who rents this place to us. He asked... so...'

I'll have to leave that sentence hanging. I took off without a place to land.

Matteo's eyes widen. 'Nacho? You're going out with Nacho? Seriously?'

I frown back at him. He's making him sound like a serial killer. 'Interesting that you're leading with that and not the cliff diving. Nacho a friend of yours?'

Matteo bristles and goes to put his helmet back on, stopping briefly. 'If you're off cliff diving then you must be fully recovered. Enjoy your date. And good luck with your performance tonight.'

Before I even have a chance to respond, he speeds off. The brief encounter occupies my thoughts all the way down to the beach. I feel disappointed that it didn't go better. And while I'd love to imagine that he seemed a little jealous, it certainly sounded like he wouldn't be coming to see me sing later. I try to put him from my mind as I approach Nacho, who lets out a low wolf-whistle, playfully making out that he's swooning over my appearance. You'd think I would go to pieces if an incredibly handsome and impressively vain man showed an interest, but all I can think of is how annoyed Matteo seemed. I summon up a cute grin for Nacho, who takes me over to a large group of beautiful people and introduces me.

'This is Connie. She is a singer. I have rescued her from this crazy group of girls I have rented the villa to,' he says, showing them a picture of the Dollz on Instagram.

Because I rarely think things through when I'm nervous,

when they ask how I've enjoyed Spain so far, I blurt out that I've been cleaning up their vomit and picking up their bags and hair all morning. Nacho looks appalled but the rest of the group laugh, calling me Cenicienta.

I must look puzzled because he explains: 'They are calling you Cinderella.'

* * *

The next two hours are among the most terrifying of my entire existence. Nacho and his friends climb repeatedly up a rock face and hurl themselves into the deep turquoise sea without a care in the world. Climb, squeal, plunge, repeat. It is horrific, and I am in danger of having a fatal heart attack just watching. Nacho emerges from the sea like James Bond and swaggers over to me.

'Your turn,' he says, holding out his hand.

I shake my head politely. 'There are many other ways I'd prefer to die, thanks.'

Nacho honks with laughter and pulls me reluctantly to my feet. He drags me over to the rocks and the crowd insist on me climbing up with them. I get to the piece of jutting-out rock and peer over the top to the sea below.

'No. No thanks. Not for me,' I say. I may as well be standing at the top of the Empire State Building. There's no way on earth that… *Aaaaaarrrrrrggggghhhhh!*

The bastard pushed me, is my last and only thought before I hit the sea, which feels like bloody concrete breaking every bone in my body. I plunge down almost to the seabed before I hover suspended in the water. I open my eyes and catch a glimpse of brightly coloured fish swarming around the rocks a few metres in front of me, before I'm thrust back towards the surface in a cloud of bubbles, crashing into the sunlight and gasping for air. Adrenalin blasts through me like an electric current.

What a rush!

'Again,' I yell, swimming back towards them. 'Again!'

I am *dying* to tell the Dollz what I've been doing. I am all but floating back to the villa having added cliff diving to my list of all-time favourite hobbies. I sent Ged and Liam a selfie of Nacho and me posing on the jutting rock with the sea far, far below. I got an instant aubergine and winking emoji back. They have little respect for comfort zones and personal achievements. As I pass by the supermarket from yesterday, I hesitate just a fraction before I swing in to buy some fresh bread, Fanta for Liberty, crisps, paracetamol for Big Mand and lemons for Tash. There's an annoying part of me that really wants the Dollz to like me. When I reach the villa, I am amazed to find no one there. The whole place is empty, and I try not to feel too deflated that they've abandoned me *again* as I put the shopping away.

I have a few minutes relaxing in the sun, thinking of Matteo and his dark moody eyes and his excellent manners and firm, muscular body. I wonder what he would make of my cliff-diving adventure. I spend some time trying to track him down on social media, searching Nacho's Instagram first before I comb the internet with every combination of 'fit, shredded, hot guys in Benidorm'. Before I know it, I am lost in a frenzy of searching for him on Tinder.

A short while later, I hear music filter through from the main house and cries of 'The Chop'. I race through to witness the girls drawing back their hips and thrusting them forward. Tash sits back down as her leg is disappearing into an angry purple pumpkin. I can't help but feel concerned.

'Tash, are you sure that ankle is okay? I know a doctor who might look at it.'

'No thanks, babes,' she says flatly. 'It's gone completely numb anyway and the shoes I have for tonight don't have straps, so I'll still get them on. The show must go on, as they say. Yaaay!'

Before I can say anything, Big Mand, who is clutching her blue arm, the bruising clearly visible against her brown skin, yells over to me that she doesn't need a doctor either as her arm is numb too. I give her the paracetamol and receive a slight nod in thanks. From somewhere, more Prosecco is produced.

'Should you... erm, shouldn't we be rehearsing and going over our song choices?' I say, acutely aware that I haven't got round to my own yet. 'Or at least testing the equipment out beforehand?'

I am met with several frowns as they continue pouring out drinks. 'So!' Liberty squeals excitedly, her face lighting up as she waves her phone around. 'The nuns have invited us to join them for prinks at their villa before we hit The Jolly Roger later!'

Tash rolls her eyes and says bitterly, 'We're not going if you just disappear off to get yourself fingered as soon as we get there.'

Liberty's face drops, making it obvious that this was her exact plan. 'I feel like the Mother Superior's really into my vibe though,' she says. 'We had a real connection, you know.'

'We know you had a connection. His hand, up your fanny,' Tash says, clearly unimpressed. This is met with giggles from the rest of the girls.

'Fingering? When did that make a comeback?' brays Cherry. 'It's like checking a camel's teeth before buying it at market. How many dinars are you worth?'

'More than he can afford,' says Liberty, brightening. 'It'll be free drinks, though.'

'Okay,' says Tash reluctantly over the cheering. 'What time?'

'Six o'clock, they said. I think their villa isn't that far from here. They dropped us the location.'

This is ridiculous. 'We don't have time for the nuns,' I say. 'It's nearly six o'clock now. We have to get sorted for—'

'Connie,' Tash says forcefully. 'Stop worrying about the gig. We'll rehearse at the nuns' villa. We'll have plenty of time. Just make sure you look the part though, eh? That's the most important thing.'

'Yeah, it's not what you sing, it's *how* you sing,' says Big Sue.

'But mostly how you look though, yeah?' says Liberty.

'And how you dance around,' adds Cherry. 'Always keep on the move and they'll not notice how terrible you look or sound.'

They stampede back off upstairs full of giggles and tales of see-through tops and spray-on glitter clothing for their spectacular, showstopping opening extravaganza on The Strip. I stand rigid for a full minute after they've gone. I am so far out of my comfort zone. I down my Prosecco in one gulp and make my way nervously back to the cottage in a daze.

Why did I waste the day cliff diving? Why?

I'd had very little time to pack and feel panicked as I rifle through what few clothes I have and pull out some black denim shorts, a black bra and a mesh black vest top that I'm pretty sure Liam must have sneaked in there, wishing for the first time ever that I had some leg tattoos to brighten it up. It seems incredibly daring for a stage outfit, so I grab a little cardigan to throw over the top. I look like I'm about to go skateboarding with a load of teens. I strip off and rummage through the case until I find my standard-issue black dress. It's a no-nonsense, knee-length number perfect for all occasions. There'll be no dramas, no wardrobe malfunctions; it is literally disaster-proof. A shout from the main house is inviting me for slammers. I make my way unsteadily to the kitchen in my high criss-cross strappy sandals – my nod to a sexier Benidorm style. I think I'll get away with them if I don't move a muscle on stage.

As I reach the kitchen, I am greeted by a blaze of colour. My jaw drops. Surely this is a joke? I'm sure it's the law that glitter is only acceptable if you are either starring in a *Vogue* photo shoot or you are eight years old. Some of the girls have opted for brightly coloured see-through fishnet tops that reveal not just a hint of nipple but nipple piercings and underboob as well. They've all opted for bum-cheek reveal and heavy make-up to hide their sunburnt faces.

I clip-clop through the patio doors.

'Oh my God. Who died?' Liberty says dryly.

I smooth the fabric down self-consciously. I might have known this would be their reaction. 'No one, obviously. This is what serious... Wait, have you just glued glitter and rhinestones over your bare breasts?' I'm distracted by the strapless bikini sprayed across Liberty's chest.

'We want to make a good first impression,' she tells me. 'So you can take that judgemental look off your face.'

'I'm not, it's not... I don't think,' I say, struggling to deny it. 'I just thought...'

I'm not sure what I thought. I've seen their videos, all of them dressed in provocative underwear on stage, but this, this takes it to a whole new level.

'I don't have the abs for that sort of outfit.'

Liberty purses her lips. 'You definitely do.'

Tash sashays in wearing a spectacular silver snakeskin catsuit that also looks sprayed on. On closer inspection, it is indeed sprayed on. She twangs an invisible piece of elastic which holds a minuscule silver thong in place. I marvel at the superior breasts bursting to be free of the tiny bra top stuck on with body glue.

'Industrial strength. I got it off the internet,' she says. 'It's illegal in most countries.'

'Ooh, givvuz summa that then, hun, for me nipple tips,' says Big Mand, enthusiastically taking the tube Tash is handing over.

'They'll *never* come off with that glue. It's used in shipping yards,' Tash boasts confidently.

I mean, they all look amazing, like extras in a Scandinavian sci-fi porn movie. I watch in awe as hundreds and hundreds of selfies, at all angles, are taken. It's the most smiling I've seen the girls do since we got here. Liberty shows the group her selfie, proudly zooming in. I marvel at the explicit image of her undercarriage and bum-cheek reveal.

'Very flattering. Huge thigh gap, babes. Amaze.'

'Great bum cheeks. So firm. Like a young boy.'

Silence descends as though they have just realised I'm still here. Tash examines my outfit and flicks her finger towards my dress. 'You're not going to be making any fashion headlines like that.' She frowns and flicks her finger upwards, indicating that I should hitch it up. 'What's with the who-died approach? You are so off-message, Connie. This sort of thing might work at a wake but not on stage in Benidorm.'

'It's a tribute gig, hun. You're supposed to be colourful and fun,' says Cherry. 'It's just too dowdy, babes. Too frumpy. You look like a woman who grows her own veg and uses her own poo as fertiliser.'

'I can't see any extra hairpieces. There's no glitter, no lashes and no tattoos,' says Big Mand, counting off her fingers.

'You do realise we *all* have to look the same? That's kind of the point? Sisterhood? We're essentially two halves of the same act,' says Tash.

'We'll need to redo you from top to bottom,' says Big Sue, brandishing a make-up brush.

I stand in silence to let the irony of their idea of 'sisterhood' wash over me, then against my better judgement I down two shots of tequila in rapid succession and let them at me.

Tash says, 'Try this, babes.'

I catch a slither of material being thrown in my direction. I hold it up. It's a brightly coloured Lycra hairband. I slide it over my forehead, slightly confused as to how this will be in any way transformational.

'That's one of my favourite dresses,' she announces.

Oh Christ.

'Now come here,' says Big Mand, coming at me with a can and some pots of glitter.

* * *

After a few minutes, they stand me in front of the mirror. I gasp. The girls have transformed me into a shiny, metallic, mythical, wood-fairy, nymph-type creature. I have face gems around my green eyes that make them seem huge and doll-like, and instead of looking foolish, they are very striking. My beachy, sun-kissed brown hair is swept over to one side, and sparkly thread is cleverly woven into a wide, ornate shoulder-grazing plait. They've given me a body tattoo in silvery blue glitter that snakes its way from my boob down my stomach to my knee. My arms have glitter armbands to match in blues and greens and my boob area has a sprinkling of purple glitter. I'm nothing if not colourful. Like a human bird of paradise wrapped in tinsel. That Lycra scrap of dress just about covers my nipples. It has a huge cut-out area to show off my new stomach tattoo and, like liquid, runs smoothly down my body to just about cover my crotch.

'Much better!' squeals Tash, obviously ecstatic that I'm now on-message and won't embarrass them all by hiding my lady parts and wearing too little glitter.

I am having difficulty breathing.

I may look incredible but there is no way on earth that I am leaving the house like this, never mind going on stage in front of people. I need to go and change immediately.

A beeping outside distracts me.

'Taxi's here! Let's go!' roars Big Sue like a drill sergeant. 'Go! Go! Go! Move it, people!'

Deep breaths.

Deep breaths.

10

As the beeping from the waiting taxi continues, the Dollz scramble around for bags, cigarettes, vapes, Greek yoghurt for sunburnt shoulders and hairspray, and my thoughts immediately fly to Matteo. What will he think if he sees me on stage like this? He'll think I'm ridiculous. I feel a panic attack coming on. I exhale slowly, chanting inside my head that I can take my black dress with me in my bag and change back before I go on stage. The Dollz will be too busy to stop me.

Talk turns to the nuns as we inch our way to the door.

'If I was single, I'd deffo go for Sister Hugh Huge Ones,' says Cherry, confiding in us that his arty tattoo sleeve makes her foof twang. Tash and Liberty confirm that a major minge twinge has also occurred in their lady bits too.

'I thought Sister Kevin was okay,' admits Tash. 'But he is a bit hairy for my liking. I am so *over* these hipster beards and the Jesus-waves they all have now.'

'I'm deffo getting off with the Mother Superior,' says Liberty, boldly staking her claim and receiving a cold glance from Tash.

'Actually, I'm not bothered which nuns I get off with,' Tash then decides easily. 'I'll be too drunk to tell them apart anyway.'

My stomach plummets. Another beep outside alerts us to Jorge waiting patiently to take us to the villa full of nuns. A feeling of dread overwhelms me. I quickly emergency WhatsApp Ged and Liam a photo of me and a screaming message saying there is no bloody way I can go on stage dressed like this.

Ged is the first to get back.

> You're very blue. You remind me of my favourite cocktail.

Liam says:

> Mermaidesque. Simply fabulous, fabulous, fabulous.

Easy for him to say. This is probably his dream outfit. He then messages:

> Are you all going in drag or just you?

Am I insane? What am I doing?

The minibus outside beeps for the third time.

'Maybe I should give the nuns' villa a miss and head straight to the venue for the soundcheck?'

They all glare at me.

'No way! We've gone to a lot of effort,' Tash says, giving me the once-over. 'It's a bloody miracle really. Come on, you'll have a great time. Like last night.' She winks a big, elaborately made-up eye at me. 'Right, babes?'

Where to begin?

I drag myself out to where Jorge is picking his jaw up off the floor. His eyes are out on stalks as they roam slowly over each of us in turn. To make matters worse, the girls are gyrating around and jiggling their boobs for him. He is so beyond excited that he can barely get the minibus started. It takes several attempts as his hands are shaking and he can't tear his eyes away from us to concentrate on getting the keys in the ignition.

Liberty gives him the address and his face drops instantly. He fixes us with pleading eyes. I understand why when we drive to the end of our street, turn the corner and come to a stop. We have arrived. The thirty-second journey is over. Jorge is gutted. He looks like a man who has just been told he owes a fortune in back tax. I hand over a five-euro note and tell him to keep the three euros change.

'*Quiet!* It's Nancy! *Nancy!*' Big Sue bellows as she holds up her phone. We listen to her make agreeing noises, her face serious. 'Excellent first impressions... yes, uh-huh, yep, sure, new clients, a lot at stake, yep, uh-huh, make sure that... miserable black robes?' Big Sue's head whips round to glare straight at me. 'No, definitely not. Happy songs, yep, no, yep, we will make sure of it, yes. No worries, Nancy. No worries.'

Big Sue lets out an enormous sigh.

'What did she say?' I ask.

She shrugs. 'Nothing much. Only that she's got a lot riding on our performance tonight and if we fuck it up, she'll come over and ram her Louboutins right up our flanges.'

I gulp.

'Oh, and Connie? She says stick to the happy songs tonight or she will kill you with her own bare hands.'

With my nerves on edge, we pile out of the minibus and into what I assume will be a monastic nightmare of biblical proportions. I am petrified that the Dollz will drink too much, we'll turn up late to the gig and have no clue what we're doing. It's all far too slapdash for my liking and once again I'm so far out of my comfort zone I could puke. The girls are all giggling nervously, which doesn't help.

The door swings open with a flourish, and Sister Kevin greets us with a loud, 'Fuck me!'

We all troop in. As we are ushered to the pool area, we are greeted by a group of twelve wide-eyed, open-mouthed nuns, some of whom drop their drinks as we walk through. I am trailing unenthusiastically at the back as Cherry roars, 'Slut Drop!'

Oh Christ.

We all drop professionally in perfect formation, rising tantalisingly slowly to a deafening cheer. The music is cranked up and suddenly, thanks to some impromptu pole dancing round a parasol by the Mother Superior, Liberty and Big Mand, the party is in full swing. All the girls are immediately approached by nuns fighting to light their cigarettes and fetch them drinks. I stand back with my hand on my hip, surveying the area. Now, where best to put myself so I'm out of harm's way and barely visible? Just as I am casting a wary eye around, a nun interrupts my surveillance. He has tucked the hem of his habit into his shorts. He is sweating with the heat, and he is as red as a tomato. I notice that most of his waist-length hair has done a runner down the back of his head, but he has wisely collected it into a ponytail for safekeeping. I can't help but wonder what his purpose might be in approaching me. I am giving off powerful 'Do *not*, under any circumstances, come forth and hither me' vibes.

'Hello there. Would... would you like a drink?' he asks nervously. I shake my head. I'll be keeping my wits about me tonight, thank you very much. 'Or would you prefer to get high? I know you girls and your fear of sugar.'

Sugar is the least of my concerns right now.

'No thanks. I have to perform on stage in a short while.'

'Perform?' he says, his eyes lighting up as though I'm going to pop out some ping-pong balls like Sticky Vicky.

Oh yes indeed. I did my due diligence the night before I flew out here, only to later regret it severely.

'I'm a singer. A sort of avant-garde, musical fusion of classical and spiritual but with a melancholic feel...'

'Oh,' he says, backing away with a look of disappointment. I might as well check over my backing tracks while the girls writhe around like they are auditioning to get into a Playboy Mansion pool party. They are having heaps of fun knocking back drink after drink.

My phone beeps with a message notification. I peer at the broken screen, which is getting worse as the day goes on. It's from Liam saying he hopes I'm having a good time and not moping by myself, refusing to join in the fun like some boring, stuck-up prima donna under a cloud of doom and gloom. Standing apart from everyone like this suddenly feels very lonely. Maybe I *should* worry less and join in a bit more, instead of standing here on my own. I edge a bit closer to the pool area where Tash is dancing with Sister Kevin.

'I love a man with a beard,' she says flirtatiously as she reaches out to play with his face. Noticing me lurking nearby, she suddenly barks at me, 'Connie, feel his beard!'

Luckily, I am saved from the embarrassment of declining as one of the nuns puts on a Beyoncé track and we all line up ready to do some formation dancing. The nuns are reacting as if we are putting on some major Las Vegas show and whooping and cheering like Americans.

I'm in bits wondering how long all of this is going to take.

'I'm a real woman's woman,' I hear Big Mand say. 'I much

prefer the company of a powerful, intelligent woman to a man. We're so much better at stuff, you know?'

Her making a stand for strong, independent women everywhere is just what I need. The nuns are encouragingly transfixed and agreeing with everything she says. It isn't until I reach the group that I notice her glitter top needs a touch-up. Both nipples are protruding from the faded glitter, having clearly lost their shipping-industry-strength stick-on tips, her boobs jiggling with each wave of her arm. I dig into my bag and root around for the glitter stick that Tash gave me for such emergencies. I hand it over to Big Mand and flick my eyes discreetly down to her nipples to indicate the reason for it. She'll be humiliated.

She follows my gaze and lets out a tinkling laugh that has the nuns mesmerised even further before she slowly opens the glitter stick and smoothly applies some sparkle. Every pair of eyes follow the stick round and round as Big Mand makes a huge sexual show of circling her nipples as she rubs the stick over them, cupping first one breast then the other. The nuns are open-mouthed and salivating. So is Big Sue.

'Mandeep! You big hooahh! Leave them poor bastards alone and make us all some of those cocktails, pet!' Liberty yells.

The nuns follow Big Mand over to the drinks bar like little ducklings. Elaborate cocktails are handed around to the girls, who are getting off their trollies. Everyone is dancing flirtatiously by the pool while a few of the nuns splash around, showing off.

Oh my fucking God. We should be at The Jolly Roger rehearsing by now and the Dollz are showing no signs of being even remotely bothered.

'I'm going to head over to the venue,' I shout over the music when I can't bear it any longer.

'No need,' yells Big Sue, checking her phone. 'Hoargghhhay is on his way. Just chill, will you, Connie?'

Suddenly there is a stampede to the toilets and much talk of touching up. As I queue outside the bathroom, I peer down at my appallingly skimpy outfit, thankful that I will soon be able to change back into my sober black dress rather than go on stage looking like a glitter bomb accidentally blew off all my clothes. We hear Jorge beeping his minibus impatiently outside, which creates a flurry of panic to hurry up.

When it's eventually my turn, I go into the bathroom to see if I can't somehow stretch a few more inches out of this dress. It would seem that I definitely can't. I'd desperately like to change now but as I hear the frantic beeping, I stuff my black safety dress back in my bag, quickly touch up my bright pink glossy lipstick and head back to the pool.

The first thing I notice is that it seems very quiet. The second thing to hit me is that there are no girls here. I cast my gaze frantically around as a dozen nuns turn in my direction.

My chest instantly tightens, and I struggle for air.

Deep breaths.

Deep breaths.

'You've just missed them,' says Sister Kevin, his voice full of surprise. 'But you're more than welcome to stay here with us. Isn't she, lads?'

I sweep my gaze across the twelve nuns, varying in shape and size, all roasting in the sun as they cast their drug-addled, boozy eyes towards me, hold their pints aloft and let out an enormous cheer.

I am literally going to have a heart attack.

11

I race out of the nuns' villa as though the place is on fire and head straight back to my cottage. With shaking hands, I wrench open the main gate to our villa. I can't fucking *believe* they've done this to me *again*. I mean, anything could have happened to me. *Anything.* Not to mention I'm going to be horrendously fucking late!

I need to take stock. I will google a taxi number and order one to come immediately. My lungs are billowing in my chest as I walk towards the pool. The Dollz are on stage before me, so I might even have time to change out of this ridiculous outfit, and I can take a moment to get into performance mode. I can do this.

Deep breaths.

Deep breaths.

I'm just rounding the corner when I see a large figure emerge from the pool. Our private pool. Our safe haven. I'm at the end of my tether with soaking wet, near-naked men every-where I go. His hands are clutching a sandal and a large clump of hair. Perhaps because I'm in a high state of stress, I let out a blood-curdling scream.

We lock eyes.

I keep screaming.

It's Nacho. Thank God. I've never felt so relieved to see anyone in my life, but he shakes his head disapprovingly. He waves the hair at me, saying in a disappointed tone, 'You will break the pool if you do things like this.'

'It wasn't me,' I protest, pressing my hand to my chest. 'It was the Dollz.' I really don't need these experiences. I've never screamed so much in my entire life as I have over the past two days.

'I thought you have singing performance tonight,' he asks.

'Yes,' I say in a rush. 'They left me. I need to ring a taxi. I'm late.' I point to the hair dripping water onto the tiles. 'I'll make sure that doesn't happen again.'

Nacho brightens, nodding to my outfit. 'Very blue, very small.'

After a minute of chit-chat, me explaining that I need to get changed, him insisting that there's no need, Nacho is adamant on driving me to the venue to catch up with the girls.

'I'll just get changed and do hair and shave legs,' he says, winking at me and waggling an impressively smooth, tanned calf in my direction. 'I come back in one hour.'

'That's so kind, Nacho, but really, I need to get there quickly. I go on in less than twenty minutes.'

I simply don't have the time or the patience for the Spanish and their lazy *mañana, mañana* approach. Not today. I'm in need of some ruthless German-type efficiency. I frantically jab at my phone, searching for a taxi number that isn't Jorge. I'm not in the mood for his lecherous approach either.

Nacho stands watching me with interest.

'Hola, taxi por favor. Immediatemente. Emergencia grande.' I wait for someone to take a fucking age to reply.

'Emergencia? Sì, dos horas.'

'Two hours!' I wail. 'No, gracias.'

Jorge it is. I dial the number, conscious of the minutes ticking by. Jorge picks up but tells me he is with the Dollz. 'They are very, very, very excellent. I no go. I wait for end of show.'

Hopeless. Effing hopeless.

I turn my pleading eyes to Nacho, who swiftly grabs my hand, pulls me towards the gate and, before I know it, I'm clutching on to his soaking wet torso as he valiantly kicks up the stand of his moped with his flip-flop and we set off.

'Don't worry, I will get you there, Cenicienta!' he says, laughing like a maniac.

I'm going to die. It's so unfair. Bits of glitter are flying off me as we pelt round corners at a 45-degree angle and hurtle down a series of narrow backstreets. Not so much as a helmet or knee pad between us.

Jesus Christ. I am genuinely petrified.

'Naaaachoooo... Caaaaan... you... slooooooow dooooooown?' I yell into the wind, only to immediately regret it as he turns round to face me, taking his eyes off the road for what feels like an eternity.

He is a raving lunatic. I cling on for dear life as he veers across two lanes of beeping traffic, all thoughts of ever fancying him cancelled out by fear. We suddenly screech to a halt after what could be seconds, minutes or hours. I get off the moped and stare blankly at Nacho. His handsome, reckless face breaks into a huge grin.

'Fun, yes?'

I have no words.

With sweat beading on my forehead and legs wobbling like a newborn calf, I make my way over to The Jolly Roger. It is a huge, sprawling pub with doormen managing a crowd of people wanting to get in. It is nestled between two open-plan bars, both of which have topless women twirling on poles where a window might once have been.

They begin to touch their breasts provocatively as soon as they catch sight of Nacho. I can't help but notice they have perfect jutting nipples, twinkling as their diamond piercings catch the light. They swing their hair around like two theatre curtains swishing together, their lips a glossy red to match their skyscraper heels and their tiny red thongs stuffed with euro notes. Nacho yells over to them in Spanish and they blow him kisses.

Desperate to get in, I squeeze through the crowd. There are hundreds of people here and much excited talk of Ted Sheeran and many posters and life-size cut-outs of the actual Ed Sheeran as though he's actually performing live on The Strip tonight.

Deep breaths.

Deep breaths.

Nacho waves to the doormen, who let us straight through. As he chatters away next to me, I can barely hear him for the panic coursing through my veins and the ear-splitting sound of the Dollz belting out a rendition of 'Salute' by Little Mix. It's no surprise to me that none of them noticed that I wasn't on the minibus, and as Tash and the girls gyrate and execute their moves in perfect synchronicity, all I can do is stare with my jaw hanging open. They are saluting the crowd, and the crowd are saluting back. The girls have the entire place eating out of their hands, and the atmosphere is electric.

Nacho distracts me by pointing over to where his large

group of friends are all dancing along in their seats. The Dollz look stunning up on stage with their outlandish costumes, the glitter sparkling against the spotlights. They exude confidence and a sexiness that I could never attain in my wildest dreams. I glance down at my costume in despair. Has it shrunk? I pull it down to an inch below my crotch and feel immediately self-conscious and out of place. I swivel my eyes around for the toilets so that I can get changed and lock eyes with Matteo, propped up against the bar. He takes a moment to squint at me as though he can't quite place me. He seems slightly shocked at my glittery appearance but manages to hide it. Then he slides his gaze to Nacho hovering next to me and turns back to the barman.

I'm so late I feel sick. To my terror, the Dollz announce to the crowd that it was their last song, and the crowd erupts into enormous applause while the barman who Matteo was talking to grabs a microphone and invites everyone to cheer even more loudly for them as the girls cartwheel and shimmy off stage. He leans in towards Matteo before they both stare over at me.

My instinct is to bolt for the door. I very much regret ever getting on that bloody plane as a man who I assume is the manager walks towards me with the microphone, weaving in and out of tables packed with drinks and punters out for a good time, and makes a loud announcement.

'Ladies and gentlemen.'

I try not to have a mild stroke as he gets closer. A hush falls. I really want the ground to swallow me up and never let me go.

'If you think the Dollz were good... then you are in for a real surprise because tonight...' he says, elaborately sweeping his arm across the crowd towards me as though he were in court, pointing out the accused.

'Because tonight... ladies and gentlemen...'

It's all very unnecessary but the crowd seem to be enjoying the build-up as they gawp expectantly at me.

'...we have one of the *top* tribute acts in the UK singing for you.'

I do wish he'd not go on.

'She's been hailed as *even better* than Ted Sheeran. Can you believe it? Ladies and gentlemen, please give a huge Benidorm welcome tooooo... Connie Cooper!'

Oh. My. God. I am going to kill Nancy.

Everyone in the entire bar looks at me expectantly while I stave off a catatonic seizure. I feel my organs ready to shut down one by one. There's no time to think so I smile weakly as he thrusts the microphone in my hand and leads me up on to stage. Feeling sick to my stomach, I quickly bring up my backing track playlist with trembling fingers and give him my broken phone to plug in to the enormous PA system behind a curtain just off to the side of the stage.

'Erm, hello,' I say gingerly into the mic.

The crowd erupts into cheers as though I've just announced the drinks are on me. There's much whooping. It's quite intimidating, made worse by my heart beating three times its normal speed.

'I think maybe there's been a slight mix-up.'

The thunderous roar immediately subsides. The mood in the room has deflated like a balloon. Who would have thought one could pop an atmosphere so quickly? The manager is wearing an understandably perplexed expression.

'I mean, I'm not one of the top acts... near the top maybe... top thirty perhaps but definitely not better than Ted Sheeran. I know how much you like him,' I say in a high, strangulated voice, trying to lighten the hostile vibes I'm getting. 'But I'm more of a, how should I put it? I'm more an avant-garde fusion between, let's say, soul and the great classics.'

The crowd seems disappointed, which makes me even more nervous. I yank my dress down and signal to the manager to play the first track. It takes forever to load up as my phone goes into constant buffering mode.

Gaaaah!

'I hope you enjoy the show.'

I walk over to the phone and twiddle the knobs on the loud-speaker, stalling for time, only for it to emit a high-pitched screech which has the audience wincing.

'I'll start with one of my, erm, favourite, erm, hits from way back in the eighties.'

Now I just can't seem to get the tuning back where it was. I should never have touched it and, judging by the lack of response, the crowd don't seem to give a shit about hearing any hits from the eighties anyway.

'Just get on with it,' someone shouts in a bored voice.

Now there's an atmosphere. An awkward atmosphere. I feel the sweat running down my face. I swipe at it with the back of my hand, causing a smear of glitter, some black eyeliner and a smattering of rhinestones to come away. At the side of the stage area, the Dollz are looking at me with horrified confusion.

Luckily, the twinkling notes of my first song float lightly out of the speaker. Had I known that the Dollz were ending on such a banger, I would have rethought my choice and now I severely regret choosing such a slow pop ballad to open with. I sing along to the haunting melody of 'You Are the Reason' and luckily the tremble in my voice is barely noticeable. I manage to get to the end and, while it does show off my vocal range, there's an almost collective sigh of frustration from the audience as what's left of the energy is immediately sucked from the room.

I wipe my face again to stop the sweat pouring into my eyes. It's bad enough having to force a whole bar full of punters to listen to music they hate, without looking like a Picasso. There's a smattering of polite applause afterwards. If they didn't like that, then they definitely won't like the next one. I signal wildly at the manager to skip the next track but he's busy serving at the bar, too far away to help. I reluctantly start singing and sidle over to the PA system to change it myself. I wouldn't normally change songs halfway through but literally the whole bar has gone back to talking and drinking and no one seems to be listening to me anyway. I can barely bring myself to look at Matteo, or Nacho or his friends, or Jorge and definitely not the Dollz. This is beyond humiliating.

Fumbling with the microphone, I stop the track mid-flow and search for something else. The crowd is growing restless, and the bar manager is giving me a warning look. He has been joined by a dark-haired beauty who is frowning at me under her thick fringe.

'Siri! Siri, search previous playlist!' I yell in panic while I try to make sense of why my fingers have become as much use as cocktail sausages.

My phone blares into the handheld mic in a robotic tone, 'Previous search: hot guys in Benidorm.'

Fuck!

The whole place suddenly goes quiet as everyone turns in my direction. 'Searching: hot guys in Benidorm called Matteo.'

Fuckety fuck!

The crowd bursts out laughing. Like lightning, I flick to my music library. I hit select on the first track to appear and

suddenly the opening notes to 'Somebody to Love' immediately blare out.

Of all the tracks! Shitting, shitting hell. He'll definitely think
I'm desperate for him now. It's as though I've been possessed by
an evil spirit hell-bent on ruining my life.

'I can be your Matteo if you want, love!' a red-nosed man in
socks and sandals jeers. The Dollz, oblivious to the heckling,
are chatting to the nuns who have turned up just in time to
witness how diabolical I am being. Nothing short of an exor-
cism will get me out of this mess.

It's no use, I'll just have to brazen it out. I blink slowly and
start singing. I just won't make eye contact with Matteo. It's a
big tune but I carry it comfortably and by the time I reach the
chorus, I've surprised myself by moving around on stage,
encouraging everyone to sing along. It's completely out of character for me, but the bar manager seems relieved and says
something to Matteo that he doesn't quite find funny. He's
standing rigidly at the back of the bar, staring at me. He must
think I'm a crackpot. The only upside being he'll think I'm a
crackpot interested in him, rather than Nacho.

I try to ignore that my dress is sliding up my backside as my
make-up and jewels are sliding off my face, and I belt out the
tune to get the crowd back on side. It was a shaky start, but I
think we'll all be able to get past it and salvage the show.
Thankfully, I get significantly more applause for that song and
babble at the crowd while I fiddle with the phone to find a suit-
able song to play next. The pressure is excruciating.

'How about a bit of Ed Sheeran?' I say hopefully, despera-
tion permeating from my skin. Once again, I flick my eyes over
to Matteo, who is speaking on his phone while the dark-haired
beauty is talking rapidly at him, in between firing me evil looks.

It's like the last five years of failed auditions for the Sinfonia all rolled into one. I click on the only track I know all the words to: 'Perfect'. Like a lullaby soothing an angry baby, the opening notes float out across the sea of bald heads. Adrenalin is pumping through my veins, so when it comes to singing the gentle harmony, I sing in Italian. I totally fucking forgot that I knew how to do this. Italian! It was one of my final year projects at university.

For a moment, I manage to block out the nightmare of Benidorm and lose myself in the lyrics. The Dollz are beaming as they slosh their cocktails in time with me. Matteo's face is unreadable. His eyes are darker than ever. I put everything I have into this performance. In fact, the song is hurling out of me as if my life depends on it. I end up turning away from the crowd to sing the rest of the song directly to Matteo.

People are turning round in their seats to see who I'm singing to. I think he must be getting a bit embarrassed at the attention, so for the final line of the song, I concentrate on the crowd, when suddenly the unthinkable happens. My phone battery dies and with it the music. I finish the final notes a cappella as though it was all intentional, refusing to be thrown by a technical hitch. I press the palm of my hand to my solar plexus and hold the note, climbing higher and higher to the fade.

What does throw me, however, is that out of my peripheral vision I notice Matteo leave the bar. He weaves quickly through the crowd with his phone clamped to his ear, the dark-haired beauty hard on his heels, and disappears. It's like a punch to the guts.

There's a second of silence as I stand there catching my breath before the crowd erupts into applause.

'Thank you,' I say, glancing over to my phone, which is completely and utterly dead. As the crowd bellows requests at me, I nod, smiling brightly. 'Erm, does anyone have an iPhone charger I could borrow?'

There's a confused sort of period where everyone starts patting down their pockets and looking around them and under tables as though iPhone chargers could be lying randomly about.

'What model is it?' someone asks, which gives way to a group discussion about cable lengths and battery life. The manager approaches the stage and hands me a charger with a look of incredulity.

All in all, the mood deflates again, and I limp through the rest of the set after that, unable to sing any of their Ed Sheeran requests. I'm a mess. It's a relief when it comes to an end. I return the charger to the manager.

'I'm sorry about that. I'm usually much better and much more organised.' He simply tuts and walks off.

My phone springs to life. It's Nancy.

'What sort of bollocks was that?' she barks hoarsely. I listen to her tearing strips off me. Nothing I don't deserve. 'So basically, you've been showing off your vocal chops instead of giving the crowd what I promised them, and you've embarrassed me in front of Spain's biggest talent promoters, Connie.'

I wince at how angry she sounds.

'I'm furious with you,' she rasps. 'I'm putting the Dollz in as the headline act for the rest of the week and you as support. And you're lucky to get that. If there was anyone else to replace you with I would. Do not let me down again!'

'It was my phone,' I say weakly, knowing there's absolutely no excuse I can give. Not the dress, not the glitter, not the Dollz... not the phone. I failed to prepare and behaved very unprofessionally. Perhaps Nancy is right. I haven't got what it takes.

'How did you find out so soon, anyway?' I ask. 'I've literally been off stage for two minutes.'

'Because the promotors were watching.'

Argh! Perhaps I can go and grovel my apologies.

'What do they look like? What are they called? I'll try and catch them.'

'Alex is the one who hired you on the phone, and the other is Matteo. He's the head of Jezebel Music, and from what I've seen of him, he's a total fanny magnet. If you've lost me his business, I'll never hire you again.'

Oh no. No. No. No. No. No.

12

After a night of tossing and turning and chastising myself over and over for such a dreadful performance, I haul myself out of bed. Nancy's sour tone and harsh words are still ringing in my ears, and each time I close my eyes, all I can see are the disappointed faces in the crowd as I bombed on stage last night. I heard the Dollz' noisy return in the early hours and not one of them came to see if I was all right. Lord knows where they think I sleep. Under the kitchen table?

I drag myself into the bathroom and shower off the remaining glitter and gemstones. Apparently the industry-strength glue does work on some parts of the body: those sensitive parts that should not have glue anywhere near them. Then I contemplate going back to bed to hide for the rest of the week. My head is swimming with negativity. I rerun those moments where I'm inviting people to the gig as if I'm something special.

Come and see me. Come and see how great I am. Come and see me, the greatest thing since sliced bread, at The Jolly Roger.

My phone rings.

'How are you feeling? Did you get much sleep?' Liam asks,

his warm voice steeped with years of friendship and comfort. He didn't bat an eye at my hysterical late-night call. It's like falling into a cloud of cotton wool and just what I need.

'I'm honestly not sure I can face the world ever again,' I say, while Liam makes soothing noises back at me.

'Sometimes you need to hashtag fail at your goals in order to hashtag realise your true potential,' he says.

'I bared my soul to Matteo. We shared a truly emotional moment and yet he failed to tell me a very significant detail about himself, namely that he was in *charge*.'

'Hmm, with the power to make or break your career. Yes. The gig could have gone better, babes.'

'Thanks for the reminder.' I can't help but raise a tiny smile. We both know I have brought this on myself.

'Well, don't look on Facebook, whatever you do,' he warns, making me frantically scroll through Facebook.

There are endless images of me at the gig in a wide range of anxious poses. I look lost and troubled in each and every single one. A quick swipe down the comments leaves a lot to be desired. I have not exactly been a hit on The Strip.

'I can sense you scrolling, hun. I told you not to look at it. Just ignore it. People only have one-minute memories these days. They'll have already forgotten.'

This is the worst I've felt in a long, long time. I have no idea what to do with my life. I've spent the last six years coasting from one lame job to another as I stayed by my mother's side and then stayed trapped in a bubble, not knowing what to do with myself other than try to follow in her footsteps to sing with the Sinfonia. Five times I've been rejected. I'm technically perfect but don't quite have the X factor apparently.

'Don't give up, Connie. This is just a blip. I know you. You're capable of great things when you choose to be. Don't let that negative energy cause you to spiral. Rise above it. Do something fabulous to counteract it. I'll ring you later. Love you, honey.'

He's right. We've been here before.

I clear my mind and concentrate on my breathing. A melody floats through my brain and comes to me in humming form. I scribble down words into lyrics and thoughts into verses, and a chorus emerges. I didn't get a first in my music degree for nothing and, like a whippet, I add musical notes and play around with chords. I have no instruments with me so I imagine a guitar and some drums and what they might sound like before I remember the big white piano in the lounge.

* * *

Lost in thought, playing the piano for longer than I realised, I look up to see the Dollz crowding around me.

'Are you okay?' Big Sue asks. 'You feeling lost and lonely, are you, pet?'

'A bit,' I say, feeling self-conscious. 'And no, I'm not okay. I'm far from okay. Didn't you see me last night? I totally sucked.'

They all stare at me, nodding in agreement.

'I can't go on tonight. I just can't. It's too embarrassing.' I get up from the piano stool and stand tall, gathering up my notes. It's important to stand my ground.

'Yes, you will. You're our warm-up act,' Tash says forcefully. 'We did a great job for you yesterday and today you repay the favour. It's time to get your big girl pants on, okay?'

I plonk myself back down on the stool with a thump at her harsh tone.

'Not that she gave us any thanks for it,' says Cherry sharply. 'If it wasn't for us, the whole gig would've been a complete bloody shambles.'

She's right. My lip wobbles. I swallow and sniff up the threat of tears. I feel like such a loser. A huge, colossal waste of space.

'No offence, babes,' Tash says with a slight unfriendliness to her tone, 'but I get the distinct impression that you think you're too good for Benidorm. Too good to be singing with the likes of us?'

'Yeah,' chips in Big Mand. 'You've looked down your nose at us since we got here. It's like you think the audience needs you to "teach" them about "proper" singing with your avant-garde this and your vocal range that. Well, let me tell you, Connie, pet, the audience knows what they want and what they want is not you wailing gloomy tunes at them. They want happy, uplifting melodies because most of them are on holiday from their humdrum lives and just want to get pissed.'

'That's right. Those fatties in the audience have earned it,' Tash says. 'They've retired here to escape their families and to dodge childcare duties. And your job is to help them forget the guilt.'

I nod understandingly. She's right.

'Yes. You're right. You were all brilliant.' I cast my mind back to their dazzling performance. 'Awesome, actually. It was a great show. I'm sorry I let you down.'

'It's simply a matter of being organised, if you ask me,' says Liberty.

Well, maybe if you hadn't fucking abandoned me to twelve fucking nuns at their villa with no way of getting to the gig, I too might have been better fucking organised, part of me wants to scream, while outwardly I smile and suck it up. I need to be better than this. I really do.

'Now, what are we all wearing tonight?' Liberty continues. 'This Red Bull event we're doing tonight has a very strict dress code. You are warming up the crowd for us, so we need you to dress up, sound alive and get them in the mood for dancing. Just like we did for you. Understand?'

'What sort of dress code?'

While I'm unable to disagree with a single word, I'm praying that I don't have to dress like a Berlin nightclub dancer. I'm not sure I can take any more humiliation.

'Cocktail casual. There'll be famous artists there. Proper singers and lots of talent scouts,' she reminds us. 'Plus, Nancy has her spies keeping a close eye on us now, thanks to Connie's disaster job last night. Who thinks they'll be able to give her a hand getting ready?'

The group eyes me up and down, sucking in air and shaking their heads in the manner of car mechanics pricing up a job.

'Thanks, but I can get myself glammed up for tonight. What is cocktail casual exactly?'

When they show me pictures of the glamourous dresses and shoes they are wearing, I feel panic rising again.

'It's almost as though she's never done a real show before,' says Cherry, seeing my alarmed expression.

'I wonder what Nancy was thinking? She usually sends us someone top-notch,' says Big Mand. 'Not some first-timer. Connie, how long have you been singing in clubs?'

'Erm,' I hesitate. 'Seven years.'

'*Seven feckin' years?*' Tash all but screams. 'Jesus. How have you lasted this long? Seven years? Seven actual years? Or do you mean seven dog years?'

They all howl with laughter.

'What time are we leaving?' I ask tightly.

I'm going to stay civil and polite. After all, I am here to develop a healthy and lasting week-long professional relationship with these attention-seeking, shallow, nun-obsessed boozehounds that just happen to be much better on stage than me, even though they put far less effort in and have been doing it for less time. There's no point explaining that the last five years were spent nosediving, as I helped nurse my mother through cancer and became consumed with grief.

'Hoargghhhay is booked for 8 p.m.,' answers Tash. 'We'll pop to Tiki Beach for a confidence drink before we go on stage tonight.'

'Fine,' I say, checking the time on my phone.

I can do this. The show must go on.

As they stampede away, I think wistfully of Ged and Liam, always there to support me, and importantly, to advise on my fashion choices to keep me in touch with my inner truth, or as they like to say, to keep me from looking like a village librarian. I could really do with a fairy godmother about now. Suddenly, an idea pops into my head. I will text Nacho for help. He seems the type that would know all about grooming. Within minutes he has dropped me the location for a salon and the nearest Zara. I have a quick shower and head straight off.

* * *

As I rush into the salon, I am greeted by one of the girls I recognise from cliff diving. We exchange cheek kisses before I show her pictures on my phone of the nails, hair and make-up I need done. She hurries me to a seat, and I hear comforting words that sound like lift, tone and highlight as she picks up strands of my hair and rubs them between her fingers. She frowns, deep in thought, as she pulls my hair down the sides of my face before messing about with side partings as she makes eye contact with me through the mirror. Almost as though she is telepathically suggesting it is time for an exciting change.

While another beautician deftly works her magic on my neglected nails, I check online for dresses in Zara. All the while my thoughts flash back to Matteo and the way he looked at me while I was making a fool of myself on stage. I feel a surge of panic swilling in the pit of my stomach. Trust him to be the head of Jezebel Music. It's like the universe has really got it in for me.

I fight back the instinct to run away from it all, fly back to Newcastle and hide in my bed. I need to turn this negative spiral around. I sit upright and square my shoulders as I stare at myself in the mirror. It's time to be the woman I know I *need* to be, not the invisible woman I often *want* to be. When it is time for my hair to be washed and conditioned, I turn my phone on to 'do not disturb' mode, close my eyes and force myself to daydream that I'm excellent on stage. And at the end, Matteo is so impressed he asks for my bloody number. In fact, he's desperate for my number; he begs me for my number. *Begs!*

Two and a half hours later and I can't believe what I am seeing. The woman in the mirror is sophisticated, elegant, and really quite stunning. The girls at the salon have managed to make my black eye disappear behind professional make-up. They've given me extremely flattering contouring and have styled my hair with subtle highlights. It shines as I swing my head from side to side. I leave in a cloud of coconut-scented hair mist and air kisses and, even though they protest, I leave the girls a huge tip.

I walk on air across the bustling square, almost strutting as I pass tables laden with tourists sitting outside in the sunshine having tapas and drinks. People are laughing, chatting, sharing time together. It's such a happy and uplifting environment, it's infectious. I check my phone map and see the store I need is just up ahead.

In Zara, I pick out a sparkly, dark ruby-red dress which complements my newly sleek and glossy hair. It has shoulder cap sleeves that show off my toned arms and is short enough to show off my legs without being tacky. I also treat myself to some high black shoe boots that finish the outfit off perfectly, and some pretty underwear because I need all the confidence I can get.

I send the girls at the salon a photo as requested, and a *huge* thanks and some emoji love hearts for squeezing me in to make sure I was ready on time. I send the same photo to my father, Ged and Liam with the same emoji love hearts. I have *never ever* looked this good in my entire life. This is confirmed in capitals by Ged and Liam almost instantly. I feel like I might just be able to pull this off.

Once back outside, the warm air hits me. Luckily, the evening sun is low, and the heat is not so harsh. I peer down one of the narrow cobbled lanes towards the sea twinkling away. I have just enough time to make it to Tiki Beach for 8 p.m. I can't wait until the girls see me. Not that I need their approval in any way, obviously. I am a strong, resilient woman, as of an hour ago.

I walk along to the bar we've arranged to meet in to find it is rammed full of (I'd love to say boisterous and good-natured) lager louts. I stand outside to wait for the Dollz.

And wait.

And wait.

And wait.

I suddenly remember my phone is on 'do not disturb'. It beeps the second I turn it back off. I have thirteen missed calls, all in the last five minutes.

Shite.

I feel instantly panicky as I return the call.

Tash screeches down the phone, 'Connie, I've been trying to ring you for fucking ages!'

Five minutes.

'What's wrong?' I yell back desperately. 'Is it your ankle? Has it burst?'

'Who switches their phone off before an important gig?'

I wait to hear what the emergency is, hovering on the verge of hyperventilating.

'We have no tequila,' Tash whines. 'Or lemons. We have no lemons.' She sounds drunk.

'That's it? That's the emergency? You've rung me thirteen times over a lemon shortage?' I ask tentatively, unable to fathom her out. It's as though I've volunteered to be in charge of lemons.

'Yes... No! Wait. No, it wasn't about that at all.' I wait for Tash to search her memory. 'I got the times wrong for tonight. Yes, that's it. Nancy rang, you're on in half an hour.'

'Half an hour?'

Tash giggles.

'Yes. And it's not on The Strip. It's on a boat. Some big boat down at the marina. Fuck knows where that is, but anyway, go on ahead of us and cover until we get there. Hoargghhhay can take you. He's outside.'

'Tash. Where do you think I am?'

'Didn't I just see you waxing in the kitchen, babes?'

I hang up.

Jesus wept. Where do I start?

I run out of the bar into the street to hail a cab. As I'm flailing my arms around, I do a double take when I notice Matteo walking down the other side, deeply engrossed in his phone. The dark-haired beauty from the bar last night is scampering along beside him trying to keep up. I can't believe it. I need to hide.

Unfortunately, the bearded nuns suddenly round the corner and make a huge fuss about me standing there.

'It's the Dollz!' they yell excitedly. 'The Dollz!'

'It's not the Dollz,' I say tightly, trying to keep them from making a scene as they break out into The Shopping Cart.

Their heads swivel wildly about before their eyes come back to rest on me and their faces fall.

'They're not here! *They're not here!*' cries Sister Kevin, sounding bereft. *Ridiculous really for a group of grown men.* 'Where are they?'

'They'll be along later,' I hiss out of the side of my mouth. This only causes them to cheer as loudly as though England had just won the World Cup. Everyone in the vicinity turns to see what the rumpus is about.

13

Matteo clocks me standing there amongst the nuns. The dark-haired beauty says something to him before giving me daggers with her eyes and stomping away, her thick hair swinging down her back, her wedges making a slapping sound on the pavement. I'm like a rabbit caught in the headlights, frozen to the spot as he strides over. Like the waves parting for Moses, the nuns disperse as Matteo reaches me.

'Aren't you supposed to be on stage about now?'

He's so masterful.

'Yes. Yes, I am. But listen, I can't apologise enough for yesterday,' I blurt, feeling very nervous around him. 'I'm mortified. I really am. I didn't know you were him. I mean the boss.'

We take a beat to stare at each other.

'Would it have made any difference?'

Good point. Probably not.

His expression is unwavering. His beautiful mouth set in a tight line. His eyes thunderously dark. He is a powerful man. Like a panther in human form. Graceful but lethal. He has this undercurrent simmering under his skin, signalling delicious danger. I snap out of my trance. There must be a way that I can defuse this tension and regain some professional dignity.

'Turning up late was inexcusable. And the costume choice. And the whole thing with Siri. The search for... hot guys called... that was unforgivable. Simply bang out of order.' *Yes, Connie. What he really needs is to be babbled at, but in a much higher pitch.* 'And the song choice! Then the phone dying!' I look briefly away before meeting his gaze. 'I'm not sure I've got time to list everything I did wrong to be honest, but... well, it's very out of character for me. I'm not usually that hopeless or unprofessional.'

'It has been a strange couple of days,' he says.

I nod, getting lost for a brief second in his eyes, framed with thick lashes. I take a closer look at him. He is dressed in a very smart and expensive suit. His dark longish hair is very European and sophisticated. He very much has the upper hand with his striking features and his mysterious ways. He is way out of my league.

He continues to stare at me.

I'm wondering if he's thinking about that almost kiss when I leaned in or whether the fiasco at The Jolly Roger has cancelled it out memory-wise. He is breathtakingly beautiful from this close up, and I'm finding his clean, soapy scent a veritable pheromone. I wonder if he is single.

Pull yourself together. He is the boss. Show some respect.

'I would have stayed around last night to make sure you were okay but...' He shrugs and exhales loudly without bothering to finish the sentence.

'I suppose you would have had angry customers to deal with. And an angry girlfriend?'

There, I said it. Now tell me who the dark-haired beauty with the mean eyes is.

He cocks his head as though to say, *What do you think?*

'Apart from being late, do you think you are going to be as bad tonight?' he asks, ignoring the question about an angry girlfriend. 'Just to give me a heads up, that's all.'

Quite right. My nosiness smacks of insecurity. His private life is none of my business.

'I'm on my way there, right now. I'm really sorry,' I tell him. I think I'll be apologising for that until my dying breath. I lift my arm to wave down a taxi, but it flies past without stopping. So does the next one. I blow out my cheeks. This might be harder than it looks. 'I promise. I'll get there somehow. There won't be a repeat of last night. Otherwise, I'll ask Nancy to give you a full refund. I'll probably get sacked but to be honest, the way I'm going on, I probably deserve to be.'

The corners of his (deliciously kissable) mouth lift slightly as he shrugs. 'Don't be too hard on yourself. You messed up, so what? It happens. And if I remember rightly, you actually warned me not to go see you. And you made your feelings about this place pretty clear from the off.' His eyes are suddenly sparkling with mischief.

The sheer cockiness only adds to his appeal.

'Oh God,' I groan, my hands flying to my face. I peek at him from between my fingers. 'Please forget all those things I said about Benidorm.' And all those insults about the people who live here. His home. I am outwardly cringing.

'It's easy to judge a place if you don't get to know it properly. By the way, Nancy has sent a playlist through to the venue manager. She insisted he set it up ready in case you fly in at the last minute and bombard the audience with some horrendous mix of distressing tear-jerkers. Her words, by the way.' He smiles at me. 'I hope you know all the songs on it, with you being so new at this.'

Ah. Awkward.

'I'll sing whatever she wants. We'll put on a great show tonight, don't worry,' I say, praying I can get there on time and the Dollz won't turn up pissed.

'Have those girls left you again?' he asks astutely.

Christ Almighty, what sort of amateurs must he think he's dealing with?

'No. Well, yes, but it's fine. I'll be there on time.' I try to act casual. 'Where is the gig exactly?'

'You don't know where you're going, do you?' He sighs. 'Come on. I'll take you.'

Thank fuck.

'Watch out for these cobbles,' he says, holding out a hand for me. I force myself to relax because he obviously only sees me in a platonic way so there is no need for my imagination to run riot at his close proximity. He takes my hand and leads me down a narrow, deserted street shaded from the sunshine. A breeze flows through it, cooling us down. Our fingers are loosely entwined, sending shoots of electricity up my arm. I must not read anything into it. The Spanish are a very handsy people.

'Is this where they find me naked and a bit murdered?' I ask, trying to lighten the mood.

'No, you're thinking of the next alley along.'

He's sharp, isn't he?

We keep moving along the street until we reach a busy cobbled square, drawing lots of stares from people. We are spectacularly overdressed for this part of town as we make our way across the square to a huge park bursting with greenery. It's magnificent, crowded with families and children playing. A far cry from the Benidorm I have seen so far, which is littered with drunks and mobility scooters. I feel instantly guilty at having been so judgemental about the place.

'This town is beautiful,' I say, admiring the wide central avenue stretching for miles, flanked by trees and benches.

'Yeah. Not bad for a shithole full of pickpockets and naked Germans,' he says.

I nod, embarrassed to my core. 'I have a problem with trying new things. Being out of my comfort zone can make me defensive. My flatmates say it can be very off-putting. I'm sure this is a wonderful place to live and work.'

I hope I don't sound disingenuous. I give him a sheepish look by way of apology and pray that he doesn't ask me where I live or what I do for a living. Unemployed with no clue what to do with one's life doesn't quite have a glamorous ring to it.

Matteo emits a husky laugh. It's got to be one of the sexiest laughs I've ever heard. 'Have you ever thought of living abroad?' he asks.

I shake my head. I've suddenly become mute as we hurry along. I'm due on stage in twenty minutes and I have no idea what songs Nancy has picked out for me or any time to do a soundcheck. Nerves are beginning to spiral around my stomach as I try to focus on what Matteo is saying and not on how much his presence is interfering with my pelvic floor.

'You probably have a busy career back there?'

I think about the three endless years I've just spent as a data input cleaner. It really is as boring as it sounds.

'I've recently taken a sabbatical,' I say, suddenly remembering that I told him all about losing my job. 'So now I'm on a sort of spiritual journey.'

These are Liam's words. He recently qualified as a mixologist. He takes us on what he calls a 'spiritual journey' most nights, while we are glued to *Bridgerton*.

Matteo stops walking to regard me with interest. 'What sort of things do you do on this spiritual journey? Are you searching for the answers to life's profound questions?'

Christ but he's persistent.

I can't tell if he's genuinely interested or terribly amused by it. I need to put an immediate end to this interrogation. I think about my recent pursuits over the last two days. I've been in a permanent state of anxiety and there's been a lot of screaming. I've also committed my deep-rooted, childish fantasies about him to paper.

'Erm, for a start, poetry... No, not poetry, it's more experimenting with words and sounds... and thoughts. A spiritual journey of thought.' *Phew.*

He tilts his head to one side. He's probably thinking that this is not a very long or very spiritual list, or very normal behaviour.

We carry on walking.

'I mean, songwriting is what it is,' I admit, my cheeks flaming. 'I write songs and, well, I, erm, sing them to myself.' I can't believe I'm admitting to this. I should say something more exciting. 'And I do extreme sports, of course.' *Who could forget I'm a cliff diver now?*

He looks impressed. 'Right, right. And when did you... How long have you been doing all that for?'

'Let me see,' I say, staring into the middle distance as though I almost can't believe it's been so long. 'Gosh. Wow. Since... since, well, since yesterday.'

I slide my eyes sideways to glance at him, but he's staring straight ahead. He thinks I haven't noticed, but he's biting his lips together. I stop talking. There is no defence. I'm boring. Until two days ago, I lived a boring life.

He stops walking and turns to face me. He has such kind eyes. He's wearing his Sunday evening eyes. The listening ones.

'I'm boring,' I blurt. 'I've done nothing with my life, and I'm embarrassed about it, okay? Happy now?'

'Connie,' he says, stepping toward me and putting a finger under my chin to gently lift my face. 'You are anything but boring.'

I shake my head. He's being polite.

'It's only been a couple of days since we met, and you've seen me through my first panic attack. I ran you over. Very much a first for me. You've introduced me to a classy new game called "Tash or Gash". And last night you revealed to an entire bar full of people, most of whom I know personally, that you've been stalking me on the internet.'

I blink worryingly at him. Nothing he's said is inaccurate.

'Tell me what's boring about that?' he says, his face breaking into a huge grin. 'They'll never let me forget it. Plus, you've been through a really tough time. Your mum died. Cut yourself some slack.'

In a heartbeat, he's taken me from zero to hero. I have an incredible urge to hug him. I think my eyes must be heart-shaped, because he studies me intensely. He probably has no idea what to make of me. I'm sure women throw themselves, emotionally, at him all the time. He opens his mouth to say something then shuts it again. He gives my hand a reassuring squeeze. We continue walking in silence, me trying to stem the rising tide of romantic thoughts about him and him probably pretending not to see me looking dreamily at him. By the time we reach his old-lady scooter, he's composed himself. I, on the other hand, am a quivering mess of unrequited lust.

'May I?'

I nod as he comes in very close. Our bodies are almost

touching. The moment is fraught with tension as he slides his hands very slowly from my ribs down to my hips, taking me by surprise. I seriously hope I am not misinterpreting his actions.

'Checking for concealed weapons?' I ask. My eyes close briefly as I focus on his hands starting their slow, teasing re-ascent, this time taking my dress with them. His touch is as light as a butterfly flapping against my skin. I gasp when he pulls my dress up to the tops of my legs.

He picks me up and sits me astride his moped in one fluid movement. The whole thing feels like foreplay, especially now I'm sitting with my bare legs akimbo, new lacy knickers boldly on display. And just like that, there's an instant shift in tension. Matteo gives me a distinct look of lust that sends pangs of desire shooting through me. I chew my bottom lip as I stare up at him. For a moment, neither of us moves. His gaze slips from my eyes down over my body. As if in a trance, I widen my legs a fraction. This seems to send him into a spin. He inhales sharply.

He clears his throat. 'Helmet,' he bellows, breaking the tension. 'Safety first.'

We put on our helmets and fly through the streets. I cling on tight and feel the warmth of his taut body under my hands. It's no use. My every nerve ending is on fire. My hands feel as though they are literally burning through his suit. I take a moment to convince myself that this may all be one-sided. All in my head.

After all, he has not mentioned that magical almost-but-not-quite kiss we shared. I think back. Was it alarm on his face, or did I misread the situation? Our lips were almost touching. It was a sort of magical lip hover. And it *was* magical. Totally fucking magical, and he must have felt it too.

Unless he didn't. And I've got it all wrong because I am so

out of practice. My nerves are unbelievably fraught. I must behave like a grown woman and stop this obsessive fantasising. But it is much harder than it sounds. When we come to a stop at a set of traffic lights, he casually twists round to check on me. He takes his hand from the handlebar, palm up, and nods as though to ask if I'm okay. Can he not feel my crotch burning into him? My legs squeezing against him in a provocative manner? Feeling uncharacteristically brave, I take his hand and place it on my thigh in answer. My breath catches as I wait to see what he does. I can see nothing of his face through the helmet.

If he's not single, or interested, then he'll move it off my leg and I'll simply dismount and make my way straight to the airport.

As the lights change to amber, and the moment stretches on with me thinking about hurling myself from the bike to avoid the ensuing embarrassment, he lightly strokes the entire length of my thigh before returning his hand to the throttle. I freeze.

I feckin' knew it!

We wind our way through the streets down to the sea and along towards the marina with me barely able to think straight. We park up and I wait, shuddering at the thought of what I want him to do next. He slides easily off the bike. I hand him my helmet and swish my hair free as though I'm in a hair commercial and doing a hard sell on him. He steps towards me, not breaking eye contact, and we do the sexy, slidey body thing where he lifts me off the scooter and we are inappropriately touching each other until my feet touch the ground. I feel the electricity crackle between us. His dark eyes are full of promise. I lick my lips – they're not even dry! – and bat my eyelashes – like I'm in a *Fifty Shades* film! – another thing to thank the girls at the salon for: the flamenco-fan lashes. He holds me close with one arm, clamping me to him tightly, while his other hand roams my back and then cups my bottom, and I melt as he pulls me even tighter against him.

He seems almost bewildered. 'You do something to me. I can't explain it. I feel drawn to you.' He swallows and runs a hand through his hair.

My entire body is on fire. I am in immediate danger of actually panting, my lust for him reaching critical levels. The sun is setting over the mountains, and the air is heavy with fresh salty sea and the aroma of palm trees and olives and distant garlic and herbs. It's intoxicating.

Matteo takes in a deep gulp of air. 'I'm about to do something very unprofessional.' As if to make absolutely certain that I get his drift, he cups my face with his hands and gently kisses me on the lips. We take a beat to let his actions sink in. Technically this is a murky grey area. It could have disastrous repercussions from a client-manager point of view. And I'm sure Nancy would be the first to disapprove. I tip my head, eager for more. As soon as our lips touch again there's an unmistakable charge of energy, like he's lighting the fuse to a firework. 'This could complicate things,' he says.

'Could it?' My voice is huskier than a phone-sex worker just back from the night shift. I am trembling from head to toe and very much of the opinion that this could be one of those relationships that can become quite physically sexual yet still retain a certain modicum of professional distance. Before either of us changes our minds, I reach up to return the kiss. As our lips melt together, we struggle to pull apart. It feels so wrong yet so, so right. Matteo looks as startled as I feel, with his hair a bit messed up from me manhandling it and his cheeks flushed.

'I'm never this spontaneous,' he says, blinking a few times as if to get himself together before leading me over to the marina. I float alongside him, admiring the brute force of his stride, his long legs, his firm grip on my hand and the sexy way he keeps looking at me as though to check I'm real before he shakes his head as if he's wondering if he's lost his mind. It feels like a wild dream. If I'm Cenicienta then he is totally my Prince fucking Charming. The water twinkles like it's covered in sparkling jewels, reflecting the last of the setting sunlight. It's enchanting and dreamlike.

'Is this where they find me at the bottom of the ocean wearing concrete boots?'

'No,' he says. 'Concrete is so bad for the marine life. We only use kelp now.'

I find his passion for the future of the planet a huge turn-on. I'm about to tell him when we suddenly reach an imposing yacht rising majestically out of the marina. It's straight out of a music video, complete with supermodels in bikinis serving trays of drinks.

I gasp.

'I had no idea you had such a... big one...' I trail off, making myself sound filthy dirty yet suddenly overwhelmed at the same time.

'Come on, let's get you on stage. Just follow the playlist, interact regularly with the audience and try not to do any avant-garde stylings,' he says briskly like he's arranging a military coup. 'Then I'll give you a tour.'

I find this sort of professional adeptness enormously engaging. I gaze up at him moonily, wondering if he can see the twinkling stars bursting from my eyes.

I'm in a perfect moment.

I allow myself to fast-forward and imagine us being together. An actual couple in a fully functioning relationship. Him, not minding my lack of joie de vivre and my frequent teary outbursts, and me, able to ignore his too-perfect looks and the fact that he is my boss.

14

He sweeps me on board and takes me straight into the VIP section. The celebrity DJ for the night spots us immediately and greets Matteo like an old friend. I listen to them chatting in French. *French!* The party is already in full swing. The music is thumping, and there is a frisson in the air. Overwhelmed and out of my depth, I hover at the edge of the circle before heading over to prepare for my set. I am suffering from a permanent flutter of butterflies in my stomach since the kiss. I can think of nothing else. I just want him to kiss me and put me back under his spell with those gorgeous dark eyes of his.

While Matteo is networking, he makes sure to glance over to the stage area where I am checking the equipment and scrolling through the songs that Nancy has chosen. I hear a commotion and witness Nacho strutting in like a magnificent prize peacock, with some of the cliff divers who are dressed equally as glamorously. He comes over to say hello and tells me his friends at the salon WhatsApped him the Cinderella photo I sent them.

'Cenicienta,' he says, 'are you doing the same comedy routine from last night or different?'

Christ alive. I will be forever haunted.

I laugh it off and catch Matteo staring over at me. He doesn't seem too happy that I am chatting with Nacho. Both men exchange a determined smile. First, it seems ridiculous that these two Greek gods are even giving me the time of day, let alone paying me this much attention, and second, it probably is high time I did some cyber-stalking of Matteo if we are to continue heavy petting like we have been.

'How do you two know each—' I'm cut off mid-sentence as the manager comes over to ask if I'm ready to start.

'We need you on quickly. Amy Housewine has run out of songs to sing.'

I send a quick prayer up to my mother. *Please let me be good.*

* * *

An hour later, I'm still light-headed. I don't know quite what came over me, but somehow, I did exactly what I was told. As if on automatic pilot, keen to get the show over with and to stick rigidly to Matteo's plan of *nothing* going wrong, I have breezed through every song in a technically perfect manner. I went through each one without dropping a single note or upsetting the audience with my preference for reducing grown men to tears. All my years of training have kicked in to lead to this very moment as I keep my nerves and feelings for Matteo at bay, to concentrate fully on the job at hand. And while I do like to take my audience on a journey with me, I have to admit they look like they have enjoyed happy songs being sung to them. I'm on the home straight and on to the last track. I glance down to see what it is.

Oh no.

I look across the dance floor with alarm. Thankfully, Matteo seems to have disappeared. I've noticed him talking to lots of people throughout my set, meeting and greeting. He has a very firm handshake, it appears. I'm relieved he's not here to witness what I'm about to do. After seven years of singing basically the same songs over and over, this one is only ever reserved for the last song at a wedding, not on a yacht full of promiscuous, fun-loving twenty-somethings. They are going to hate it. It's going to ruin the vibe completely.

Who should I tell? I cast about anxiously for the manager, but I can barely remember what he looks like.

'This last song is for,' I say, lowering my voice, 'all you lovers out there.'

Trust bloody Nancy to sneak this in. It's like she's done it on purpose. I have no option but to start singing 'The Power of Love'.

I'm singing about a body and holding on to it and doing all I can to bring it pleasure. How embarrassing. Name a single lustful woman on the planet who could sing this song and not think about their Mr Window Seat. Soon, thoughts of that delicious kiss flood my mind as I close my eyes and belt out the tune.

When I eventually open them, I see Matteo edge closer through the crowd, watching me. The way he fixes me with his dark look ignites a feeling of something new. It is spreading through me as I stare back, entranced. I feel the thump of my heart drumming against my chest in time to the music. Without breaking eye contact, I carry on singing. Suddenly, the song takes on new significance, my voice sounds thick with emotion, and I feel my lungs ready to explode as I proclaim rather loudly that I am his LAY-DEEEE and he is my MA-AAAA-AAAAN.

I feel my face go beetroot red as I sing. I wish I could rip my gaze from his, but like a driver with their eyes glued to a pile-up on the opposite side of the road, I just can't. Couples are smooching on the dance floor between us. The tempo is suitably chilled, lots of people are lounging around, swaying in time. Somehow, I've managed to create a sexy, romantic sort of vibe. It's like a penny dropping. This is how I used to be. Before I became covered in cobwebs and dust.

I focus my attention back on the crowd and sing about heading for something, somewhere I've never been, until the music fades and I'm clapped off stage. The DJ has followed my lead, and the mood of the club has come down a notch to give people a rest before he builds it back up.

I make my way down the steps at the side of the stage and am walking shyly over to Matteo when Nacho swoops in out of nowhere, like a bird of prey, snatches me by the waist and swirls me onto the dance floor as though he's a professional flamenco dancer about to administer an advanced masterclass.

'Much better singing, Cenicienta,' Nacho says, giving me a flirty wink. 'Much, much better. Very hot.' He stretches his hand out towards me and pulls me into him before thrusting me out again. 'Now I give you dance lesson you never forget.'

He picks up my hand and places it on his shoulder, and we do a sort of awkward two-step back and two-step forth, as Nacho raises himself onto his tiptoes, thrusts out his elbows and bores holes into me with a stern but simmering gaze.

'I am bull,' he says, landing a heavy hand on my shoulder. 'You are matador.'

Maybe the dance is sexier than it sounds, but I've never been one for animal cruelty. The next few minutes drag by while there's all manner of facial expressions going on and a lot of unexplained eye contact and touching. I try to look over to

Matteo, but each time, Nacho puts a finger to my cheek to bring me back to face him.

'Feel the music,' he insists, beating his breast. 'Feel it.'

He twirls me dizzyingly about, not breaking eye contact while I stiffly try to follow his lead. He very much reminds me of Cherry. Very intense and stressy. The two seem cut from the same cloth. He's all fluid movements while I jerkily sashay about, embarrassed to my core that Matteo is witnessing this clumsy display. The whole thing feels wrong, like a long and intimate sexual encounter with a hot neighbour while your husband watches on disapprovingly.

Thankfully the song ends and just as Nacho leans in to whisper something in my ear, Matteo cuts in to sweep me away, laughingly saying something in Spanish to Nacho that I don't catch. I give Nacho a shy wave as he shrugs, pretending to be heartbroken.

'Thanks,' I say, sagging against him, relieved. 'Latino dancing can be very taxing, can't it?'

Matteo is staring down at me with a serious expression as he pulls me gently into his arms. 'Then let me show you how to do it properly,' he says.

Oh my. My stomach flutters.

His dark eyes hold mine, and in time to the slow thumping beat of the music, he twirls me leisurely out, then in again before pressing me up against him. We sway in perfect time, shifting our weight from foot to foot in harmony with the music. Our hips connect and grind to the deliberate beat. There's no jerking or flinging, just a natural feeling that we fit together flawlessly.

He leans in close. I can barely breathe with lust as I feel his hands holding me firmly. His body feels tight and muscular, and he is the perfect sort of tall with perfect shoulders to hang on to, and he behaves like the perfect gentleman. I am lost with desire for him. For a long while, we are oblivious to anyone else on the dance floor until at last the DJ signals a change in tempo and lifts the beat. It seems to break the spell.

'I suppose I should get back to work,' he says, sounding ruffled. The attraction between us is hugely strong. It's almost a bit out of control and unnerving, the way we seem to want each other.

I nod, not trusting myself to speak. I am gutted our magical moment has come to an end. Matteo leads me off the dance floor and then surprises me by leading me through a narrow doorway into a storeroom full of kitchen supplies and a window out to sea. He pulls me roughly to him, his eyes dark and intense. His hands take my waist as he presses me against the wall. I instinctively loop my arms round his neck and look up at him through my huge lashes. We are both panting as he lowers his mouth to mine. I hear him groan, a primeval sexual sound, the split second before our lips touch and an exquisite sensation floods my body. We explore each other's mouths, our tongues moving feverishly through our lips while a surge of white-hot heat explodes within me from the connection. After an eternity of bliss, he pulls back a fraction and we stare goofily at each other. This definitely feels like the start of something.

When he finally slips away to continue working, I go to the toilets and check myself in the mirror for signs of lipstick over my chin or forehead or ears. I take a moment to stare at my reflection, no longer recognising the woman staring back. I like this new me. I like her a lot. Lustful Connie is fun and vibrant. I quickly reapply my lipstick, smooth my hair back into shape and race away from the mirror before the feeling wears off.

As I reach the VIP lounge, I hear someone yell, 'Stanky Legg!' at the top of their lungs, and instantly freeze. Sure enough, Tash and the girls are gyrating each leg in a circular motion on the dance floor before they swivel, bend over and begin to elaborately dry-hump each other. Everyone around them stops to stare. The tone has been considerably lowered.

Oh dear Lord.

The Dollz spot me mid-hump, and wave. I wave back from behind the safety of the VIP rope. They've obviously forgotten all about ditching me before the gig and didn't even have the decency to come and see me do my pitch-perfect warm-up set. And they are incredibly late.

'Connie. BAAAY-AAAY-AAABES, get us seven free bottles of Cristal!' Tash yells over to me.

Not a chance.

'And make sure they givvus bottles with straws, not friggin' glasses,' yells Cherry.

Nope.

They totter over to the VIP section and are stopped by a burly doorman in a black suit. There's an awful lot of low-cut spandex dress and tattooed thigh on show and I'm failing to see where the five hours in hair and make-up have gone. Mostly on strong, angry eyebrows by the looks of things. While they do still look spectacular, Tash is hobbling, her swollen ankle spilling over the straps of her shoe, Big Mand's arm is swinging loosely by her side as though it has been recently sewn on and has yet to take properly, and Liberty has a single, water-filled blister running the full length of her nose, fried hair extensions and dry, severely cracked lips. They are making a right scene, and I imagine it will be only a matter of minutes before things turn ugly. I catch Matteo trading worried glances with the DJ.

'Tell the *free* bar people we're with you, Connie. Why aren't we on the friggin' VIP list? Tell them we're the main headliners and you're *our* support act.'

I go over to the girls. 'Tash. I think you'll find you're actually supposed to be on stage. You're late.'

Tash, to give her credit, looks all confused. The Dollz dutifully back her up. 'No, I don't think we are, hun. We're on after you.'

'I've already been on,' I say. 'And I was great. As requested.'

'Have you?'

After an uncomfortable silence, while they all flick their eyes drunkenly from one to another, blaming the time difference, I take a beat to wonder if I've been reading the situation all wrong. I'm suddenly not sure if the Dollz do have their act entirely together.

Matteo swoops in behind me. 'Dollz. You have three seconds to get on stage,' he barks. 'You're thirty minutes late, so there's only time to do four songs. Make it quick. And up the tempo.'

Their faces drop as they take him in.

'Who's the bossy, hot Latino?' Cherry says to Liberty as they click-clack their way to the stage, eyeing up Matteo as they go. 'I wouldn't mind a piece of that. Christ, I love a domineering type who knows exactly what he wants.'

'Yes, I know what you mean,' agrees Big Mand.

'Showtime!' bellows Big Sue, looking at her. 'Bossy enough for you?'

It's almost as though a switch has been flicked as the Dollz go into entertainment mode. The opening notes of 'Push the Button' blare out from the speakers, commanding instant attention. The Dollz strut onto the stage with all the crackling energy of a sold-out arena show. There are only five of them and yet they fill up all the space, travelling from one end to the other in perfect formation. Their moves, the timing, the twisting and turning is choreographed in such a way it's hypnotic. Their body movements are so fast and light and in sync with the music that you can't tear your eyes away in case you miss a bit. Hips are gyrating, leg splits are executed, they are making sexual shapes with their body parts. The upbeat singalong music choice, the costumes and the vocals combined create a sizzling performance.

They might be exasperating but they are impressively in time with all the harmonies and dance routines, and they go down a storm with the crowd, who have been singing and dancing along with them. They finish on a real banger, 'Dancing in the Dark', a high-octane dance anthem by Mickey Modelle. The lights go out and strobe lights flicker on the stage, giving us dramatic glimpses of their incredible routine. Even with only half a show, the mood is electric. They have nailed it. As they come off stage, I go over to congratulate them. They are barely out of breath.

'Connie, where are the bubbles?' Tash yells as Big Sue answers her phone. She comes to an abrupt halt, causing the Dollz to pile into the back of her. 'Shit,' she says to them. 'It's Nancy. She's docked half our pay for doing half a show and demoted us back down to support. How does she find out so quick?' Big Sue is shaking her head and tutting. 'We've got one last chance. She's very disappointed in the lot of us. She says to remember we are a team. A double act and we need to support each other. She also blamed Connie for not getting us here on time. Apparently, you're the most experienced and should know better.'

They all look deflated.

Welcome to my world.

'Follow me to the VIP section,' I say. 'I'll get you some fizz.'

They don't need telling twice. We crowd into the roped-off

area and the Dollz go to work introducing themselves to the celebrities. They are scampering about like excited puppies.

'Ooh, I love that French DJ. David whatshisface. Do that song!' threatens Cherry, eyeballing him. 'You know the new song with the... what's it now? It's a bit like that one about a car but norraz good. Play it anyway and we'll do our TikTok dance for you, pet.'

The DJ flicks her an amused look.

'The Nae Nae!' she yells, suddenly thrusting her arms out.

Everyone stops to stare. Out of the corner of my eye, I see Cherry knocking Liberty off balance. I try to catch her, but she flails, hurling her drink right into Tash's face. And in slow motion, a chain of unpleasant events unfolds.

Tash falls back, taking much of the VIP rope and the majority of the golden bollards with her. We watch helplessly as one of her pointy, chopstick-heeled stilettos flies off and slices through the air towards the DJ booth, hitting the Frenchman squarely in the throat. He stumbles back, upsetting a table full of flaming sambucas, which immediately sends the tablecloth, and nearby stage curtains, up in flames.

You couldn't make it up.

The whole place gasps at the same time, as bouncers leap into action spraying fire extinguishers at the dancing blue flames while people race from the VIP area in panic. I look over at Tash and the other Dollz, and they are howling with laughter. They all think this is the funniest thing they've ever seen, until the barman flees past them, and they realise there is no one to serve them their bubbles.

Nancy is going to go ballistic when she hears about this.

15

We are all herded out of the area. Although it seems like forever, the fire is put out in just a few minutes, and the fuss dies down. A quick glance back to the main deck reveals Matteo busy ordering people around, yelling instructions and masterfully trying to contain the crowds of revellers keen to get back to partying. He seems annoyed at the rumpus we have caused.

My face is aflame with embarrassment.

'What about my shoe?' Tash asks.

'Exactly. Where there's blame there's a claim!' agrees Cherry. 'I think I'm a little traumatised by this. PTSD, it's called. I'll sue whoever is in charge. I'm not a paralegal for nothing.'

Just as I'm hoping Matteo can't hear her, his head spins around to give us all a withering look.

'Let's give him some space,' I suggest, shepherding the girls further outside onto the deck.

There's much moaning about stilettos being caught in the decking as we are joined by a throng of partygoers also being herded outside.

'And what about the free bubbles?' Tash wails. 'Do you think they'll bring the drinks out to us?'

Hundreds of people pour out of the entrance, bumping against us in their hurry to evacuate, pinning us to the railings. I hear a shriek come from the middle of our group, followed by a huge splash.

'What was that?' I ask.

There's a faint gurgling sound as we peer over the side of the gangplank into the water six feet below. A bread bun pops to the surface followed by a handbag.

Jesus Christ.

'Head count!' booms Big Sue, towering above us to take charge. 'Head count right now!'

The girls start to bicker about who it might be and whose fault it was.

'Wait. Where's Cherry?' Big Mand yells.

'Quick! What's the Spanish for lifeguard?' Big Sue bellows.

They all turn to stare at me.

Shite!

'Lifeguard! Spanish! *Think*, Connie, think!' yells Big Sue.

'It's, erm... well, erm...'

It's no use. My mind is a complete blank.

'Use your A level Spanish, hun! Your A level Spanish!'

Oh my fucking word.

'You've done nothing but go on and on about it since we got here!'

I have no idea. My mind is blank. I cast my eyes about to see if there are any lifeguards around, but all I see is the crowd chatting and vaping without a clue that one of the Dollz has fallen overboard. Without thinking, I kick off my shoes, hop up onto the railing and jump in.

I free-fall for what seems like an eternity before I crash into the sea, plunging down just like the cliff diving yesterday but with none of the fun. I sputter to the surface to get my bearings.

'Here, Connie!' screams Tash, frantically grabbing at a nearby arch of golden balloons. She rips a bunch of them away and thrusts them down to me. 'Catch!'

We watch them bob around on the breeze, before they fly efficiently away, up, up, up into the night sky. Undeterred, she spins around. The Dollz, following her lead, immediately leap into action, scooping up anything close at hand that might help – some flippers, a champagne flute, a tray of canapés and some-one's beach towel. Tash throws them all down to me while a crowd of expectant faces leans over the handrail to watch them float away before disappearing beneath the water.

Pointless. Utterly pointless.

Thanks to my cliff diving, I've become something of a Navy SEAL, and I dive under. The water is much darker and colder away from the lights of the yacht. I resurface to gasp some air and dive back under. I can't see a thing. On my next go, I glance about.

'Connie! Behind you! Two o'clock!' bellows Big Sue.

Another bread bun floats to the surface a few feet from me with some air bubbles. Within seconds, I've located Cherry and hauled her up to the surface, coughing and spluttering. The security team have galvanised at the sound of the girls shrieking and have thrown us an assortment of inflated rings.

I grab on to the nearest ring for support and pull Cherry towards it. When she has tight hold of it, I reach out for another ring and guide Cherry to the dock wall, which is only a few feet away.

'Don't forget her bag,' yells Big Sue.

I spot it glistening on the surface, just about to sink. 'Okay,' I yelp, swimming towards it.

'And the chicken fillets if you can, babes. She borrowed them from me!' Liberty shouts down.

I see them floating nearby.

'And that hairpiece. That's mine,' yells Big Mand. 'Over there, Connie. Quick, grab it before it disappears.'

FFS.

There's a metal ladder bolted to the wall, which we attempt to climb while trying to manage the bag, the buns, the hairpiece, and the enormous safety rings at the same time. It's easier said than done and makes a real climb of shame out of it as Cherry, a few rungs above me and still wearing very high-heeled slingbacks, slips a few times, almost sending us hurtling back into the sea.

There's a huge gasp each time from the girls, which does nothing to help but seems to amuse the gathering crowd.

'Mind you don't break your nails, love,' yells Liberty. 'Or your heels. Or your neck.'

When we reach the top, Matteo is standing there, ready to lift us up, with a look of disbelief on his face. Once Cherry is safely standing on two legs, he reaches for my hand. 'Are you okay?'

'I'm not doing this on purpose,' I say as he puts an arm around me once I'm up. 'I'm really not.'

'It's like there's a huge drama everywhere you go,' he says with an incredulous tone, taking the ring, the soaking wet bag, the straggly hairpiece and the fillets from me. I cringe. He's not wrong.

Cherry sputters beside us. 'Thanks, you two.'

I take in the thick black streaks of make-up running down Cherry's face, her hair strewn all over, her skimpy clothes riding high up her waist, and I assume that I must be pretty much in the same bedraggled state. *Oh well. It was nice while it lasted.* I yank my dress back down and remove a glob of seaweed from my shoulder as Matteo returns the bag and chicken fillets to Cherry. She gives me a grateful smile.

'Eeh, I must learn to swim at some point.'

By now, we have attracted a huge audience, and they have all seen fit to capture it on film. I am *mortified.*

'Well, I better go back in,' Matteo says formally. 'The security guards will want to assess the damage before the event can continue.'

I pick up my shoes, feeling overwhelmingly deflated. That's two nights on the trot the Dollz and I have ruined his gigs. Not to mention the first night when he had to stay and keep me company and make sure I didn't die from concussion.

He must surely have had enough of us getting in the way of his work. That passionate and unforgettable kiss we shared is probably a distant memory already.

'Bye then,' I say, watching him leave. 'And sorry again.'

He doesn't even acknowledge me as people rush at him from all directions, bellowing hysterically in Spanish and carrying on as though there's been a major threat to national security. A blare of sirens announces the arrival of a squad of cars screeching to a halt on the dock. Dozens of Guardia, the national police and two trucks of firemen spill out, ready to charge onto the boat and determine the exact cause of the fire, probably for blaming and insurance claim purposes.

I groan loudly.

What did I say about being jailed for something the Dollz have done? Despite my best efforts to remain calm, the weight of what just happened falls heavily on my shoulders as a wave of disappointment envelops me. It's a new low of professionalism. I swiftly weave in and out of the crowd, away from the yacht. Away from the Dollz.

'Connie, wait up!' yells Big Sue.

The Dollz are clambering down the plank after me. I hesitate, taking in their serious expressions. The girls are probably distraught at the chaos they have caused. They'll be petrified of going to jail. Probably wanting me to represent them in a court of law with my A level Spanish. I studied long and hard for that prestigious qualification. Therefore, I should be able to explain to the judge, should he ask, what our hobbies are, what our favourite lessons at school were and how many pets we have between us. But outside of that, very little. They will be disappointed.

I wait for them to catch me up. They may be looking to me for comfort and reassurance. I will do my best.

They crowd round me, linking my arms.

'All that smoke has put us in the mood for some barbequed chicken,' says Big Mand. 'Fancy something to eat?'

I take a beat to eye each of them in turn. They were unbelievably late for their headline performance. They almost set fire to a yacht worth millions. Cherry almost drowned in front of our eyes. How can they contemplate leaving the scene of the crime like this?

I glance back, but I can't see Matteo anywhere. I run my hands down my wet dress and pick off the kelp stuck to my filthy, streaked legs.

'Sure, why not?'

Once we get to the beach on the north side of the Old Town, it takes us only twenty minutes to walk its full length with our dresses hitched up and our shoes clenched in each hand. The twinkling lights of the beach bars light our way back up on to the promenade and we cross the road in bare feet. As I walk along, I think about Matteo. I only met him a few days ago, and already I feel like we have shared a whole relationship on the one hand, but that he is still a complete stranger to me on the other.

My heart sinks. I can't believe this is how my holiday romance ends. As quickly as it began. With me spoiling it and embarrassing him. He'll want nothing to do with me after this.

'Hopefully it'll blow over, and Nancy won't get to hear of it,' says Big Sue. 'We'll all be for the chop if she does.'

'Ooh, look,' says Liberty. 'We're trending on Twitter.'

16

It's the following morning, and quite honestly, it hasn't been the ideal start to the day I was hoping for. We all awoke to a text from Nancy. I swim up and down the pool mulling over the shambles of the previous evening and how we are going to explain it to her. She wants to speak to us all later today because she is still too angry to speak to us this morning. The Dollz are lounging on the sunbeds. They have been unusually sheepish.

'I think the real problem was that last cocktail we had while we were getting ready,' says Big Sue, her eyes closed. 'It was just that bit too strong.'

'Hmmm. Yes, you're right. Who made it?' says Tash accusingly, without moving a muscle.

'If it was The Skanky Lady we had in the kitchen, then it definitely *was* too strong because Cherry made it,' Big Mand says, rubbing her arm. 'But to be fair, I needed it for the pain.'

'I genuinely think it was the faulty shoe, Tash. There would have been no fire if the strap had been doing its job properly. As a paralegal, I should know,' says Cherry confidently, not rising to the bait. 'We can probably sue whoever makes those Gucci knock-offs in China.'

'If you ask me...' begins Liberty.

There's a collective groan.

'Well, excuse me for having a PhD,' she continues. 'But the real issue here is our deep-rooted desire for validation. Our crippling need to hear people clapping every single thing we do. We obviously need a major overhaul of our belief system if all it's built on is praise.'

'She's right,' says Cherry. 'It's like my marriage counsellor says. We need to revisit our shared values regularly, otherwise I find I'm nagging Tony so much that he doesn't know which nags to focus on.'

We all murmur agreement as this creates much discussion with words like 'changing mindsets', 'managing partners' and 'life goals' being bandied about. I hear Tash, a university lecturer, suggest they do some revisioning so they can hone their act to achieve their ambitions.

'I hate to say it,' adds Big Sue, 'but maybe we need to take this little side hustle of ours more seriously. Take this hobby to the next level?'

I rest at the side of the pool, flabbergasted at what I'm hearing. All of the girls have careers. Like, proper careers. They are probably even a bit younger than me, and they all have their shit together. Singing is only their hobby, an excuse for them to be together and enjoy each other's company, and they're better at it than me, who has been slogging away professionally for years. I clamber out of the pool. If I was depressed before, then I'm totally and utterly floored by their revelations.

'What do you think, Connie?' Tash asks. 'You've been doing this for an extraordinarily long time, and yet you still seem incredibly focused. Is this a sideline for you too? What's your actual job?'

Is this a trick question?

'I... I don't have another job. This is it. I have to impress Nancy enough to trust me again while I'm waiting for my big break. I guess I just want to sing for the Royal Northern Sinfonia and then perhaps the London Philharmonic and take it from there?'

'Why?' asks Liberty.

I'm incredibly shaken by this very simple and straightforward question. A blast of grief surges through me. 'I've always wanted to do that,' I say, forcing a bright smile. 'My mother was a classical singer with the Philharmonic. It's what she would have wanted for me too.'

'So how come you're not singing with them? You sound good enough to me.'

'Too technical. Not enough... I don't know, not enough emotion or sparkle, I guess.'

'How many times have you tried to get in?'

I'm not revealing that.

'Sometimes failing to achieve your goals helps you fulfil your destiny. Maybe the Sinfonia or Philharmonic is not the right path for you,' Liberty says, sounding exactly like Liam as she nods at the girls.

How dare she! What does she know? I am immediately incensed. 'I know what my path should be. And I certainly know all about failing. Is that what you mean? I'm a failure?' I say through tight lips.

'I think what Liberty means, love, is that you probably need to experience life a bit more. Fall in love, fall out of love and back in love again,' Cherry says gently, sounding exactly like Ged.

'Be brave then be a mess. Be a warrior then be a wimp. Do things, *life* things, and share the ups and downs with the people around you,' says Big Sue. 'Do you think you've maybe closed yourself off a bit?'

I lower my head so they can't see my eyes filling up with tears and blink them away.

'I didn't mean to upset you. We all carry our deepest scars on the inside,' Liberty says softly, her eyes full of sympathy.

That's all it takes. One look. One apology. My lip wobbles as hot tears spill down my cheeks. 'It's fine. It's fine,' I say as the Dollz lift their sunglasses. 'It's just that I recently lost...'

'Your mother?' says Cherry.

I nod. I was actually going to say my job. I'm not sure I want to open up to this lot.

'That explains it then,' says Liberty. 'That's why you don't sing properly.'

Excuse me? I wipe away my tears, the tidal wave coming to an abrupt halt.

She continues, explaining herself to the Dollz as though I should already be aware of the answer. 'Connie is doing that classic bereavement thing where her grief has become her comfort zone. Following in her mother's footsteps will make her feel her mother's still with her, and because she's not chasing her own dream, it's why she'll find herself stuck in a loop, never going anywhere.'

I can't fucking believe this. I glare at her before I grab up my towel and stomp off. I hear instant bickering behind me.

'You and that bloody PhD,' Cherry calls out.

* * *

An hour later, I'm clutching my notebook to my chest and muttering into the wind. Liberty has thrown me completely with her casual remarks and insensitivity. How dare she assume to know anything about me or my relationship with my mother? So what if I'm still grieving? So what if I'm stuck in a loop of failing audition after audition?

I take a beat to listen to what I'm saying. When did I decide that I needed to be a classical singer and follow in Mum's footsteps? Is that what I really want or what I thought she wanted me to want? I shake away the confusing thoughts. It might help if I get them down on paper. Good old-fashioned pen and paper. I trudge down to the beach towards a small alcove and find to my delight that it's empty and there's a shelf of rock for me to sit on and stare out to sea.

I have questions for myself, starting with what in the name of fuck am I doing with my life and why? I scribble away.

* * *

I have no idea how long I've been sitting staring out to sea, writing things down in my notebook or singing random bits of tunes that disappear with the lapping of the waves, but it has soothed me. I am going to release all these musical notes onto the piano keys and see if I can't Elton John the fuck out of them. I get out my phone to record the basic melody for later and see Nancy has texted. She is ready to give us all a joint bollocking and is going to FaceTime us shortly.

I take myself back off up to the villa. As soon as I walk through the door, the Dollz crowd round.

'Sorry, Connie, pet,' says Tash. 'Liberty was bang out of order.'

'I wasn't,' says Liberty sharply. 'Owning your own truth can be one of the hardest things to do, but are you okay, Connie, love?'

I plonk my notebook down, nodding.

'We'd hate to upset you,' says Cherry. 'For a bunch of women in customer-facing professions, we sure do antagonise people a lot, don't we?'

This makes me smile. A few home truths for these girls are in order. 'All you've done is leave me behind or leave me to sort you all out. There's been no sisters before misters.'

'You're right,' Tash says, hanging her head. 'We've been awful.'

'Sorry if we haven't made you feel like one of the girls,' says Cherry.

'And if we've made you feel bad, sad or mad,' says Liberty.

All three.

'Shame because I usually have such a gift for lifting spirits, don't I?' Tash looks to the girls, and I see some of them agree.

'You have a gift for lifting *spirits* all right,' I say, pleased with myself that I'm still able to be quick-witted at such a trying time. 'Especially tequila.' They've been mortal drunk since before we even arrived.

'It's my job,' explains Tash. 'I have to deliver up to four hours of lectures per week. It's exhausting.'

There's a murmur of understanding.

'And to be fair, *I* only drink because I'm a mother. It can be horrendous,' Cherry tells us.

Ah, yes. Cherry's children, aged one and three, are demons sent from hell to torment her and her long-suffering husband.

'I drink between births. It's the only way. I'm a huge supporter of fanny,' admits Big Mand. 'But there's a limit to how much fanny a person can take in one day.'

No one seems to know how to react to this.

'And another thing.' I sniff, beginning to calm a little in the face of such empathy among the girls. 'Those photos of me on your Instagram were hideous. I was humiliated.'

Suddenly, I'm joined by Liberty, Big Mand and Big Sue, who didn't like their photos either and accuse Tash of never asking their permission first. Especially as some of them have important jobs and wouldn't want drunken photos of themselves or their undercarriages splashed about the office.

'You're right. I only ever post photos where I look fabulous and you all look less... fabulous,' Tash says, leaning against the kitchen table. 'I suppose it's my one flaw.'

They all lean in towards me with caring expressions. I suddenly wonder if I've horribly misjudged them.

'Shit. Incoming!' yells Big Sue, straightening up and waving her phone around. 'It's Nancy. Look alive, people!'

* * *

'I can't believe she's making us do this,' complains Tash as we make our way into the Old Town.

'She's treating us like children,' agrees Liberty. 'It's your simple power play. Well, it won't work on me.'

'Connie,' says Big Sue, 'I think you're probably the best one to take the lead on this, seeing as you've been promoted back up to headline act.'

Nancy tore strips off us all for our unprofessionalism and our holidaymaker attitude to what is essentially a work trip and nothing else. She ended the call yelling, 'Don't you dare let me down or else you'll all be coming back in body bags.'

I check the directions on my phone and stop abruptly outside an old building in a bustling, narrow street. There's a sign above the ancient wooden door saying *Jezebel Music*.

'We're here.' I hesitate, not looking forward to seeing Matteo under such disgraceful circumstances before pushing the door open, allowing the Dollz to troop through. Once inside, the reception area is surprisingly modern and spacious. The receptionist greets us in English.

'Here are your passes for the festival tomorrow. Your maps for the site and the details of timings,' she says, efficiently handing us a pile of papers. Her smile fades as we hear a clip-clopping sound approach. We all turn to see a very glamorous woman wearing a less than impressed expression. I recognise her instantly. She's the dark-haired beauty from The Jolly Roger who stood next to Matteo and followed him outside and who was with him yesterday outside Tiki Beach.

'Hello,' she says coldly in a thick Spanish accent. 'I'm Alexandra. Co-owner of Jezebel Music.'

Nancy's instructions were very clear. We were to come to Jezebel Music and essentially grovel an apology to the two owners of the company, Matteo and his business partner, Alex.

'Hi,' I say. 'I'm—'

She cuts me off. 'You're the singer who lied to me over the phone, ruined the gig at The Jolly Roger and,' she says, pointing to the Dollz, 'you're the ones who ruined the gig last night. It's like you have come here to purposefully put me out of business.' There's a slight pause as none of us are quite sure what to say. She's spot on with her assessment. 'Follow me.'

We follow her into a sparse office and crowd in as she sits at her desk. There aren't enough seats for us, so we stand awkwardly around the room.

'I would have fired you after The Jolly Roger gig. What was that? It was embarrassing,' she says to me. 'We expect much better. We have a reputation to uphold. We are the biggest promoters in Spain and building our reputation across Europe. We can't have artists like you making fools of us.'

My cheeks are on fire.

'To be fair,' says Tash, 'it wasn't Connie's fault she was late. We accidentally left her behind at the villa with all those randy nuns. They can be a real handful.'

'Which is why she turned up looking like she'd been standing in a wind tunnel,' says Liberty, trying to be helpful.

Oh my word.

'But more so because I got a lift on a motorbike afterwards from our landlord,' I say. 'Not because of anything I got up to with the nuns. Although Nacho's driving was a bit wild.'

Somehow, this explanation doesn't sound very convincing. It makes me sound like I was late due to bonking my way through half of Benidorm, but I'm grateful to them for trying.

Alex raises a pencil-thin eyebrow. 'Yes, we all know how wild Nacho can be.' She says 'wild' as though she means slutty and effectively ruins my case for the defence. 'That doesn't explain why you embarrassed my business partner by singing love songs and staring at him all night.' She gives me an evil glare. 'And you've obviously been stalking him on social media. He's the boss. He's paying you good money to do a job. Show some respect.'

Even the Dollz are rattled and, for some reason, I've lost my voice.

'But she was great on the boat,' says Cherry, leaping to my defence. 'Apparently.'

She only has my word for it.

Alex sighs elaborately. 'I know exactly what happened.' She points angrily at me again. 'We rented that yacht at great expense, and don't get me started on how much damage you girls caused with the fire. You ruined the event. We lost a serious amount of money because of you.' Our heads hang down as Alex tears strips off us. 'If I had been there, I would have sacked you all, but Matteo seems to think we can't replace you at such short notice. He is furious with you all, of course. Furious.' Alex sweeps her disapproving gaze across us, resting it on me. 'I advise you to stay away from him. Is that clear?'

She continues to stare at me.

'I will be at the festival tomorrow to personally oversee your performances. Your only job is to warm up the crowd and create a good vibe before the real acts come on, understood? The real singers. The ones with *real* talent who write and perform their own music. All you have to do is show up on time and do your job. It's not much to ask, is it?'

We shake our heads.

'She's going on a bit,' Tash mumbles.

'If you let me down, you will never work outside of the UK again. Is that clear?' Alex tuts and waves us away as though we are naughty children being dismissed from the head teacher's office. It is humiliating.

Once we are back outside, we all look sadly at each other. 'What is her problem with you, Connie?' Tash exhales loudly. 'Christ, babes, she really had it in for you.'

She really did.

'Does anyone want to eat their feelings? Who knows where Tapas Alley is?' asks Big Mand. 'I could do with some comfort food.'

'I hope they do kebabs and chips, dripping in garlic sauce,' Liberty says as I lead the way.

You can take the girl out of Newcastle...

17

After a few hours in the Old Town, sitting in a quaint tapas bar, we have successfully dissected and analysed what we think Alex's problem is. 'She's unfulfilled. She has a crush on her business partner, and after the way Connie threw herself at him on stage, she now sees her as a threat and is determined to get her off the scene.'

I swallow, amazed at how astute Liberty is with her observations. It's incredible. Just goes to show you shouldn't judge a book by its cover.

'Yeah,' says Tash. 'Connie, do you have a massive crush on the boss?'

What sort of question is that to ask? We're not twelve.

'No, of course not,' I lie, my whole face burning up.

'He's definitely a hunk of spunk,' she says. 'And he looks super shredded to me.'

'Does he?' *Christ, I hope they don't probe too much.* 'I hadn't really noticed.'

'It's just that we heard you singing earlier in the shower. Your voice really carries. And you were singing a love song.'

'So?' I say, aware of the defensive tone creeping into my voice.

'It was about a moody, dark-eyed fella who refuses to love you back.'

'No, it definitely wasn't about him.'

'And you mentioned the name Matteo quite a lot. It's a difficult one to rhyme, isn't it? Mind, you gave it a good go, didn't you, pet?'

Crap.

'The way to a man's heart is through his loins,' says Liberty with some authority. 'It's all about confidence. Not size, colour or shape.' She sweeps an eye over our group, stopping at me. 'Connie, you have no confidence.'

While the Dollz discuss my inadequacies at great length, I fight the sinking feeling that Alex is surely more Matteo's type. She's sophisticated and well groomed and successful.

'I say we finish these cocktails and take Connie shopping,' says Big Mand.

'She needs to find her own style,' agrees Tash. 'And I know just what that should be.'

'And maybe some leg tattoos,' says Big Sue.

'And definitely some sex appeal,' says Cherry. 'We should teach her how to move her body properly. She's all legs and no rhythm. Like a drunk on stilts.'

The Dollz discuss the pressing issue of what I should wear to the festival tomorrow and the shortfalls of my ability to lure men.

'What time are we meeting the nuns?' interrupts Liberty, glancing at the time. 'They've really made the holiday – I mean, work trip – haven't they?'

Tash rolls her eyes and accuses Liberty of being unable to

take two steps outside the villa without getting fingered by one of the nuns.

Liberty goes a bit red. 'I have experienced an unusually high amount of fingers up there this week compared to normal.'

Delightful and charming.

'Come on then, let's get Connie sorted out with some decent clothes.'

'Yes, that a woman of her age would wear.'

'I'm only twenty-seven,' I protest.

They raise their eyebrows as if to make a point.

'A woman who cares about how she looks.'

'A woman who has regular and satisfying orgasms. Men can't tell but women can. It'll give you the glow that you currently lack.'

I blink rapidly. 'Or how about clothes that say *I'm classically trained, come with me on a spiritual journey*?' I say in a feeble attempt to regain the upper hand.

Cherry glowers at me. 'That's the musical equivalent of cock-blocking, pet.'

'Connie, love, if you want us to transform you into a sex kitten then you'll have to loosen up,' insists Liberty impatiently. 'You want Matteo to find you sexy and exciting, don't you? And you want to bring some sparkle to your performance, don't you? Well, the two things are intrinsically linked.' She points a mani-cured nail at me. 'But *you* have to find *you* sexy and exciting first.'

I nod warily. I mean, that is definitely true and it does seem like the next natural step in my bid to stray out of my sexual comfort zone. 'But Alex has warned me off him, and to be honest, after last night, I should really just back off and leave him alone. I'll be gone in a few days.'

They look at me aghast.

'A few days is a few days,' bellows Big Sue as we troop off through the cobbled streets of the Old Town. 'Anything could happen. You could fall in love tomorrow, pluck up the courage to act on it and elope the day after that. Who are we to deny our fate?'

We all stop to stare at her.

'She's right,' Big Mand says, turning the colour of tomato soup.

'Yes,' says Tash. 'Anything could happen. Connie, you need to be more optimistic, honey.'

All this loud bickering and braying is making me nervous. We are dangerously near the Jezebel Music offices as we coast by the main shopping lane and its window displays showing all the latest fashions from Zara, Mango and several Spanish boutique shops with lovely colourful prints and clothes that swish.

'No. No. No,' mutters Cherry as we pass by. I scurry along, keeping my head down as we pass Matteo's office and duck down an alleyway. Along we go until she yells, 'Here we are.'

I take in the neon sign swinging above the door and instinctively step backwards.

'No way,' I say as they crowd in.

'We're telling you, Connie. This is where to buy all your stage costumes. It's where we get ours. Stop being such a prude.'

Sweet baby Jesus.

I look at the huge sign that says *SEX SHOP*, and after glancing surreptitiously around to make sure that no one is watching, I follow them nervously in. I can hand on heart say that I've never been in one. Ever. But once inside, I'm immediately surprised as I gaze around the shop.

'See?' says Tash. 'It's just like Ann Summers.'

Like I would know that.

I wander surreptitiously down the aisles trying not to gawp at the display of sex toys and weird-looking objects lining the shelves. I may not be very experienced when it comes to these things but I'm now feeling way out of my depth.

'I've had to resort to one of these,' says Cherry, picking up a large vibrator.

'There's an even bigger one over here,' says Liberty, brandishing something the size of a two-litre bottle of pop.

'Fashionable sex these days involves a minimum of two or three people,' says Tash knowingly. 'Filming on their phones as they go. It's all about completely hair-free bodies, waxed skin and bleached bumholes.'

I freeze with alarm as the girls nod their heads in agreement.

'But I have to say, girls,' Cherry warns, 'always get some sort of disclaimer signed otherwise some twat will post it online once you break up with them. Take it from me. I'm not a paralegal for nothing.'

'What about this?' shouts Tash, thrusting a small black plastic doggie poo bag at me. 'It's a jumpsuit.'

I take it cautiously from her. It's very thin and clingy. And small. Very, very small. 'Thanks,' I say, praying they have something in a more substantial material; a viscose, a loose cotton, anything that won't give me thrush.

It takes only a few minutes for the girls to grab items of clothes and sling them over their arms. 'Here,' Big Mand says. 'These will look great on you. Try them on.'

There follows what can only be described as an X-rated, bondage version of *Say Yes to the Dress* as I wrestle with a series of laces, straps and rubber and parade in and out of the changing rooms to cheers and boos. The Dollz insist on me trying on each item, some of which are carefully crafted out of nothing more substantial than dental floss while others ensure my boobs are hovering by my chin.

I'm finding the Dollz' sense of frivolity and carefree attitude to all things 'fetish' increasingly infectious. I have never tried on clothes like this in my life, and after a short while, all my anxiety disappears.

'You can't put a price on sexual confidence,' says Big Sue. 'Well, you can at these cheap prices.'

'So true,' agrees Big Mand, handing me some egg-shaped ornaments. 'Pop these in, hun. You'll not regret it.'

'We need to make her look like someone you'd want to have sex with on stage,' adds Tash. 'Your Latino hunk of spunk is going to die when he sees you in this lot. You look amaze, babes.'

That does it. An exhilarating feeling of confidence rips through me. So much so that I agree to buy all of them on my credit card with the gusto of a high-class escort who can easily afford the investment. I leave the shop wearing a tiny, figure-hugging, strapless playsuit in faded blue denim, the least rubbery of my purchases. It goes well with my white trainers and makes my legs look like they belong to a baby giraffe. It is doing wonders for my confidence.

I step outside feeling bold and brave. Until I hear, 'Cenicienta!'

Shitting hell.

Nacho is waving at us from down the alleyway. He is looking at the *SEX SHOP* sign and raising his eyebrows. The Dollz are very excited by his unexpected appearance and charge towards him like a herd of rhinos. It's only when I trail after them that I realise Matteo is with him. I peep at him over the top of the girls' heads. My toes are curling, my whole face is glowing, and I could die of embarrassment as he tilts his head to eye my many, many bags baring the *SEX SHOP* logo.

How to explain? How?

He walks around the outside of the group towards me. It's more of a prowl. He has a dangerous aura about him. Rough, stubbled and ready for sex, that's the only way to describe him. Unless he doesn't, and I'm simply under the twin giddy highs of being in a sex shop while under the influence of the Dollz. I am mesmerised by the muscles rippling beneath the soft fabric of his T-shirt and the way his denim shorts are clinging to his thighs. He's staggeringly beautiful. He doesn't break eye contact with me the whole time, and I can't tell if he is angry about the yacht incident, as his face is giving nothing away. In a few strides, he reaches me.

'They're not mine,' I blurt, holding up my bags.

He raises a questioning eyebrow.

'Well, they *are* mine, but they're not for sex. I didn't buy sex things.'

I must clarify.

'They're for the show. For stage. Costumes.'

It's no good. I've become lost in his incredibly sexy eyes as he sweeps his hair from his forehead.

'About last night and the fire,' I say hesitantly. 'I'm so sorry.'

Matteo shakes his head. 'No worries. It's been dealt with.'

'Alex told us you were very angry.'

Matteo's eyes widen. 'You've been to see Alex?'

I nod. 'Nancy told us to go and apologise. Did Alex not tell you?'

Matteo looks away as though he's hiding his annoyance.

'She told us you were furious and that I should...' I blink. 'I should stay away from you. Which, under the circumstances, is probably... wise.' A thought occurs to me. 'How do you all know each other? Nacho, I mean. Does he work for you?'

He hesitates for a moment. His fingers reach out and lightly graze mine, but before he can answer, we hear the girls shrieking and making a fuss of Nacho, pleading with him to come to The Strip tonight to 'celebrate' our night off.

'We're helping Connie find her true sense of self,' I hear Liberty saying to Nacho. 'A sort of fast-track professional development for beginners.'

Beginners at what?

'And we're showing her how to move properly on stage,' adds Cherry. 'She'll be benefitting from my many years of TikTok choreography.'

'I'll be transforming her look,' says Tash. 'Contouring, shaping, smudging.'

Good Lord.

'We'll be in charge of making her sexy,' says Big Mand, grinning from ear to ear at Big Sue. 'She'll be a total wang-magnet by the time we've finished.'

Oh my God, they are so not helping.

Nacho lets out a small laugh. 'Wouldn't miss it, Cenicienta.'

I blush instantly.

Matteo looks impassively back at me. 'Sounds like you'll be very busy.' That chemistry between us is suddenly gone like a puff of smoke.

'No, it's very not what they are making it sound like. I won't be attracting any *wangs*. None. No *wangs*,' I blurt in panic. I'm horrified. My eyes flick once more to the bags I'm holding. I feel they are giving out the wrong impression. 'I'm as far from a good-time girl as you could possibly hope to get!'

The Dollz groan and start protesting.

'We'll be on The Strip at 9 p.m. You'll not miss us,' Tash promises the men.

Nacho looks briefly at Matteo before confirming that he will see us there.

'Try not to burn anything down, will you?' Matteo says in a cool tone. 'I'll see you at the festival tomorrow.'

'What? Aren't you coming to see us tonight?' yells Cherry, not making it sound obvious in the slightest. 'I mean, you don't have to. But if you want to, then Connie will be there. I mean, you're the boss so you probably should come. Not that I'm telling you how to do your job or anything.' Cherry is the colour of the tomato she shares her name with. 'But if you could please come that would be great. You won't believe your eyes.'

Pathetic. Utterly pathetic.

She's crumbled even faster than me, making out that there's going to be some big reveal that simply must not be missed.

'Fine. Can't wait,' he says dryly before his phone rings and he mouths 'work' before disappearing off into the crowded lane, Nacho running after him.

'Well,' I say. 'That didn't make me look desperate at all, did it?'

Big Sue checks her phone and barks at us, 'Look at the time. Let's go! Move it, people. We only have until twenty-two hundred hours to complete the mission.'

18

Back at the villa, I rummage through the pile of new clothes for the least sexy outfit to wear tonight. My decision-making this afternoon has left a lot to be desired as I sift through the Barbie-sized garments. I want to give Matteo the right impression. I fear I may have come across as sex crazed. I must also under *no* circumstances make a right fool of myself by drinking too much. I wander into the kitchen to see the girls have outdone themselves in the competition for heavy make-up, their lashes like industrial street sweepers.

'Connie, that dress looks like a second skin. It leaves nothing to the imagination,' says Tash approvingly. 'Just hitch it up a bit, babes. Fabulous!'

Oh dear Christ.

And before we know it, we've all had four slammers each! My eyes are wide with liquor, and I feel invincible. Tonight, I will be putting all these embarrassing episodes, that happen literally every time I come within an inch of Matteo, well and truly behind me.

'Hasn't the trip been great so far?' asks Cherry. 'So much

has happened. I haven't missed Tony or the kids once. Not once.'

'Yeah, remember how funny it was at the airport when Tash brought down all of those shelves in duty-free and we couldn't get away quick enough?' says Big Sue.

'I've still got that bearded paramedic's number,' says Tash with a wink. 'But he's no Sister Kevin.'

I remember Matteo having a panic attack on the plane and me helping him, and us getting lost in a crazy, private moment here at the villa.

'I still can't believe you all thought I'd been out with you on that first night, when I hadn't,' I remind them.

'Where were you?' asks Big Mand, screwing her eyes to remember. 'What happened to the wheel of Brie?'

'Matteo ran me over with his moped on the way back from the supermarket,' I sigh. 'It was incredibly romantic.'

'He ran you over?'

'Uh-huh,' I say, distracted at how so much has happened in such a short time. 'He was tracking me because I'd stolen his phone by mistake. He was very courageous. I could have died.'

They roll their eyes theatrically.

'You might have that Stockholm syndrome. Here, have some more,' says Big Sue, pouring another round. 'You'll need it for where we're going.'

I frown.

'Don't worry, babes. I'll be your role model and mentor for the rest of this trip,' volunteers Tash. 'Now repeat after me. I am a confident, powerful, sexually ambitious woman.'

'I am a confident, erm, sexually, yes, sexually ambitious, powerful woman,' I say to the girls, sloshing tequila as I wave my glass around.

And I'm sure I will be once I've convinced myself.

'Exactly,' agrees Cherry, knocking back her shot and wincing as she sucks on the slice of lemon. 'Yes, we are beautifully flawed women with runaway libidos, but we don't need men to feel good about ourselves.'

We drink a shot to such profound wisdom.

'We just need each other. Sisters before misters!' yells Liberty.

This also sounds wise. We drink another.

'Hoes before bros,' Big Sue cheers.

We couldn't agree more. And another.

'Keen women of substance!' I join in, feeling myself spiralling as the alcohol rushes to my head. I slam down the glass, narrowly missing the bench, and it smashes on the floor. And even though it's hilarious, they all seem exasperated. Another shot is hurriedly placed in front of me just as I have a light-bulb moment.

I gasp loudly. I've just realised something very important. 'I am a confident, powerful, *sexually ambitious* woman!' I say, perhaps for the first time. 'And you.' I point at Big Mand. She will want to know this about herself. 'You are a powerful, sexy woman, and you.' I point at Big Sue. 'You are a powerful giantess, a huge, powerful gladiator.'

'Great. Come on, bitches, let's go!' Cherry barks at me.

I should tell Cherry how much I admire her directness. No messing. She tells her absolute truth. I sling my arm around Cherry's thin, bony shoulders. 'I love you, Chezza. You're so bossy.'

'Big Sue,' she says. 'Can you carry Connie out to the taxi, love?'

* * *

The Strip is buzzing. There are gorgeous women swirling around gracefully on poles and tabletops. It's too hot to wear anything but a G-string. It makes complete sense, especially in this heat, with the disco lights whizzing round and the music pumping out. There's a strong party vibe and people are spilling out from the bars on to the pedestrianised square where bartenders with beer kegs on their backs are refilling drinks with a hose. All the men seem to be wearing their T-shirts tucked into their back pockets, allowing the air to cool their armpits.

Big Sue returns from the bar with a huge fishbowl full of bright green liquid and a dozen straws and plonks it down on our table. We all take a slurp. It's delicious.

'What's in it?' I ask, admiring the neon glow.

'Everything,' she says.

'Right,' barks Cherry. 'Up you get. It's time to show you how to dance.'

We make a dance floor out of the area next to us and I join in with the girls as they do their signature routine to a Spice Girls classic. I'm told many times to loosen up, make my body pop, use my arms and make love to the crowd.

'Make love to them, Connie!' Cherry orders forcefully, watching me twerk awkwardly to a group of frightened teen hipsters. 'But not like that!'

It takes another round of drinks for me to finally get the hang of sexy dancing.

'Connie, I will show you how to pole dance, now you've got a grasp of the basics,' says Tash, clambering up onto the table to grab the pole. Her swollen ankle is now level with our eyes, and I can appreciate how bulbous it is. Just as she hooks her leg round it, there's a big cheer from the girls as the nuns swoop into the bar, their eyes lighting up when they spot us. They come tearing towards us like overgrown, hairy toddlers. Tash squeals with delight and leaps off the table in the direction of Sister Kevin.

We all hold our breath as she soars towards him like a flying squirrel. He catches her expertly, her legs straddling his waist, their mouths colliding in a somewhat violent-looking kiss.

We watch, mesmerised.

They kiss.

And kiss.

When she starts to bounce provocatively up and down, one bum cheek nestled firmly in each of his hands, I realise she might not be coming back from this adult cuddle to finish her demonstration anytime soon.

Meet Tash, everyone, my role model and mentor.

To our surprise, the Mother Superior leaps nimbly up onto the table, grabs the pole and within seconds his tattooed head and legs are gracefully whizzing round the pole. We all gasp as he expertly lifts his body sideways, perpendicular to the table, using only his reedy tattooed arms.

'The trick is to change your perception,' he tells us, flipping upside down. 'This is the swan.'

Liberty is ecstatic at such gymnastic prowess. He is making it look effortless. I feel prickles on the back of my neck and turn to see Matteo has just walked in with Nacho and a gang of the cliff divers. Like a submarine periscope, Big Sue cranks her neck up to peer over the crowd. She clocks who is in my line of vision. Like lightning, she scoops me up and plonks me on the table with instructions to grab the pole and start dancing like a nun.

Shitting hell.

'Do it!' roars Cherry, drawing attention to me. 'Do it now!'

The Mother Superior hoists me up the pole by the waist. I slide immediately back down. 'Forget everything you ever learned about gravity and just let yourself go.' He then pirouettes off the table to land in a balletic pose.

Matteo is looking around. It won't be long before he spots me standing on top of this table full of drinks. My chest immediately tightens, causing me to squeeze my eyes closed and grab the pole. I am greatly disappointed to find that, when I open them, I have not been magically teleported far, far away from here. I stand rigidly while the group makes its way towards us. I have been spotted.

My skin prickles with equal measures of nausea and excitement as Matteo's gaze travels from my strappy sandals, up my bare legs, to my tiny animal-print see-through body-con dress, underwear clearly visible. I glance over to the professional dancers twirling around, making this strenuous art form look easy. I cross my heart and hope for the best. I shift my weight, hooking one leg round the pole, and swing for dear life. I see the bar full of people blur as I spin round and round. I grab tightly on to the pole, closing my eyes to stop the dizziness.

'I'm going to nail this,' I chant silently. 'Be confident. Be powerful. Be sexy.'

I lean seductively out from the pole, arching my back, nipples like Greek olives pointing skyward as gravity spins me in circles. My thick mane of glorious hair swishes behind me and before long I'm wondering if I look as fabulous as this feels. It takes all my upper arm strength to clamp my thighs to the pole and lift both legs off the table while I swoosh sexily for all I'm worth.

I risk a quick peek over to Matteo. We lock eyes for a long

moment, him walking towards me in slow motion, me gyrating for him, oozing sensuality from my every pore. The music pumps out, and the buzz of people chattering in my ears and the reckless feeling that Matteo is watching me be a total goddess is flooding my veins with adrenaline.

I. AM. NAILING. IT.

He stands right in front of me. I stretch my legs out so that he can appreciate the lean muscle, honed by years of jogging.

He gives me a shy, appreciative smile. It floods my soul with confidence. I close my eyes and wonder if, like me, he is imagining my thighs wrapped around his neck.

I bend over backwards, my boobs somewhere down to my chin. Even upside down he's incredibly handsome. I pull myself up as provocatively as I can and swing like a performing chimpanzee.

Whoosh.

Whoosh.

I am all woman, I want to roar as I fling my legs out behind me. It's like a primeval spirit has taken control of my limbs. I am as light as air.

Whoosh.

Whoosh.

Oof!

At the same time as one foot connects with something solid, throwing me off balance, the other sweeps the table surface as I hear the systematic crashing of drinks to the floor. My eyes snap open. The world stops spinning as I survey the damage. I've emptied the table of the giant fishbowl and pint glasses, and they have smashed into millions of tiny pieces across the floor, creating a huge puddle. But no one seems remotely bothered about this small lake of broken glass and beer. Everyone has turned towards Matteo. He is standing nursing his eye.

We stare at each other as the horror of the situation sinks in. It would appear that someone, there's a worryingly high chance of it being me, has kicked him in the face. He is giving me the look that you'd give someone you were perhaps thinking of strangling with your bare hands. It sends immediate shivers of remorse down my whole body.

There's a trickle of blood crawling down his cheek. He bends down to retrieve his phone from the wet floor where it is lying smashed and stomps away shaking his head.

'Oh, my fucking God, Connie!' howls Liberty. 'That could not have gone any worse, pet.'

* * *

Finally, somehow, it's three thirty in the morning and most of the girls are struggling to stay awake and are slumped over the tables back in The Knee Trembler. I'm still sitting bolt upright in a traumatised daze. I have been unable to speak since the pole-dancing incident.

'Connie? Connie, are you able to take Liberty to the toilet while I mop up after Cherry?' Big Mand croaks.

'It's no use, she's still zoned out. Big Sue? Big Sue?' Tash squeaks. 'I'm ready now, love, if you can help me over to the... to the... What did I say I wanted to do?'

I snap briefly out of my trance. 'I will not be broken. I don't need a man to complicate me.'

Gosh. I've just coined a new phrase. I wonder if it will catch on.

'You mean to complete you,' says Cherry. 'You don't need a man to complete you.'

'Yes. That's what I mean. I don't need a Matt to complete me.'

Why do I have this huge pain in my chest? As though I have

disappointed myself yet again. Always with the disappoint-ments. The unfulfilled feeling. The empty, pointless point of existence.

'There's no point to me, is there?' I say sadly. 'No point.'

'Connie. Stop being so self-obsessed, will you?' yells Tash, jolting me out of my depression. 'It's not all about you.'

She's right. No good will ever come from being excessively preoccupied with one's own life and thinking everything and everyone in this world should be focused on oneself. I give her an admiring look. Tash is enormously enlightened.

She stands up, throwing her arms wide and bellows, 'Look at me! Someone look at me!'

The Dollz all turn towards her while I try to work out how this shameless cry for attention is any different to me being so self-obsessed.

'No. The real me,' she says, pointing to her heart.

Ah. Perhaps that's it.

'Finally. She's owning her own truth,' says Liberty. 'Show us who you really are, babes.'

Tash swipes away at her phone and demands that the manager plugs it in to his speakers. She is having a brief second wind and gets up on stage to perform her much talked-about version of *Riverdance*, which I remember we were very much looking forward to.

She hobbles onto the shallow stage, leaning against the wall to get her balance. And as if possessed by the spirit of Michael Flatley himself, she's off. We marvel at the speed with which she jiggles her feet about on stage despite the swollen ankle, only to see her pass out in the middle of it. She's mid-air one minute, executing a perfect split, and the next, her eyes clang shut and she's crumpling to the floor.

Luckily, Big Sue has the reflexes of a cheetah and swoops down to catch her just in time.

Beep.

Jorge is pulling up in his minibus. He has come to our rescue. We have never loved him more.

19

'He's never going to speak to me ever again,' I moan the next morning, padding through to the main house in search of paracetamol. My brain is clanging like a set of church bells. They've been ringing incessantly from the moment I awoke.

'No, he probably won't,' agrees Cherry. 'What in the name of fuck were you thinking?'

What was I thinking? I was thinking, *You would have killed me if I didn't get up and dance on the table, you scary witch*. That's what I was thinking.

Deep breaths.

Deep breaths.

I tossed and turned all night, tormented by images of Matteo and my strappy gladiator stiletto karate-chopping him in the face. Then, rather disturbingly, I was plagued by erotic imaginings of what would have happened had I not high-kicked him but instead had, as planned, performed a sexy, hypnotic dance to draw him captivatingly in. I may have accidentally altered the true course of destiny.

What if fate is doggedly trying to throw me and Matteo

together and I, in some warped feat of self-sabotage, am getting in my own way? What if I am to blame? This needs to be debated immediately. I flinch at the sheer pain of thinking.

'What if he's the love of my—'

'Never mind that. I think I might ask Sister Kevin to marry me,' Tash says, interrupting me as she wanders in with a dreamy expression on her face. 'It's the beard. It does things to me.'

'*Yes*. You should do it on stage at the festival, in front of thousands of people,' says Cherry. 'That way the proposal is both incredibly romantic and legally binding.'

And just like that, my mammoth philosophical predicament is usurped as the Dollz find this new turn of events extremely exciting but also, it would appear, extremely tiring. They trot out of the kitchen to discuss marriage proposals and how best to capitalise on them on social media, from the comfort of a sunlounger.

I'm restless.

Too restless to be left alone with only my thoughts. Flashbacks are haunting me: Matteo's lips, his eyes, his biceps, and of course his quick and intelligent mind and his flair for business. I'm not one of those shallow types who is only interested in someone for their looks or their wealth.

As I follow the girls outside, my phone pings. We all stop dead in our tracks.

'Is it Nancy?' Big Sue hisses, her eyes darting around as though Nancy may have installed CCTV in the pool area.

'No,' I say, disappointed it isn't Matteo. 'It's Nacho.'

'Who?'

'Enreeky. He wants to know if we are up for going jet-skiing this morning?'

The girls are now lying flat out on the beds, eyes closed, expensive sunflower oil dripping everywhere.

'We have a marriage proposal to organise,' Tash bellows from her lounger before slipping her glasses back up.

'We probably don't have time to go anyway. We should start rehearsing soon,' I say.

There's a collective groan.

'Connie, you should go and represent us. Let him know we are still definitely *interested*. Just be back two hours before the festival and bring some lemons with you, babes.'

This is just the sort of distraction I need to take my mind off Matteo and the humiliation of last night. I will also be able to drill Nacho for information as to what happened to Matteo afterwards and whether his eyesight is still intact. Another wave of shame sweeps through me. I will text him to see if he is all right.

I tap out a short message and press send.

★ ★ ★

I make my way down to the marina to see Nacho and the cliff divers hanging about in a large group. I am warmly welcomed with much chuckling and mimes of karate chops and high kicks. Nothing I don't deserve so I laugh along with them and assure them they are all safe as long as they stay at least two metres away from me.

'How is Matteo?' I ask. 'Have you seen him today?'

'Yes. He is good. No worries. We can hire a jet ski each from the kiosk and go out to the caves just along the coast because the water is beautiful there and crystal clear,' Nacho tells me in Spanish as we troop over to the tiny cabin to strip down to our swimsuits. I pay my money and get fitted with a life jacket. We leave our clothes and bags in a big heap and are all shown down to the jetty and given jet skis. Nacho takes a selfie of us all smiling and waving in our life jackets. I take one too and send it to Ged and Liam or they'll never believe it.

Ged responds:

> Cliff diving. Pole dancing. Jet skiing. Who even are you?

I glow with pride. He's right. I would never have thought it possible last week and yet look at me.

The group are obviously used to hiring the jet skis and jump straight on them. They do circles and fancy tricks in the marina while they wait for me. The instructor takes me over to a demo jet ski and tells me how simple they are to use, in both Spanish and English.

'We have only this two-seater left,' he apologises, pointing to a massive tank-like beast of a machine. He clocks my eyes popping in terror. 'But you share, so is okay. No worries.'

'Share? Who with?' I ask.

He points to the cabin just as Matteo emerges with his life jacket on. He stops suddenly when he sees me standing with the instructor.

My heart skips a beat. *Maybe exceptionally good-looking men tend to stick together for safety reasons.*

'Connie, what are you doing here?' he says, rattled. 'Are the Dollz here too?'

I point to Nacho, who is showing off on his jet ski by balancing on one leg and steering with his foot. I swallow a huge lump in my throat. 'No, they're not. Nacho invited me.'

'Yes. Of course he did.'

'He didn't tell you? Aren't you friends?'

'I'll let him explain.'

The mystery simply adds to the charm.

I take in the wad of bandage stuck above his eyebrow and the black eye still at the purple and green stage and wince.

'How's your eye?'

'About as good as your pole dancing.'

'Yes, I'm so sorry about that. Did you get my message?'

Jesus. Has there been a time when I haven't started a sentence to him with an apology?

'Forget it. It was an accident.' Matteo shrugs. 'At least I hope it was.' He looks sternly at me like I'm a naughty schoolgirl. Or maybe I'm imagining that. Tiredness seeps through my veins as I stifle a yawn. 'Big night, was it?' he says, unimpressed. He's probably thinking ahead to me being half-asleep on stage at the festival. 'Looks like I'll have to drive the jet ski then.'

'Presumptuous of you.'

I am not loving my tit-for-tat tone one bit, but I'll be buggered if I admit to going to bed pissed at four this morning.

Matteo blows out his cheeks. He doesn't seem overly keen on the alternative. Come to think of it, neither am I, but I've made the point, so I best stick with it.

'No offence,' I say, 'but I've seen your driving and it doesn't always end well for me.'

Matteo seems put out for a moment before he starts to laugh, holding up his hands. 'Fair point. You drive.'

Two seconds later, as we float slowly towards the others, I realise I have not thought this through. The jet ski is supremely powerful, and I have not yet built up the courage to give it some throttle. Worse still, Matteo is sitting behind me so once we start going faster, he will have to put his hands around my waist. My actual body. My bare skin. I have gone to pieces, and it is greatly affecting my command of this whopping, great machine. My thighs are splayed either side of it, and I'm leaning forward as far as I can to reach the handlebars. I try not to picture my buttocks poking towards him in an inviting manner, rather like a baboon in the wild, presenting her bloated, vibrant red backside ready for mating.

Matteo is sitting patiently as I glance over my shoulder. While I'm relieved that he has grabbed on to the two side handles for support rather than my waist, I do feel his eyes are saying, *Connie, for fuck's sake, we won't even get out into open sea at this rate.*

So far, we've managed to share many monumental experiences in the last week, giving each other matching black eyes, smashing each other's phone screens and all but ruining each other's livelihoods, which is bizarre enough without ending up on a jet ski together.

'I'll turn this handle, shall I?'

He nods encouragingly as I give it a twist. The jet ski roars to life and almost throws us off as we speed out of the marina at a lightning pace. I get a rush of adrenaline straight to the head as the wind whips up my hair and seawater sprays out to the sides.

It is thrilling! I *love* it. I could squeal with excitement, but I should try to play it cool. I'd like to appear as though this isn't the most exhilarating thing I've done in my entire life, even though it absolutely is.

'This is so amazing, isn't it?' I yell over the roar of the engine.

Matteo says nothing.

He's either sulking or incredibly blasé, perhaps because he does this every day of the week. Unless he isn't and he can't hear for the noise? I slow down for fear of going too fast and crashing into one of the other jet skis and become immediately conscious of not being able to see Matteo's hands on the side handles. I swivel round and eye the empty seat behind me with dismay.

Sweet baby Jesus.

I frantically scan the immediate vicinity. I can't see him bobbing in the water nearby. I retrace my steps as it were, back into the marina, and spot his head bobbing up and down metres from the departure point. I reach him just as he climbs wearily out and up the ramp. He stands with his hands on his hips, his head tipped accusingly to one side.

'I didn't do it on purpose,' I yell over, cutting the engine, allowing the jet ski to float up to him. He's got fronds of sea kelp in his hair. His bandage is lost at sea. He's picked up some engine grease from the thin layer of petrol lying on top of the water. Looks like it'll stain his shorts. I best not mention it. Not after what happened on the plane. I try not to stare at how ripped he is. Or how the tattoo sleeve on his arm moves with every muscle. Even half-covered in slime, he's magnificent.

Credit where credit's due, he wades back in and hops on without saying anything. I put my hands nervously on the handlebars. I turn to give him a reassuring grin. I hope he can't tell that I'm now shitting myself. Just as I twist the throttle, his hands cover mine. I glance down at his tanned fingers. It feels very intimate, and a white-hot shoot of electricity runs through me. I wait to see what he does next. He applies a tiny amount of pressure, guiding me to twist the accelerator slowly, and we gently pick up speed and expertly glide out of the marina.

Suddenly, I can think of nothing else but his hands on mine. His skin feels hot, and it's making me prickle all over.

'You might want to watch where you're going,' he says in my ear. It sends delicious currents down my neck.

I nod, not trusting myself to speak. My whole body has started to tingle.

'Seriously. Watch where you're going.'

I nod, daring to glance back at him so he can see my big cow eyes from close up. Water is spraying over him.

'Left, Connie, left!'

He has such dark eyes to match his thick, dark hair, which is swaying very attractively in the breeze.

'No, other left!'

Gaaaah! He sounds so masterful as he leans in and gently swerves the jet ski so we can avoid a boat coming in and a group doing doggie yoga on paddleboards.

We don't go as fast as the others but make sure to keep up at the back. I am finding the experience invigorating. I cannot believe I'm doing this. By the time we reach the caves, I am ecstatic. The others have already jumped off the jet skis, leaving them afloat in the cove, and are swimming into the caves. The water is so clear it's almost fluorescent with vividly coloured fish of all shapes and sizes. It feels as though I'm in an exotic dream. This can't be me. I wish my mother could see me now. She'd never believe it. The rest of the group disappear deeper into the darkness to explore the nearby caves.

'You coming?' Matteo asks.

Now is not the time to tell him I've developed a crush on him that is so overpowering it has affected my ability to swim. My body has literally turned to jelly. I need to get a grip. This is ridiculous. He can't be interested in me after the show I've made of myself, and I shouldn't be interested in him either. It's too soon. Or maybe it's been too long. Either way, he is way out of my league and I'm going back to my humdrum life in a couple of days.

'I'll catch you up,' I say.

He dives off the jet ski and swims into the dark depths while I slip into the water and float on my back at the cave entrance to let the experience soak in. I stare up to the cave roof high above me and wonder at the rock formations twinkling away. The Dollz' words echo in my brain. *I'm a strong, powerful woman. I deserve happiness.* I must keep reminding myself of that. I should put these affirmations into the universe, so they come true. I check to make sure I am alone.

'I am a strong, independent woman!' I shout up to the ceiling and listen to the echo.

What else do I need to be?

This is the most at peace I have felt in a long time. I've been in Spain less than a week and have already felt more emotions than I have in the last couple of years. In a way it feels as though I'm being shaken awake.

'I am a confident, powerful, sexy woman!'

No, that sounds too much.

I hear Ged and Liam in my head telling me that life doesn't always turn out how you expect but that doesn't mean I have to remain so bitter and miserable about it. I have been bitter since my mother passed. This is very true. Perhaps I should be more honest with myself.

'I am a sometimes lonely, often bitter woman with the ability to cope adequately when the need arises!'

Hmmmm. More accurate but far less punchy.

My voice echoes off the cave walls as I float with my ears submerged, listening to the vibrations of sea life humming through the water. I do believe I'm being in and of the moment. My busy mind is cleared of thought as I focus on each breath, my chest swelling before I exhale slowly. I am calm. I am thankful. I am going to try and be more accepting. I must not harbour this resentment of how my motherless life has turned out, as it will only hold me back.

A niggling feeling gnaws at my serenity as thoughts of the

gig later this evening and performing to the Benidorm festival crowd flood into my mind. Nancy has not been backwards in coming forward. The main thing is to keep her happy. I will make sure to impress. I have yet to get a playlist and backing tracks together, never mind quickly learning some of Ed Sheeran's hits. It will take some time to sort out and do a run-through. Nerves get the better of me just thinking about Matteo coming to hear me and me making a mess of it.

As though he has read my thoughts, he pops up right next to me, causing me to suddenly lose my stride, my arms flapping. Matteo grabs me firmly by the life jacket. We stare at each other for a few moments.

'Sorry to startle you like that. Fish whispering or whatever it was you were doing,' he says.

'Vocal warm-ups,' I splutter, focusing on the light bouncing off the sea, the rocks, anywhere but his glistening skin as droplets of water drip tantalisingly down his neck. 'I was doing vocal warm-ups for tonight.'

I brace myself for an eye roll. *He doesn't need any further proof that I'm mental.*

'Why? What were you doing?' I ask.

Swimming, Connie. He was swimming.

'I was looking for lonely, bitter women with the ability to cope adequately,' he says. 'I hear the caves are full of them.'

Cheeky fecker.

Matteo laughs, raking his gaze from my eyes slowly down to my lips, which, as if on command, part ever so slightly. Suddenly there is an unmistakable charged current flying between us. I must give him a signal of some sort because he leans towards me and then thinks better of it and stops. We are mere centimetres apart.

'You are very cheeky. You should be punished,' I purr, sounding like a dominatrix.

Where is this coming from? I should hop on a plane to Amsterdam. I could make a fortune.

His eyebrows raise a fraction. He likes it. Time feels as though it is standing still. Our mouths are hovering dangerously close together and the air between us is crackling with unresolved sexual tension, as far as I'm concerned anyway. He may well be thinking of doing his taxes, getting a puppy or what he's going to have for tea. When it comes to men, especially this man, I'm lost at sea, quite literally.

He does not move a muscle, so neither do I. I briefly worry if the attraction is all one-sided. As he tilts his head, I can see his mind racing to make sense of me. He's clearly unsure. It could be an opportunity for this strong, independent woman to take the lead. I should lean in and place a salty kiss gently on his lips, but I can't. The rejection would be crushing. Snippets of all the times I've humiliated myself in front of him sap my confidence. Matteo will have to make the first move. My eyes drill into his, willing him to do it.

Just as I think he's about to move in, I hear my name being called.

'Cenicienta!' Nacho is bobbing in the water just outside the cave. 'Cenicienta, come! Come! We go back to shore now.'

'Your date is calling for you, Cinderella,' Matteo says. 'The name suits you,' he says before he swims away from me, slicing through the water like he's part dolphin.

Date? Why would he think... *Oh.*

I swim over to the jet ski. Matteo hauls me up onto it and straight into the driver's seat. I immediately twist round.

'There's no date. We're not on a date,' I say. My heaving chest causes the life jacket to swell. My boobs are almost touching my chin. 'There have been no dates. It's very, very platonic. Nacho is like my brother.'

'Oh?'

'Like my newly discovered, foreign, given-up-for-adoption brother. And this excursion would be like meeting for the first time. Or a second time, if the first was arranged by the agency and we met for coffee. Then we decided to meet again and do something more fun.'

There's something very wrong with me.

Matteo's eyes give nothing away in the face of such madness. Maybe he has come across my kind before.

'So, he's like the brother you never knew you had?'

'Yes.'

As if that makes any sense.

My whole body grows tense as he leans in to cover my hands with his, the muscles on his arms rippling every time he pulls the grips on the handles towards him. I lean back ever so slightly, pressing against him. I feel the length of his body against mine and experience pangs of wild, out-of-control lust.

It is almost like I'm dreaming this whole thing. In fact, I might be. It is bizarre, after all, isn't it? It's not like my dull, boring, grey life has suddenly become a fairy tale in full Disney technicolour, with an evil queen and handsome princes fighting for my attention, in some beautiful far-off land...

We rev up the engine to head back to the kiosk. I am high with anticipation as we zip along. Matteo has my nerves on end. He knows everything about me, and I know nothing at all about him.

I yell over my shoulder at him, 'Tell me all about you.'

It's probably not the time, but like I say, I'm really not myself.

'Seriously?' he bellows. 'Can't it wait?'

I shake my head. I need to know where this gorgeous man comes from. What he does. How he got here. What sort of woman he goes for.

He throws his head back to laugh just as we are hit by a massive wave. In one violent motion, the jet ski topples to one side, throwing us into the water with a thud. I'm momentarily disoriented as my head smashes into the sea as though it was concrete, and a swirl of waves instantly sucks me under.

20

When I surface, I hear much yelling and shouting. I search for Matteo and spot him doing the same. Relief floods his face when he sees me bobbing up and down.

'Stay there. I'll come get you!' he yells.

It's hard to know what's happening. I swallow a huge gulp of salty sea as the waves crash over my head.

Matteo swims over, pointing to the cause of the waves. A speedboat manned by lunatics is dangerously close to snorkellers, families in kayaks and paddleboarders, many of whom have been thrown into the sea like us. The lifeguards are blowing whistles from the beach and people are waving angrily at the revellers on board. Music is pumping out of the boat, and they seem oblivious.

'Dickheads,' Matteo says, grabbing my life jacket to pull me to him. 'You okay? Enough drama for you? Bet you're loving it.'

He's got a dangerous twinkle in his eye as though he's enjoying this moment. Our noses are practically touching. His eyes are glistening and dark. His arm feels like a vice. Without thinking, I hook my legs around his waist and cling to him. Our life jackets are taking most of our weight.

It's one of those special moments that will be recorded in my memory banks and replayed over and over. It may even be deserving of its own eighties-style power ballad.

A scream alerts us to danger, and we see a young girl, at the top of the slide on a large pedalo, knocked into the sea as the waves throw it off balance. The parents and young siblings scream as she's pulled under. Both Matteo and I instinctively swim over to help. The large pedalo looms above us, rocking out of control. Children are panicking and clutching on to the sides. The parents struggle to get out of the seats as it causes more imbalance. Everything happens in slow motion. The parents are screaming. 'Where is she? Where is she? Lucie! Lucie!'

The pedalo is too close to us, pounding down with such a force it makes it difficult to stay above the waves, and we are in danger of being sucked underneath. A terrifying wall of sea rises up and curls away, the white foam making it impossible to see anything below its surface. I thrash my arms to swim away from the boat bashing down beside me when I spot something pink under the water.

It's the child's life jacket.

She's hidden amongst the thrashing waves. I reach under to haul her up to me. The girl must only be about three. Her eyes are wide with fear as she coughs out some water. She feels tiny in my arms and she's instinctively clawing at my head to reach above the water, which pushes me under. My life jacket is giving me some much-needed buoyancy but between the waves crashing over our heads and the sheer panic of the situation, I'm fearing for our lives.

Matteo spots us both struggling to keep our heads above

water and reaches us in seconds. He tries to pull the girl from me but she's clinging on to me too tightly. We swim her over to the pedalo, but it's too choppy and dangerous to lift her on board. The hard plastic is a ton weight as it smashes against the waves. The parents are screaming, the girl is crying, the speedboat is thundering past unaware that it's creating tidal waves of panic as it circles around us.

'Matteo!' I shout, pointing to the jet ski, which has floated away from us. He slices through the water over to it. After a few attempts, he makes it up on board and drives it towards us, wave after wave beating him back.

The waves make it difficult to swim towards him, especially as I can only use one arm, the other clamped to the girl. It takes some effort to fight the continual surge of waves and I'm instantly tired once we reach the jet ski. I make several failed attempts to clamber on board as Matteo struggles to keep balance. Luckily, he puts his magnificent strong arms to good use and reaches down to pull up first the little girl and then me as though we weigh nothing at all. I clutch her closely, making sure she's okay.

'It's okay,' I croon in her ear. 'I've got you. I've got you.'

She sags against me, exhausted. Matteo signals to the pedalo to go ashore. The coastguard races towards us to check if we need assistance before they speed off to administer a severe reprimand to the irresponsible louts on the speedboat. A kayak with two lifeguards comes over to help guide everyone back to the beach.

There's much crying when we reunite the little girl with her family. The parents are beyond thankful to us. The father shakes our hands many times, repeating over and over how grateful he is. The mother is clamping the child to her while the siblings cling to her legs. A whole crowd of sun worshippers has gathered to help lug the pedalo out of the water, and more lifeguards have raced over to offer support.

Matteo and I step back to let them recover. My legs are wobbling and I'm swaying slightly as my muscles go weak.

'You were magnificent,' he says, reaching out a hand to steady me.

I gawp back unattractively. No one has ever said that to me before, ever. Water is dripping down from my hair as I stare back at him.

'So are you,' I say, catching myself. 'So *were* you.'

'You're a very strong swimmer,' he says. 'The way you coped with those waves. The way you dived under to save her. That was awesome. And when Cherry fell off the yacht, you went straight in to get her without hesitation. You're fearless.'

Me, fearless? This makes me instinctively embarrassed. I'm nothing of the sort.

'The way you got back to the jet ski and lifted us to safety,' I say, throwing the spotlight back on him. 'Totally awesome. Unbelievable upper-body strength. Incredible. You're the one who's fearless.'

I sound like I'm about to give him marks out of ten. I force myself not to stare at his body glistening in the sun, his shorts clinging to his muscular legs. His biceps are bulging like small watermelons, and his wet hair is dripping down his tanned face. He's simply heroic-looking. There's no other way to put it.

'I mean it. You are very brave,' Matteo says.

'No. No, I'm really not. I swim to build up lung capacity, you know? To hold the notes,' I say quickly. This whole episode has my nerves on end. He cocks his head to one side. He's giving no indication as to warrant further explanation, but I just can't seem to play it cool. 'Take the soprano octaves. They can be especially tricky. It took years of practice, but I can now hold my breath for nearly five minutes.'

It seems like Matteo doesn't know what to do with this piece of trivia in the midst of all this high-level drama.

'Are you feeling okay?' he says, stepping towards me.

My jabbering on, repeating his words back at him, seems to instantly defuse the tension and I see the admiration quickly replaced with worry.

No, I am not okay. I think I may be in some state of shock.

'We should celebrate or something,' I say, managing to make it sound inappropriate, like we've won first prize in a hot-dog-eating contest rather than having just saved a child's life.

Yes, definitely a mild form of PTSD.

Matteo nods his head. 'Maybe we should return the jet ski first and discuss partying later?'

* * *

When we eventually make it back to the marina, Nacho and his friends are nowhere to be seen. Matteo climbs off the jet ski, turning to help me clamber off. We lock eyes for a moment as he lowers me into the shallow water so that we can walk up the ramp. I feel his hand at my back keeping me steady. We have undergone yet another unique life-changing experience which binds us. Maybe these coincidences are more meaningful than we care to admit. When he says nothing, it strikes me that perhaps we no longer need actual words to discuss the enormity of our bravery. We can simply appreciate one another's greatness with silence and hidden looks.

'See you later?' I eventually say to Matteo as casually as I can. I feel my skin burning at the effort to remain outwardly calm.

'Sure,' he says, gently pressing the back of his hand to the stiletto-shaped cut on his head. 'I'll wear a full suit of armour just in case. Do you need a lift?'

'Thanks, but I'll walk. I think I need to decompress.' I'm suddenly overwhelmed with exhaustion as I unbuckle my life jacket and head to the kiosk to get my things.

The kiosk is empty, so I spot my bag on a shelf almost immediately. I'm just about to reach down for it when quite out of the blue, the air leaves my lungs like a punch to the stomach. I feel my legs turn to jelly and a great swell of fear grabs hold of me at the enormity of what just happened. I lean against the shelf. My mind has suddenly become filled with terror at how easily a life can be snuffed out. In a split second, that tiny child could have been dragged under the boat and out to sea on a riptide. What if I hadn't been there to spot her? What if we'd left the cave just a minute earlier and been back in the marina with the others? What if we'd never heard Cherry fall overboard?

Suddenly, my body trembles at the fragility of life. The terrified look in the child's eyes takes me back to when my mother was sick. Her eyes were permanently haunted. I could never make that look go away no matter how much I assured her she would get better. I press a fist to my mouth to stop any sound escaping and hunch down to wait until this awful feeling passes. My body is wracked by silent sobs.

A noise startles me. Matteo is filling the doorway. He reaches me in three strides and his face softens instantly as he crouches down and pulls me to him. His hand smooths my hair, and the other gently strokes my back until my silent heaving settles. He cradles me in his arms until I'm ready to stand up. He says nothing as he leads me away from the kiosk and over to his lady scooter parked by the marina and takes me home. We are both exhausted. He helps me off the moped when we get to the villa and holds me close.

'Sure you're up to performing later?' he says, his face full of understanding and compassion.

'Nancy will kill me if I mess this up. I'm fine now. I think I just needed to get the shock out of my system.'

'Totally understandable. That was a big deal. I feel shaken myself.' Matteo exhales slowly. 'Life can turn on a dime, as they say.'

'She could have died. We could have died.'

Matteo reaches out to take my fingers lightly in his and we share a moment that feels so tender, so loaded with understanding. When he pulls me in for a hug, I can almost feel him transferring some sort of strength to me. After a long while, he steps back.

'I'll handle Nancy if you need to duck out. I'm sure she'll understand.'

Well, he could try. Nancy has been in the business for thirty years. She is a tough nut to crack. And besides, she's had quite enough of my 'woe is me'-ing.

'Wait. Is that why you were on my flight? You'd been in Newcastle to meet with Nancy?'

He nods. 'And seeing some potential acts. I could try to find a replacement for you. You look like you need to rest.'

'Thanks, but I'm fine. I need to do it, and I promise there'll be no more drama,' I say to reassure him. 'We'll be on our best behaviour. Totally professional.'

I see the corner of his mouth raise into a smile. He doesn't believe me in the slightest. Overwhelming desire and adoration for how sensitive he's being ooze from my every pore as I wait for him to kiss me. It feels like a kissing moment. The situation calls for one of those high-intensity, emotionally charged kisses that set your soul on fire.

My eyelids flutter to an attractive close as I wait.

And wait.

My eyes spring open.

Apparently, I'm very much in the minority because Matteo holds me at arm's length and says, 'Take care then.'

He throws a leg over his scooter and takes off.

My mouth is hanging open.

Take care then?

Take friggin' care then?

'Take care' is what you say to a friend, to your grandma, to the fella in the shop behind the counter. He must think I'm a raving lunatic. I've blown it. Spain's most handsome man is friend-zoning me because I'm an emotional wreck – which he is not finding sexy. Let's face it, the list of reasons not to be interested in me could be endless.

I am beyond frustrated with myself. But most of all, I am tired of always being sad. I need to find a way to live with it so that it doesn't swamp everything I do.

21

A few soul-searching hours later, we are on the minibus on our way to the festival just outside the town centre and the Dollz have confirmed my suspicions that 'Take care then' is definitely a sign of a fizzled-out, non-romantic attraction.

I am gutted.

Absolutely gutted.

Liberty has reached deep into my soul to discover that I do really, really like Matteo. 'Connie, pet. I think you're ready for something to happen between you that is not, as has been the recent case, anything to do with great disappointment, fear or near-death experiences, am I right?'

I nod.

'But you must acknowledge the truth that he might not feel the same way and be okay with it. You're a big girl. It happens. Even though I'm sure he *is* into you. I saw the way you looked at each other before you sliced his eye open with your stiletto.'

She is being polite. This is what any expert would call 'unrequited love'.

'We told you to be brave and bold, and you were. There are

loads of people out there for you to meet, honey. Lots of adventures to be had.'

It makes me think of my dad dipping his toe in the Lakes with Madge, and I suddenly realise that I'm finally ready. I'm ready to fully commit to meeting new people and trying new things. It feels like a revelation.

'This isn't just about Matteo,' I tell her. 'It's about being present in the moment. With everyone and everything.'

Liberty beams at me. 'Finally. She gets it. Hoes before bros.'

'Hoargghhhay, darling. You can drop us off here, pet,' Cherry yells down the bus. 'At the performers' VIP entrance.'

We arrive suited and booted to find the music festival is in full swing. We draw cheers as soon as we step off Jorge's minibus and the security guards let us through without even checking the passes we are wearing on lanyards round our necks. We crowd into a massive tent and register our names. Someone says something in rapid Spanish that I don't catch and jabs at a big chart. It's the festival layout. There are four stage areas, a food zone, a drinks zone, and a chill-out zone. He is very stressed and frantically pointing out the stage areas, pointing at me, pointing at the Dollz, pointing back at the chart then pointing to the exit and waving us to go through as a queue builds behind us.

We step outside to see the nuns have us tracked down within minutes of our arrival as though they are wearing homing beacons.

'Did any of you catch that?' I ask, scurrying to catch up with the Dollz and the nuns who are marching in a determined manner through the crowd, past the many marquees lit up with fairy lights, past the stalls with colourful bunting and the many glorious smells rising from sizzling hotplates and burger stands.

We come to a stop in a very lively area. I consult my map to see we are in the drinks zone where a band is singing drinking songs in both English and Spanish. Everyone at the festival appears absolutely paralytic. We can barely move for bodies, and I still have not worked out which stage we are supposed to be on and when. The details are all in Spanish, so the Dollz are relying heavily on me to be in charge and tell them where to go. Not only that, but because of the 'Take care then' incident, I am dreading bumping into Matteo. I am so embarrassed at flinging myself at him when he is clearly no longer interested and, even worse, his scary business partner Alex will find out and fire me on the spot and make sure I will never work within the whole of Europe ever again. I should take the hint and leave him alone.

I snap back to the job at hand. The Dollz look stunning in a matching array of black rubber suspenders, bra tops, Lycra basques, fishnet body stockings and a selection of killer heels with studs, peep toes and gladiator straps. I have poured myself into the black, wet-look bodysuit with plunging neckline and cut-out waist. To me it screams dominatrix, but Ged and Liam assured me on FaceTime that it really screams hashtag boss lady.

'Just make sure *you* wear the bodysuit,' said Ged, 'and not the other way round. Confidence, darling. Have confidence.'

An hour later, I've already been round all four stages to see when we are on and not one person has managed to tell me. The Dollz have wandered off so many times that I've had to create a WhatsApp group so that I can keep track of them to tell them where to meet. It has been like herding cats since the moment we arrived. We haven't even done our performance yet and I am already exhausted. Despite all their promises to behave, the Dollz are clearly living their best lives and are not giving a flying fuck about their intentions to focus and be prepared.

I feel myself beginning to panic. It's happening all over again. I'm going to end up late and unprepared and make a mess of the whole thing. It's okay for the Dollz. They've all got stellar bloody careers, and this shared interest in singing is simply a way of bringing the group of friends together in the same way a book or knitting club or building a gin shed in the garden might work.

But for me, well, it's all I've got. I have no money coming in, no safety net, and now no clue about career goals. I'm beyond frustrated with myself. How did I let this happen? Being jobless, soon to be homeless and on the verge of throwing away the only chance I have left of singing for a living is not where I thought I'd be at nearly thirty. Oh, and single. Very fucking single, especially after the way I have behaved this week. And even if Liberty is right, I'd be amazed if Matteo dares come anywhere near me unless he has a thing for weepy psychos.

And now I'm in a mood.

Suddenly, I hear a shriek nearby. I'd recognise that pitch anywhere. It's the closest any of them has come to a vocal warm-up. I squeeze through the crowd to find Tash.

'Connie. Over here, babes!' She draws in a lungful of air and fixes me with a wild stare. 'BAAAY-AAAY-AAABES!' she yells, even though I am clearly fucking coming, in fucking stilts, across lumpy fucking ground, full of lethal fucking potholes.

'What now?' I ask with more patience than she deserves.

Not one of them has offered to help me find the right stage or the tent where the organisers might be. Actually, to be fair, I do know where that is. It is clearly indicated on the map with a huge arrow, but I have been so terrified of bumping into Matteo that I have not wanted to go near it.

'It's gone,' she sobs.

Bug-eyed, she announces to me and Sister Kevin that she has lost her phone. She will not be able to take selfies of herself or the giant curly pink straw that came with her drink. She's already a few sheets to the wind. I'm sure Instagram can survive with fewer images of Tash doing the peace sign into the camera while holding up yet another cocktail.

'And the backing tracks. We can't go on stage without the backing tracks. They're *all* on my phone.'

Fuckety fuck fuck.

'Our selfies are on your phone!' Sister Kevin wails.

'They are, babes. I feel we have incredible chemistry, don't you?' Tash responds, clearly distracted. 'You look ready to settle down with a special someone.'

Sister Kevin looks overjoyed.

Oh Christ. Now is not the time for a proposal.

'Where did you last have it?' I butt in. 'Does it have a tracker on?'

We wait patiently as Tash takes an age to register this barrage of complex questions.

'No, but I definitely had it in the toilets!' she blurts.

'Good, Tash. Very good. This phone,' Sister Kevin demands, swiftly taking charge of the investigation. 'Were you in the toilet taking an intimate photo of yourself as promised?'

I shake my head in despair. He's as drunk as she is. Tash licks her lips extravagantly in answer.

'Right, let's get it back,' he declares as though the Hope Diamond has gone missing. 'You!' he barks at me. 'Check *every* Portaloo there is.'

He checks to see if Tash is loving how adept he is in a crisis. And from the way she is hanging off his neck, she certainly is.

'Twice!' he yells at me, milking the situation for all it's worth.

I stare at him wide-eyed. I am not checking every stinky toilet. Besides, I'm too British, I'd have to queue politely for each one. It would take days. Weeks. Tash squeals and gives me wide, childlike eyes.

'Fankoo, Connie. Luvvoo,' she says. It certainly does something for Sister Kevin all right as I observe their open exchange of saliva. He hoicks her leg up onto his hip.

'And which toilets are you two going to check?' I put my hand on my hip. '*Twice?*'

They stop clawing at each other as Tash, removing her tongue from his ear, gives me a sharp, ferrety look.

'Connie? We are clearly sharing a special moment?'

Rather than focus on Tash's special moment, which seems a lot like all the other moments that she's experienced since we got here, I search for the rest of the girls. Not one to be seen, and less than an hour before they are on stage.

I give up.

I head towards the designated Portaloo zone where a thousand cross-legged women stand chatting and vaping while they wait in lines for the loo. I make my way through the crowd, trying to ignore the ungodly smell of urinal cakes while shaking off a barrage of shouting from women who think I'm pushing in.

'*Mi teléfono en el toiletto plástico! Emergencia grande!*' I yell, beating on the doors with sheer embarrassment that I'm making this seem much more of a crisis than it actually is. *Why is the Spanish for Portaloo not adequately covered in the A level syllabus? Why?*

I keep calling Tash's phone and strain to listen out for the ringtone against the festival music blaring out.

I get to the end of the first row and press my face to the door as it opens, sending me toppling to the ground. I am cringing with embarrassment as I struggle to get up, the bodysuit reluctant to allow even an inch of movement. This is so not going to work. I put out an urgent message to the WhatsApp group explaining our predicament. I stand staring at my phone as decades pass without so much as a ping. I have no way of knowing if any of them has picked it up and will help. I take out my map of the site. The only thing I can do is suck it up and go to the management tent.

I jostle through the crowds and approach the security guards at the entrance who block my way, check my lanyard and point me towards the hospitality tent.

'No,' I yell crossly, putting a hand on my hip. 'I'm not after free drink. I'm after Matteo. The boss man. *El jefe.*'

The guard indicates that he can't hear or understand me.

'*Quiero* Matteo!' I yell. Time is very much of the essence.

The guards burst out laughing. '*Te quieres* Matteo?'

'*Sì,*' I shout past them into the tent, hoping he can hear me calling. This is so frustrating. We now have only thirty minutes to find the phone, find the stage and do the set.

'You're in love with Matteo, are you?'

I spin round to see Alex marching towards me with a startled expression on her face.

'What? No. I was telling them I want him, as in I want to see him.'

'Well,' she says, putting her hands on her hips to mirror my actions, 'you're screaming at the top of your lungs to the entire management team inside that you want my business partner both emotionally and sexually, as in you love him. L.O.V.E. Love. Now, if you could stop making a fool of yourself for five minutes,' Alex continues in a cruel tone, 'you need to get yourself on fucking stage right now. He doesn't need another groupie. He has plenty of those already.'

My jaw drops at her stinging accusation. I take in her cold, hard expression and feel my face burn with embarrassment. The only thing that could make this moment worse would be to run into Matteo. So naturally, when I see him emerge from the tent to stand right in front of me, his eyes swivelling between Alex and me, I panic.

'That's enough,' he says to her sharply in Spanish.

He has replaced the bandage covering the corner of his eyebrow, and his black eye now matches mine. It simply makes him even more rugged. He's wearing shorts and a T-shirt as though he's stepped out of a Hugo Boss photo shoot. I feel stunned at the mere sight of him.

I've just hollered to everyone around that I love him. And at that moment, I think it might be true.

'I've got this,' he says over his shoulder to Alex, waiting for her to leave before he turns back to me.

'It's not what it sounded like!' I squeak, finally finding my voice.

'Oh?' he says, stepping towards me with a frown. 'So, you're *not* in love with me?'

He's playing with me. I feel my eyes mushroom out of their sockets. His face is a mere foot from mine. His eyes roam casually over my body. He probably thinks I'm mad or drunk or both. He's so mesmerising I can barely look him in the eye.

'Listen,' I say, lowering my voice. 'Can we talk?'

He leads me into the tent.

'What's gone wrong now? I specifically remember you promising me' – he checks his phone – 'three hours ago that there was to be an evening of no drama.'

Cheek. He can be a little too presumptuous, can't he?

'There's no drama. I just need you to help me with a few technical issues,' I say in a whatever-do-you-mean type of voice, not waiting for him to respond. 'First, I need to find Tash's phone. It's got all the Dollz' backing tracks for the gig on it. I also need you to help me find the Dollz. They've gone AWOL all over the bloody place. And finally, the stage. None of us has a clue which one we're supposed to be on or when.'

There is a short silence before Matteo answers. His eyes are glinting. He is enjoying this. 'Phew, for a moment there I thought something had gone horribly awry.'

'Fine. You're right. It's another shambles. Please,' I beg. 'I can't afford for this to go wrong. Nancy will sack us all and I'll be jobless, homeless, and my life will basically be over.'

Matteo looks at me in surprise. It's probably best to keep my volatile emotional and financial state under wraps. He hasn't exactly seen the best of me since I stepped foot on that plane.

'I'm just panicking,' I say. 'Can you help me?'

'Of course.'

Relief floods through me as I gaze gratefully up at him. He surprises me by reaching over to bring me into one of his reassuring hugs.

'It's okay. We'll get it sorted.'

It's just what I need. I melt against him, giving myself over to the moment, allowing myself to feel safe in his arms, as though the cares and worries have all just faded away for a second. Unfortunately, it has the feel of a 'take care then' type of hug.

'Stay here,' he says. He signals one of the security men over. They speak in rapid Spanish. 'Where does Tash think the phone is?' he asks me.

'One of the Portaloos.' I shrug apologetically. 'And I don't know which one. It's an iPhone with a pink glittery cover with a unicorn on but instead of a horn it's a... man's thingy.'

Christ.

Matteo is not fazed in the slightest. Almost as though he'd expect nothing less.

'So, that's the phone and set list sorted. Next on the list is the stage. I can show you that myself and then there's just the Dollz to round up.'

He's so masterful and unflappable. I can't tear my eyes away from him.

'I left some of the Dollz in the drinks zone,' I explain as I back away from him and his terribly kissable lips. 'I'll start my search there.' I feel an invisible force pulling me towards him again even though he has basically friend-zoned me and we are in this tent where he conducts his important music-mogul business, and his scary business partner is hovering nearby throwing us daggers. I feel her beady eyes boring holes into my back. I'd hate to put his reputation in jeopardy.

Aware of the attention we seem to be drawing to ourselves from Alex and the crew, Matteo and I wait to see if the phone has been located in a strained silence until a woman – who would be drop-dead gorgeous, wouldn't she? – comes over and hands me Tash's phone. Matteo thanks her and she takes an age dragging her eyes away from him.

'Well, she seems nice,' I say jovially, trying to disguise the fact that I am embarrassed beyond belief to be caught yet again so unprepared. 'That was quick.'

'It had been handed in to lost property already,' he says, pointing to a table laden with boxes piled high with phones, wallets, shoes and bags.

'Oh,' I say. 'Good, good.' *Why had I not thought of that?* 'I'll let the others know we've found it.' My phone pings in reply.

'Are they on their way over?'

I show him the photo I've just received of Tash riding a camel with Sister Kevin. 'Not exactly.'

Matteo shakes his head, laughing. 'I know where that is. It's the drinks zone.' He turns, distracted as Alex approaches him and yanks his arm. She glares rudely at me before dragging him away.

'Come on, Matteo, honey. Leave her. We don't want to be late for the main stage, do we?'

He glances back at me over his shoulder. I'm sure he wanted to say something but is denied the chance. They hurry away and while I can't hear them, they look like they are arguing because she is waving her hands angrily about. My mood instantly plummets. Liberty must have been right. This is all so excruciatingly humiliating. I feel a wave of disappointment flood over me. Matteo obviously has enough drama to deal with. No wonder he wasn't interested in me throwing myself at him.

I slip away from the tent and hurry back to the drinks zone. I spot the line of camels up ahead. The rest of the Dollz have also decided to prepare for their set by riding camels. I race over to Tash, who is busy snogging the face off Sister Kevin, and yell up to them.

'Tash! I found your phone!'

Tash totally ignores me and my triumphant return and carries on licking Sister Kevin's beard. The Dollz are giggling away and I feel an instant pang of envy at their carefree attitudes and ability to enjoy life. I hear my name being called and see Matteo approaching.

'Sorry about that earlier, with Alex. She can be a bit rude,' he says, looking at me with those concerned, kind eyes. 'Are you ready to go on stage?'

I bite my lip nervously. 'Yeah. I just need the Dollz to stop dicking about on the camels.' I fan at my face. 'We're going to be late if we don't make a move.'

While it's so hot I could fry an egg on my stomach, it's Matteo that has me all flustered. I don't want him to see me as some lovesick puppy. One of those groupies that Alex accused me of being.

'Are you okay?' he asks, lowering his voice.

'No,' I say, wiping a film of sweat from my brow. How can I explain that he is so insanely gorgeous that he is making me physically sweat? 'It's just so hot in this suit.'

His eyes travel the length of my body.

Less material went into making this suit than there is in a baby's sock.

He promptly sets about giving instructions to the guys leading the camels. They immediately turn them around and lead them to the stage where we are performing. When I shout up the new plan to the Dollz, they begin fluffing their hair ecstatically and batting heavy eyelashes while simultaneously live-streaming their arrival on a procession of camels. It does look impressive. Nancy should at least be pleased.

'Won't your girlfriend mind you coming with us?' I say as Matteo and I set off behind them. I try not to show how disappointed I am. 'Alex is your girlfriend as well as your business partner, isn't she?'

When he half-smiles back and stares at me for a second too long, I know for certain that he's a taken man. 'Not my girlfriend,' he says, 'but it's complicated.'

No, I think. *It really isn't.*

* * *

A few minutes later, we arrive, the Dollz slide easily down from their camels as though they are abseiling down a mountain, and we are quickly ushered backstage to set up. Within seconds they have magically sobered up and are ready to go out and give the performance of their lives.

Matteo and I stand at the side of the stage to help them set up and to fix microphones to the back of their costumes, but before either of us know what's happening, the Dollz ambush us into a group hug.

'Luvoo, Connie. Luvoo, Matteo. Thanks for getting us here, babes.' Tash kisses me on the cheek.

'We owe you one,' says Cherry. 'Love you.'

'Pretty fucking brilliant, the pair of you. We owe you one.' Big Sue pats me on the back.

'I literally just said that,' Cherry says, turning to Big Sue.

'Love you,' says Liberty, doing a heart shape with her hands.

'And that.' Cherry gives her a disbelieving look.

'Fuck off, Cherry,' says Liberty.

'Fuck off yourself, pet.'

'Come on, bitches. Keep it professional,' Tash barks, winking at me.

It isn't until they break free and run onto the stage that I realise they have handcuffed me and Matteo together.

What did I say about false imprisonment and kidnapping charges?

22

As the Dollz run onto the stage to tumultuous applause, I look down at our wrists shackled together.

Why have they done this to me?

Matteo is staring at me open-mouthed. He's probably expecting an explanation, and the evidence is stacked heavily against me. I have done nothing but throw myself at him, albeit by accident most of the time, since we landed in Spain. He is bound to think this was my idea.

'I don't suppose you have the key to these, do you?' he asks, raising his wrist and taking mine with it. 'I need to be at the main stage in ten minutes.'

I shake my head wearily.

'I guess they'll unlock us before you go on stage though, won't they?' he asks, swinging his head round wildly as if expecting to see a passing locksmith.

I chew my lip and try to appear positive.

'It's just I have an actual job to do here.' He sounds annoyed. He does seem to take his work very seriously, I'll give him that.

'I had no idea they'd do something like this,' I say. 'I'll try to get the girls' attention. They'll set us free. I'm sure of it.'

Matteo does not seem convinced. After we stand in awkward silence for what seems like a week while we repeatedly fail to catch their eye, I attempt some conversation.

'They make it look so easy. They have the crowd eating out of their hands before they even open their mouths.'

'I doubt you'll have any problems winning the crowd over either,' he says.

And just like that, my whole body erupts into tingles as his gaze sweeps back up from my toes to my eyes. All thoughts of him being in a complicated relationship with his business partner evaporate and, without thinking, I lick my lips and run my unshackled hand down the bodysuit, pulling a few of the straps into place, just to give it something to do. I fear I might reach out and pull him into me. I'm having flashbacks to kissing him. His hands sliding down my body. I'm like an addict wanting more.

'Right. Yes,' I say, trying to think of casual conversation that doesn't make me have sexual thoughts about him. I clear my throat. 'So, tell me about yourself. How long have you been doing this? What's your full name? What's your social media handle?'

Why am I making this sound like a job interview?

He looks up from his phone with surprise. Quite rightly, he must know I am going to google the shit out of him.

'Matteo. I'm thirty-two years old,' he says smoothly after a slight pause, tilting his head to the side and eyeing me up. 'I like limited-edition old-lady scooters, music festivals and confident women with the ability to cope adequately. Not on Twitter. Don't do Snapchat.'

He goes back to checking his messages.

'No surname?' I'm not having that. No way.

He smiles at me with a slightly exasperated expression. 'Okay, brace yourself,' he says, shouting over the loud music as the Dollz launch into their opening number. 'I come from a long line of...'

It sounds like he might be saying overly sexy men, but I don't trust my hearing, what with my heartbeat pounding so loudly in my ears.

'Pardon?' I yell back. We are right next to the speaker, and I can't make out what he's saying, even from a few inches away. 'You have a long what?'

This startles him.

God help me. I have an addiction.

'Xavier Matteo George Marie-Carmen.' He tilts his head. 'I'm not finished. Torrado Grande.'

Oh my.

'It sounds like a name that you have literally just given yourself to sound, oh, I don't know... incredibly difficult to google?'

'Why would you want to google me?'

Good point. He doesn't need to know why.

'So, "Grande", that's a right mouthful,' I shout, moving swiftly on. 'What's the "big" bit referring to?'

Jesus Christ. I've done it again. He must think I've hanky-panky on the brain.

After an embarrassing few seconds, he carries on as though I'd not sexualised his name while I try to appear as though I am listening to him intently, and not, as I am currently doing, visualising his manhood and whether it is indeed a right mouthful. I just need to keep my eyes trained on his handsome face and not let them wander. I will concentrate on my set. The Dollz will be coming off stage soon and I am on straight afterwards. My mind is all over the place at his close proximity.

'It's very embarrassing, I know!' he says.

'Not as embarrassing as my first night on The Strip,' I say, blushing at the memory. 'Singing for you.'

'You don't have to do that!'

'Do what?' I yell.

This conversation is becoming quite a chore over the racket. I pull him behind the stage curtain, where the ear-splitting music is slightly muffled. We are almost touching as we stand facing each other.

'You don't have to take off your clothes for me.'

I suppress a howl of nervous laughter. 'I'm not going to take off my clothes. What are you talking about?'

'What are *you* talking about?' he says.

'My night on The Strip.'

'Oh.' He shrugs sheepishly.

I erupt into giggles. 'So, the thought of me stripping for you was repulsive? I'm not surprised. I mean, you did tell me that you are not,' I bellow, 'I repeat, *not* sexually attracted to me.'

'I lied.'

Holy feck.

'But you said, "take care then" to me.'

'Take care then?'

He's a man so he won't get it.

'Yes. "Take care then". So, I thought... Well, it doesn't matter what I thought.'

Suddenly, the temperature behind the curtain has increased, and we are staring at each other while a sexual current fills the air. I am desperate to drill down into exactly how much he thinks he might fancy me.

'Firstly, you were in bits after the jet ski incident and saving that little girl. I genuinely meant "take care". I wouldn't have taken advantage of a situation like that.'

I am inwardly swooning.

'And secondly, you don't need to act like the Dollz to impress people. Just go out there and be yourself. Don't try to sound like the people you're covering. Find your own voice. Do it your own way.'

Could he be any more like Oprah? I'm finding his thoughtfulness an incredible aphrodisiac and comforting at the same time, like someone's sexy grandpa, but a lot younger and hotter. 'And the "it's complicated" situation?'

'Dealt with.'

'Sure?' I'd never steal another woman's man. Never. Not even one this ridiculously gorgeous.

'Yes.'

We lock eyes, and for want of something to do that won't involve me trying to dry-hump him, I lift my shackled arm over my head so that his arm is wrapped around me. I am now facing away from him so that he can't see me making cow eyes at him.

As though in a miraculous dream, I spend the next fifteen minutes watching the Dollz while slowly moving as close to Matteo as I dare. I press my back up against his impressively firm abs and nearly die when I feel the weight of his hands gently rest on my hips. I am acutely aware of every single little movement. The dazzle of the lights, the energy of the crowd, the passion of the Dollz – who are absorbed in the moment, flinging themselves around the stage, owning it like the strong, talented artists they are – it's all happening right in front of me. It has a dizzying effect. It's intoxicating. Something inside me is stirring. For years, my smiles have been empty but at this moment, I could burst. I turn round to beam up at Matteo.

'You're really enjoying this.'

It's like he can see through me, like he knows I'm used to faking it.

'It's amazing. It's just exhilarating. I can't believe I'm going on stage dressed like this!' I say loudly into his ear. 'It's the exact opposite of what I'm used to. There's no way you get this sort of buzz from a club or a classical audience.'

Our faces are but an inch apart. In that moment, I lose track of my mind, forgetting where we are. I reach up on my tiptoes and kiss him lightly on the lips. It's an enchanting, barely-there type of encounter. Rather like the magical lip hover. I flutter my eyelids open in a sexy manner to find he looks rattled. He quickly casts an eye around the vicinity. The moment dies instantly, and my feeling of passion turns to mortification.

'I thought... I mean, after the other day and the whole soul baring... I assumed. I thought we were having a, you know... a moment.' I step as far away from him as the handcuffs will allow and slap on a bright smile. 'Please forget I just did that.'

'No. It's fine. It's just...' He rakes his free hand through his hair. 'I'm kind of at work?' He lifts my downcast face up to meet his. 'I didn't mean to offend you. You're not upset, are you?'

Does a bear shit in the woods? to quote Tash. *Yes, of course you have*, I want to say. *You were supposed to kiss me back and you didn't!* And now I'm humiliated and can never again face him for as long as I live. Although, it's crucial that I sound less like a fourteen-year-old drama queen and much more of a sophisticated woman of the world.

'Yes. No, of course not. Not really. No. Well, yes. A bit, yes.'

He nods his head in understanding and leans in to press his lips to my ears. 'Just to be very clear. I absolutely do want to fucking kiss you. Just not here, in front of my whole team.'

Oh my.

Matteo indicates the crew working the giant mixing desks. He nods to the stagehands on either side, pulling at cables, moving huge speakers, busying themselves with lighting rigs and band equipment. They all wave back to him, making sure to look at me, then him, then down at the handcuffs, then back to him with sly, knowing grins. They are all wearing Jezebel Music T-shirts.

Shitting hell.

'We have over sixty acts on over the four days. Things are pretty busy round here.'

I hold up the handcuffs. 'This is the last thing you need.'

'Maybe.' He shrugs, subtly brushing his fingertips against mine, instantly sending shivers down my spine. 'You seem to have a habit of making my life unpredictable. I never know what will happen next.'

That is literally the best compliment I have ever had. Assuming it is a compliment.

The Dollz take a bow and wave to the crowd at the end of their set. It has been a sheer triumph and I'm thrilled for them. Tash also seems to have forgotten to propose to Sister Kevin, who has been looking adoringly up at her from the mosh pit. The next few seconds seem to go by in slow motion as they wave goodbye to the crowd and run off laughing to the other end of the stage. Tash flicks her hair over her shoulder and blows a kiss in our direction.

Oh. My. God. They're not coming to unshackle us.

I hear Matteo swear when he realises their plan. Then there's a deafening announcement over the mic and the next act, *me*, is invited on stage. I shudder, trying not to panic. There's nothing we can do but walk out on stage together.

Matteo has gone very pale.

'It'll be fine,' I say, suddenly snapping into professional

mode. 'Come on.' I yank at Matteo, who very reluctantly follows me out onto the stage. 'Trust me,' I say.

The poor man must realise that I have done nothing since my arrival to substantiate this request. He grins back and shakes his head, a small laugh escaping from his lips as though he can't fucking believe this latest, in a long, long line, of hot messes.

'Okay, Connie Cooper,' he says. 'Let's show them what you've got.'

As I fumble with my phone, ready to hand it to the rig guy, Matteo swipes it off me, barks some instructions and, before we know it, a speaker, rig and PA system is wheeled over for Matteo to perch on, while I am almost on top of him at the microphone stand. He one-handedly plugs in my phone and swipes away at it to access my backing tracks and then nods at me.

Christ Almighty, that was so impressive. My eyes balloon in admiration at the sheer capability. And in front of a few thousand rowdy, daytime-drinking festivalgoers!

I grab the microphone and try to get the crowd on side by speaking in Spanish. I hold up our arms to let them see that the Dollz have handcuffed us together and are refusing to unlock us. I make sure to say it was not my idea to kidnap Matteo, and this is definitely not false imprisonment despite me being partially responsible for his black eye and head bandage.

As the crowd go suddenly quiet, I mouth to Matteo, 'Ready?'

He takes the microphone gently from me and speaks into it. 'Connie, you just told everyone that this is the only way you can get a man these days, kicking them in the head and handcuffing them.'

Cocking hell.

Matteo howls with laughter as he explains to the crowd what happened, points accusingly at the Dollz, who proudly take a bow, and gives me the microphone back. I lean over, press 'play' and launch into the opening track. I chose one with a thumping bass to get the crowd clapping along. It feels weird singing with Matteo so close to me but it's thrilling at the same time, forcing me to up my game. My cheeks are hurting from all the smiling I'm doing. It's like muscle memory returning to my face.

I didn't used to be so sullen and strait-laced on stage. I suddenly remember the days when I used to have fun and play with the crowd. It seems so long ago but now, unexpectedly, the old feelings are flooding back.

When the track comes to an end, Matteo leans over to speak into the mic. He's asking the crowd if they want to hear something in Spanish they can sing along to. He's grinning away like an evil musical despot. The intro to 'Reggaeton Lento' comes on and, as I sing the opening, the crowd join in and wave their hands in the air. The Dollz run onto the stage and start spinning around, twerking, gyrating and singing backup along with me. All of our outfits are coordinated, and we are a sisterhood of rampant, powerful vixens. I genuinely feel like I belong with them.

I glance at Matteo, whose shoulders are dancing along. He seems extraordinarily comfortable with all this spontaneity. The Dollz run back off stage to thunderous applause. They have brought an incredible amount of sparkle and fun to the proceedings. The next track is a bit slower, but once again, Matteo meddles with the tempo while I'm singing. His face is lit up as he reads the crowd, signals for an earpiece and fiddles with knobs on the rig. I'm forced to speed up, and the song takes on a totally new life.

Thankfully, my years of classical training kick in, and I compensate easily, flicking from one octave to another, throwing in some of my own stylings. I've never done this before, and it is exhilarating. I feel on fire.

'You are amazing,' Matteo mouths to me, and the compliment leaves me euphoric.

Before I know it, we are on the last track. Matteo flicks through the tracklist on my phone and suddenly stops to look quizzically up at me. I frown, wondering what it is. He leans into the microphone.

'Connie, what's this track?' he says, glancing out to the crowd. 'It's called "Matteo, Why Are You So Hot?"'

He turns to face me.

'Did you write a song about me?'

He's laughing, but his eyes are saying, *Should I be worried about this?*

I'm frozen to the spot. This is why you should never let other people access your phone. Ever.

'No,' I say into the microphone. 'Of course not. No. Absolutely not. And it could be about any old Matteo. It's a pretty common name, right?'

The crowd is howling with laughter, and too many of them are filming the exchange. To my horror, Matteo presses play and the piano intro I recorded yesterday floats out across the crowd.

'Well, let's see what it is, shall we?'

The crowd roars its approval.

Bloody hell.

'Let's not,' I say into the microphone, clearing my throat and trying not to fall apart.

But Matteo is nodding his head. He has wild, pretend-serial-killer eyes. He's not going to take no for an answer.

I open my mouth to sing, but no words come out. I think I'm going to have a panic attack. There's no way I can sing my own song on stage to actual people. It was meant for me and me only.

He must be able to see the fear etched on my face, so he leans into the microphone. 'Sounds nice. Come on, Connie. Let's see what the real you sounds like.'

How can he be this comfortable on stage? How?

The Dollz are leaping about, yelling for me to do it. Matteo restarts the song.

'Okay. But just to be clear,' I say, as though I've reluctantly put my chart-topping solo career on hold to treat the crowd to an impromptu, stripped-back version of my next hit, 'it's absolutely not about you.'

It starts off quite melodic, and I'm almost cringing at the lyrics because they are clearly about a girl having a huge crush on a boy who simply does not find her attractive. He can't see what's in front of him. He can't see how much she loves him.

I want the stage to swallow me up, but the crowd is being very polite and getting behind me. Matteo fiddles with the rig and out of nowhere some drums and a bass kick in to lift the chorus and give the song an edge that wasn't there before. Now I have to belt it out to keep time. It really works and as I sing the last verse, unbelievably, the crowd join in the simple chorus with me. We sing it again. And again. And again until the fade.

It's catchy.

It's simple.

It's totally and utterly all about Matteo.

23

'That was the best experience of my entire life!' I yell as we run off stage, panting.

'Totally fucking mind-blowing!' Matteo says, his face flushed with adrenaline. He is gripping my hand and wiping sweat off his face with the crook of his arm.

'The connection. Did you feel it?' I pant. 'With the crowd?'

Matteo nods in a daze. 'I've never done anything like that before.'

We are buzzing as the Dollz crowd round, ecstatic.

'That was awesome, babes,' shouts Tash. 'Totally fucking awesome. We've already uploaded everything to our social media. You might wanna do the same, love.'

'Christ, if you hit the big time, you berra take us with you, to America and that,' says Cherry.

'Of course. Of course.' I'm still cringing about the song lyrics. The Dollz continue making a huge fuss.

'It wasn't about you,' I tell Matteo earnestly for fear that, once the adrenaline wears off, he'll think I'm a deluded crackpot. 'It was about... someone else.'

'Also called Matteo?' he says in a sceptical tone. 'Right, I won't give it another thought. It's fine. It's cool. I believe you.'

He'll not be winning a BAFTA any time soon.

'Let's get these things off, shall we?' I say, changing the subject. My heart is beating like the clappers. 'I could do with a drink or five.'

I turn to the Dollz.

'Who has the key?' asks Tash, brandishing her bottle of Prosecco.

'You, babes,' says Big Mand.

'No, I don't.'

They squabble over who had the key last and where they might have put it.

'What were you all doing just before we got here?' I say, already losing their attention.

'I was doing your Hollywood bikini wax on the kitchen table, wasn't I, Cherry?' says Big Mand. 'So I'm definitely not a suspect. I had nothing to do with it.'

'She was,' says Cherry, showing off her smooth bikini line. 'But I did request a Brazilian Desert Island to be fair. Tony will be so disappointed.'

'I've had the lot lasered off. Permanently. I've got NO hair at all,' Tash says. 'It's, like, so *fresh* down there now.'

And before? Not so fresh? Matteo gives me a withering side-eyed glance.

'I like all mine off too, just in case.' We all turn towards Liberty.

Just in case of what?

Tash runs her hand soothingly up and down her friend's arm. 'Understandable, babes.' I feel a prickle of worry that the girls are once again veering off-topic.

'I prefer to go natural. How a real woman is meant to look,' says Big Mand.

'But I've had fake pubes tattooed on, though,' Tash says sharply, causing a bit of an ugly spat to break out.

'For fuck's sake. It doesn't matter.' Matteo tuts loudly. 'Sorry, but you'll have to come with me while I manage the rest of this festival.'

I swallow. He's even incredible when he's being moody. He runs a hand through his glossy locks and over his stubble as though he's thinking of how to solve this latest catastrophe we've caused.

'Let's go,' I say, trying not to sound like I'm about to rip his T-shirt off with my teeth. 'I'm sure the key will be back in the villa somewhere. We'll find it later.'

I feel like he needs some hope to cling to.

* * *

'This is Connie,' Matteo says, introducing me to his management team.

They are trying not to smirk as he makes no mention of the fact that we are shackled together. I listen as he debriefs them on what is still to do, and they feed back to him about rigging, performers, schedules and problems. It is fascinating. There is so much involved in the festival's management. I wonder he isn't more apprehensive about us being stuck together. He's so cool in a crisis. I must stop staring at him though. I'd hate to put him off.

'Here's your walkie-talkie, boss,' says the gorgeous girl from earlier, flicking her eyes down to our wrists. Probably checking to see if we're holding hands. She gives me a tight smile before he dismisses the team and orders them all to keep in touch.

We spend hours going from stage to stage, talking to performers, checking on sound equipment, lighting and microphones. It has been enlightening. For all I have a music degree, the reality of performing live at a festival is completely different to the theory and the behind-the-scenes nature of theatre performances. I am hooked. There have been pyrotechnic explosions, glitter bombs going off, ticker-tape cannons and bursts of powder paint spraying crowds as an assortment of rock and pop bands drive them into a frenzy. The atmosphere has been turbocharged and now, even with a new day dawning, it's still showing no signs of letting up.

'I had no idea how much is involved for a singer to perform on stage,' I say as we walk back towards the management tent. He has been so focused we've barely had time to talk. 'You're quite the workaholic.' I've had to take my shoes off, and when I stumble over a lump in the ground, he swoops to catch me, taking hold of my hand firmly.

'I know what you need,' he says, stopping by a stall selling flip-flops.

It's borderline heroic how thoughtful he is, isn't it?

'Pick some,' he says, taking out his wallet. I immediately realise I have very poor decision-making skills. They are all exquisite. So many pretty colours.

'What do you think of these?' I say, holding up a pink and orange pair. 'Or do you prefer the blue and green?'

'The green matches your eyes,' he says, taking me by surprise. It's like it's the first time he's noticed me attached to him for the last three hours. 'Sorry I've had to drag you round like this. I really appreciate it.'

I immediately blush and say nothing as Matteo hands over a twenty-euro note and helps me slip them on. We bend together as he gets down on one knee while I lift each foot. It's a very fairy-tale and outlandishly romantic gesture in my mind, even if I am dressed in bondage gear and look like I charge by the hour.

'They seem to fit perfectly, Cenicienta,' he says.

I feel the excitement building between us. I'm lost in the moment when a familiar voice breaks the mood.

'What the fuck is going on?' Alex glares at us from a few feet away, hands on hips.

Matteo scrambles to his feet. The atmosphere is suddenly sour. 'Nothing.'

'It sure looks like something to me.'

'Alex,' he says, holding up our wrists. 'Chill out. We're in a bit of a situation here but I'm handling it.'

'Why her?' Alex says rudely. 'I bet you're loving this, aren't you?' Her eyes flash angrily at me. 'You probably planned it.'

'No!' I protest. 'Of course not.'

Christ, I'd hate for Matteo to think I had anything to do with this unfortunate and glorious, life-enhancing, stuff-of-dreams situation.

'Seems pretty convenient to me,' Alex spits. 'First you make goo-goo eyes at him when you should be singing to the crowd, then you write a fucking song for him when you should be doing covers and now you've got him on his knees calling you "Cinderella". You barely need the fucking handcuffs!'

I feel Matteo entwining his fingers through mine to take my hand firmly.

'You've hardly done any work since the day she arrived,' she tells him, her eyes wild with fury. 'You're looking at her with horny eyes every time she walks in the room. And I'm sure you could've had those cut off if you really wanted to. What the fuck is going on between you two?'

'It's none of your business,' says Matteo. 'Not any more.'

* * *

'So that was pretty intense,' I say a few minutes later as we approach the management tent. Matteo has not so much as looked at me since the flip-flop stand, never mind with horny eyes. Which I have to admit I would be absolutely thrilled at. But I do feel being shackled together is becoming more than a pain for him. It's also about to get a lot worse.

'I'm so sorry about this.' I am genuinely mortified. 'But I really need to go to the, erm…'

Humiliating. I should have perhaps mentioned to him earlier that I come from a long line of weak-bladdered women for whom anything remotely exciting, active or cool in temperature will bring on the need to visit the restroom.

'Sure,' he says, avoiding eye contact. 'There's a Portaloo round the back of here for VIPs. Do you need to go right now?'

I'd rather die.

'No. I couldn't. I'll wait.'

'I'll stay at the door.'

'I have to take the whole suit off and I'm no contortionist.' I jangle the handcuffs to make my point.

He looks slightly bemused.

'Can we go back to the villa and find the key?' I ask, chewing my lip.

He checks the time. 'Fuck it. Let's go. That's why I have a management team, right? They can finish up without me.'

We walk out of the tent and over to his lady scooter. Without taking his eyes from mine, he runs his hands down the sides of my body. This time, his hands linger there. My breathing becomes all lustful and I notice his is the same. He picks me up to sit on the front of the bike before sliding his arm up over my head so that we can grip the handlebars together.

Sitting behind me, he closes his hands over mine and pulls the throttle. My skin is burning with longing, and my neck tingles as his chin brushes against it. We are cheek to cheek, snaking our way through the quiet back roads. We arrive at the villa to find it empty and race straight through to the kitchen to see the key lying on the table, along with a bottle of tequila, slices of lemons and some shot glasses.

'That seemed almost too easy,' says Matteo incredulously as the handcuffs spring open. He pours us both a shot. 'Shame. I got quite used to them.'

Oh my.

'You go through to the cottage. Make yourself... comfortable. I'll catch you up,' I say, flinging the cottage key at him and racing off upstairs to use the Dollz' communal bathroom. I'm on tenterhooks. I'm embarrassed for him to hear me weeing. I'm also embarrassed I told him to make himself comfortable. I'm the sort that does not do one-night stands, except maybe in extreme emergencies. This is definitely an extreme emergency. I stare at myself in the mirror.

Am I the sort of woman who can have handcuff sex? Am I the sort of woman who can have any type of sex?

It's been a very, very long time. When I said that my last boyfriend ran screaming for the hills, I was giving an accurate account. He screamed at me for not paying attention during sex and promptly moved to the Welsh valleys. To be fair, it wasn't the first time that I'd fallen asleep on him. It was a very exhausting time in my life, and he just didn't seem to understand that my mother had to come first. And now I'm like an old abandoned house with creaking floorboards, dust mites and cobwebs that should be approached only with extreme caution.

Get a fucking grip, Connie, I tell myself. *Think sexier thoughts. You've got to own your sexuality and unleash the slutty vixen within.*

I race through to the cottage, a flush of warmth spreading from my groin. Whilst I'm desperately trying to conjure up sexy images of us consumed with lust and frantically ripping off each other's clothes with our teeth, a thought occurs.

What if he's lying naked and sprawled out on the bed like da Vinci's *Vitruvian Man*? Waiting to be serviced by me. Waiting for me to administer years' worth of sexual expertise. I'm both thrilled and petrified at the thought that Matteo is hungry with lust for me, and I'm about to find out just how much. Thoughts of him doing the *Bridgerton* buttocks scene for me explode in my mind. I enter the lounge and stop suddenly at the sight before me. It's so much worse than I imagined.

My heart sinks.

Matteo is fully clothed. Not only that, but I'm dismayed to see he is currently occupied with a little light housekeeping. I'm on the verge of asking if there's anything he'd like me to do to help as he slips deftly into the kitchen to retrieve snacks out of the fridge and arranges them neatly on the table.

Like a 1950s housewife hosting a dinner party for her husband's boss and his wife, he skips about the room switching twinkling lights on, grabbing the remote to play some music on low, automatically picking up the items of clothing that have been strewn all over the floor since my arrival. He indicates to me that he'll pop the washing pile out of the way in the bedroom.

I see the 'washing pile' in his arms – the sex-shop bags, the bras, the suspenders, the stripper clothes. He emerges from the bedroom and wanders towards me carrying two glasses and a bottle of chilled wine. He hands me one and I take a huge gulp with the nerves, relieved that he isn't racing out of the door to clean and cater for another dinner party and at least intends to stay for one drink.

'Sorry,' he says. 'I do housework when I get nervous.'

Good God. Could a man say anything more perfect?

'I make you nervous?' I say, fishing for compliments. Every word out of his mouth makes me want to light up like a glow stick.

He smiles slowly as he gives me a simmering look and takes a glug of wine.

It causes me to almost whimper. 'Speaking of nervous. What about being live on stage and making up the music as we went along? That was insane. You're really good at that.'

'Being on stage totally blew me away,' he says. 'I mean, I've been managing events and bands for years from behind the scenes but actually being on stage, interacting with the audience, making that connection was incredible. Like no other feeling.'

'It was mind-blowing,' I agree. 'I loved it.'

'You're much better singing your own stuff than covers,' he says.

I am going to explode if he keeps feeding my ego in this way. 'You're just being polite,' I say, shaking my head. 'I'm way too boring to be a performer like that. You need charisma and sparkle and—'

'Connie,' he interrupts, his hand lightly touching the cut above his eyebrow. 'Since the second we met, you have been anything but boring, believe me. And as for sparkle? You really shone on stage today. Whatever false impression you have of yourself, maybe it's time to shrug it off. Maybe it's time to let yourself shine?'

I am madly in love with every single word falling from his lips. I do hope he keeps talking for ever and ever.

I must be drooling because Matteo takes my hand and gives it a squeeze. Then he glances at the time and drains his glass as though he's going to leave.

I blink rapidly.

I have three days left. It's time to be daring and courageous. It's now or never. I reach up on my tiptoes and place a kiss gently on his lips before I can back out of it.

He hesitates a brief moment, reaches out to curl a stray lock of my hair behind my ear and then leans in to kiss me back. We lock lips as my mind travels throughout all of space and time. My head is in a swirl. I feel under a spell. It is hugely hypnotic, and I never want this kiss to end. There is such a connection between us. I'm sure he must feel it too. It is electrifying. My veins are literally *bursting* with sparkles. When we come up for air, the only thing I can think of is that I need him to stay.

'Stay,' I blurt, surprising myself as I drum up a decent enough reason, in case kissing me for the next seventy-two hours isn't quite enough. 'There's a Jacuzzi here. In the garden. It's not overlooked.'

He looks slightly shocked, so I backtrack.

'Sorry, that was too much.' His confession about his current situation being *complicated* rings in my ears.

'No,' he says. 'It's not that.'

'Okay,' I say, unconvinced. I'm not surprised Matteo has a string of ex-lovers. He's totally fucking gorgeous. *Why wouldn't he? And why wouldn't I want to be one of them too?*

Thankfully, Matteo seems keen to agree that a Jacuzzi, at six in the morning, is exactly what we need and disappears off to press buttons and fire it up.

This is happening. It's finally happening.

I have *never* had sex in a Jacuzzi. I can barely get out of my bodysuit quick enough. Then I suddenly stop, doubt creeping in. Wait, how does he know how everything works? A tiny niggle grows in the back of my brain and so I squash it before it becomes fully formed. If Liam and Ged were here, they'd definitely tell me to throw caution to the wind. I'm sure of it. Almost sure. Mostly sure. Well, a bit sure.

Christ Almighty.

I now regret Matteo giving me a few minutes to get sorted. A few minutes is all it takes for me to realise that I am way out of my depth. I feel extremely shy standing in my bra and knickers. We barely know each other, and my mind has begun to spiral. He's probably had tons of fashionable sex with a whole hemisphere of supermodels, bisexual gymnasts and beautiful professors of quantum physics who escorted themselves through college, while I've had hardly any.

And the sex shop. What if he's expecting me to produce a treasure trove of sex toys or an elaborate range of cock rings?

Wait, did he even mention sex? What if when he says 'Jacuzzi' he actually means Jacuzzi? For a moment, I have no idea what to do. Then Matteo comes sauntering into the bedroom fully dressed, still looking as immaculate as when the evening began.

Shitting hell!

Before he can say anything, I babble at him. 'You don't have to have sex with me,' I say while struggling back into my bodysuit like a strange reverse striptease. The fabric is thwacking and squelching like I'm wrestling to fit inside a giant condom.

Matteo regards me with wide eyes. 'Okay.'

'But if you do...' I pause, my leg completely stuck. 'I don't know any tricks!'

'Tricks?' he says, rattled. 'What do you mean tricks?'

Maybe I'm making this sound more like something from Cirque du Soleil than it needs to be. It's mortifying, and yet that last glass of wine is making it impossible for me not to carry on in this off-putting manner.

'I mean, I have no idea what or even where my own G-spot is, never mind yours. I've no idea what the G stands for either. And God knows, I'm certainly no sexual triathlete,' I say, flapping my arms about, unable to make eye contact with him. 'I've no idea how to do the Butter Churner or... or the Rocking Horse... or the Pretzel.'

I should stop talking. I took off there, panic sex-shaming myself, without a place to land.

'I have no idea what you're talking about,' he says gently. 'We're not under any pressure to do anything.'

He's extremely thoughtful.

The thing is, sex with me is hardly going to be like wandering through a palace of ceaseless wonder, but I really hope we will do *something*. 'I just mean that I'm not massively experienced.'

'Would it help if I admitted to not knowing what the Pretzel is either? It sounds kind of scary, doesn't it? I mean, what do you do if you're gluten intolerant?'

A soft chuckle escapes my lips. I'm so relieved.

He gives me a shy look. 'You are so beautiful,' he says, cupping my face. He looks like he's stifling a giggle. 'All that glitter in your lashes and your teeth. It really sets off your eyes.'

That does it. He's funny and thoughtful, especially at times of high stress.

I wink slowly at him. 'Wait until you see how much ticker tape I have stuck to my back.' This causes him to grin widely as I reach out to trail my fingers lightly down his chest. It's so firm it's like he's wearing a breastplate. 'I dread to think how much is under here.' I lift up his top and slide it off him. Jesus Christ, he's magnificent. He is very much allowing me to take the lead, and with each touch he looks nervous, which melts me inside. I fumble quickly with the button on his shorts before either of us can back out with nerves.

'You sure about this?' he asks huskily.

'Absolutely.' I can barely speak, and my breathing is coming in bursts. 'I've never wanted anything more.'

'Well then, the Jacuzzi can wait.' Any doubts I had about me not having an ounce of sex appeal immediately evaporate as he pulls me to him and kisses the life out of me. The traitorous catsuit obeys his every command as he pulls it easily from my burning skin.

Now, we are standing in just our underwear. His gaze never leaves mine as he steps out of his boxer shorts and takes the final step. We are but an inch away from one another. I can barely breathe at this point. He reaches round to unclip my bra, while expertly dropping kisses along my shoulder before sliding the bra straps from my arms. He is such a gentleman that he doesn't even remark on the amount of glitter pouring out of it as it hits the floor. He pulls me gently to him, expertly kissing my neck to send pangs of lust shooting through my body.

He seems the type who takes his time to do things thoroughly. I slide my hands up and down his body, pulling him in even closer. I am having a huge effect on him.

I am going to pass out with the anticipation and thrill of it all. Then, as he leans in to kiss me again, I feel his hands trail leisurely down my back and over my bottom. I nearly die of longing as he slowly peels down my knickers. Each inch of their journey to the floor is a delicious agony. I step out of them and kick them aside. Matteo sinks to his knees and hooks my right leg over his shoulder. I hold on to the back of his head for balance as he pulls my pelvis to his mouth. Thank goodness I have a strong core. I arch into him as his tongue delivers an exquisite tickle right to my sweet spot. The feel of his stubble against my thighs, his soft hair in my hands, the sound of his desirous groans as he grasps my bottom tightly is making me tremble from head to toe. When he applies more pressure, it literally takes all of a few seconds for a pulsating heat to radiate throughout my body, building and building until I am utterly consumed, shuddering with ecstasy against him, his tongue an instrument of delicious torture until the very last wave of pleasure rolls over me.

He is quick to scoop me up before my legs give way and carries me to the big four-poster dream bed. It is built for lovers. Built for making love. I sink into the feathery soft duvet and feel his weight on top of me. His knee nudges my legs apart as he nestles between them. I am in a complete daze. The aftermath of such a forceful orgasm must do that. I have not one single thought in my head. I am a contented sigh in human form.

Matteo smiles at me, a soft look on his face before our lips slide gently together. It feels other-worldly and magical, like a perfect symphony. My heart is drumming to the beat of his. His kisses are like musical notes tinkling in my brain, his fingers playing me like a fragile instrument. There's a wild sweetness to our passion. This is new and exciting, and I am desperate to explore every single part of him. The feel of his hot skin on mine is making every nerve in my body scream out for him. He trails kisses down my neck and across my collarbone before venturing tantalisingly slowly down to cover my nipples, one at a time. I gasp as he takes each peak in his mouth, flicking the tip with his tongue. It sends a spark shooting to my groin. I need him. I crave him. I undulate into him, our bodies entwined, my fingers stroking every inch of him. I feel him shiver under my touch. He feels as ready as I do. A rough moaning sound escapes from his throat as he presses his erection against me. His breathing is ragged as his hungry lips find mine.

'I want you,' I whisper, meeting his darkly desirous gaze.

24

As the sun rises, we are still craving each other. We've hardly said a word since our naked Jacuzzi because we've been locked in a frenzy of desire for each other. Every time we'd try to fall asleep, one of us would get a lustful urge to go again. I've come over all insatiable for this man. He only has to touch me and I get stirrings to make love to him. Our lips are swollen from all the kissing, and I feel swollen down below, and I bet he's sore, but we don't seem to care. I feel drunk with desire for him and I'm pretty sure he feels the same. He's made it abundantly clear several times. I don't even want to sleep because I *never* want this dream to end.

When it gets towards midday, Matteo says, 'I better go or I'll never be able to function later. I'll be walking with a limp as it is.'

He's so funny. And dreamy.

I blink slowly and try to act cool, convincing myself that's fine, of course he should go. I mean, this is just a holiday fling. It doesn't mean anything. I can't seem to keep the disappointment from my voice. It seems unthinkable that we should separate as we lie wrapped around one another.

'Of course, you should go to work,' I fib smoothly, 'and don't feel, you know, that you have to call me or anything. I understand.'

'No,' he says, stroking my cheek, 'you don't.'

He kisses me so gently I am immediately lost in a swirl of feelings. We move rhythmically together, never once breaking eye contact, and soon he is slipping on a condom and slowly entering me again. We lose ourselves in each other as our orgasms build from this slow, grinding pace. This must be making love in that very painstaking, tantric way that Ged and Liam told me about, but that they haven't got the actual patience to do. It is tender and loving and I've never felt anything so all-consuming in my life.

I am smitten. I have completely and utterly fallen for him.

When we are done, he slips out of bed and leaves me with the promise of seeing him later as we exchange numbers.

'I'll come for the start of your set,' he says, which has me tingling all over.

We have our final two gigs on The Strip tonight and tomorrow, at Voices. It's the biggest entertainment venue outside of Benidorm Palace. It is a big, *big* deal. My phone rings, interrupting us. It's Nancy.

'I saw you weren't yourself yesterday at the festival,' she rasps.

'Not myself?' I echo.

'No, thank goodness. We all noticed the huge improvement, so whoever it is you're bumping bones with to get your pipes to sound that good, keep it up.' She cackles out a gravelly laugh.

How does she find these things out? How? Dark magics?

'Now put him down...'

Matteo and I look at each other in alarm.

How could she possibly know?

'...and get yourself round to do a soundcheck at Voices because the manager has heard the rumours about you and the Dollz being a right handful. He's not happy.'

'Has he?' I say, feeling shocked.

'Yes. It was me that told him. Meh. Meh. Meh.'

While she's trying to laugh, Matteo gives me a lingering kiss to remember him by and disappears out of the cottage. I am high on endorphins, and I don't care who knows it.

'I just feel so different,' I tell Nancy. 'It's like he has flicked a switch in me and now my drab, grey life has burst into glorious fireworks just like the festival last night. I want to fling open the creaky doors to my mind palace and let in the light.'

'Jesus Christ, mind palace? Are you on drugs?' She pauses to wheeze between puffs on her vape. 'Well, whatever it is, glad to hear you sounding full of beans, pet. I knew Benidorm would be much more up your street. Give me two more brilliant shows and I'll have a surprise for you and the Dollz when you get back.'

I squash down the dread of going home in a couple of days. I'll definitely need a selfie to remind me of Matteo and that this is not a dream. It could be my wallpaper for everything. I will get a quilt cover and matching pillowcases made with it on and perhaps a rug and a lampshade and definitely some mugs for Ged and Liam.

Unless, a thought pops into my mind, *I want to stay.*

I slide into denim shorts and a vest top and go through to the main house, stepping carefully round the pool area strewn with clothes, bags, shoes and hairpieces. It is completely silent. I take a moment, wondering whether to wake the Dollz. They won't have got back until after me this morning, so it is probably a bad idea.

* * *

As I approach The Strip, I see an army of cleaners picking up bottles, cans, serviettes, burst balloons, tinsel and various items of discarded clothing in a bid to restore it to glory for the night ahead. I spot Voices immediately. It's taller than the bars around it and has a ginormous red sign spelling out its name in light bulbs. The doors are wide open, the walls plastered with posters of bands, tribute acts and singers from all over the world. It appears very professional from the outside and I feel nervous excitement race through me as I walk in. I'm immediately staggered by the size of the place. It must easily hold a couple of thousand people. Its vast floors and mezzanine levels are crammed with wooden tables and chairs with several bar areas specialising in cocktails or beers, or both. There are signs everywhere advertising drinks packages, performances, food menus, themed nights. There is something for everyone, every night of the week, every week of the year. It is a very busy place. There's a huge circular stage in the centre, and I make my way to it. I've never performed on a circular stage before.

'You have to make sure you turn around regularly otherwise people think you're ignoring them. It can take quite a bit to get used to.'

I spin round.

'Hi, I'm Dan, best known as Jolly Murs,' he says, pointing to a huge poster of himself. 'And you must be the Ariana Grande tribute act. You look just like her. Loving your high pony.'

Shrieks distract us both as a horde of children races in our direction. I assume they must be huge Jolly Murs fans but, as they thunder towards us, they leap at me, almost sending me flying. The last to arrive, panting, is a little girl I'd recognise anywhere.

'It's you,' I say, grinning from ear to ear as she leaps into my arms. 'Hello there. How are you?'

'Mammy, it's the woman!' she screams at the top of her lungs. 'It's her!'

I see a glamorous woman approach, battling her way through the children to scoop me into a hug.

'How did you find us?' she asks, looking me over in wonderment. 'We've been hoping to run into you so we could thank you properly for what you did. For saving Lucie's life. You and your boyfriend.'

'Boyfriend?'

'Oh, I see. He's your husband, is he?' She winks at me. 'I wouldn't step over him to get to Ryan Reynolds if you know what I mean. What a pair of heroes you are.'

I nod vacantly.

Why am I not correcting her?

I imagine being married to Matteo. I'd get nothing done on a daily basis. It would be one continuous loop of wake up and make love. Wake up and make love. Wake up and make love. Over and over for eternity.

'Why do you look all funny?' Lucie is asking me, an inch from my nose, her small hands ruffling my hair. I must get a grip.

'I was performing at the festival last night,' I say, shaking myself out of the trance. 'I haven't been to sleep yet.' Not the most professional thing to admit. It causes a flurry of admiring comments from the children.

'Oh, you're the singer for tonight?' Lucie's mother says. 'What a coincidence! Connie, is it? I'm Martha. I own the place with my husband Rody.' She turns to the children. 'Okay, you lot back to the kitchen for lunch.' She looks back at me. 'You want to do a quick soundcheck before you go back to bed?' Martha laughs. 'Oh, to be young and in love.'

I blush. I should correct her. I really, really should. But before I know it, Rody is bounding over to scoop me up in a bear hug.

'Thank you,' he booms. 'Thank you so much.'

'Connie's singing here tonight. Can you believe it? Is your husband coming? We'd love to thank him personally. Maybe have you over for dinner some time?'

My husband. Okay, this time I am definitely going to put her right. I open my mouth to speak when they are distracted by some squealing and fighting.

'We'll leave you to it,' Martha says, grabbing her husband. 'Don't leave without giving us your number. Dan, can you sort Connie out, please?'

'You're like part of the family here,' I say to Dan, smirking.

'That's because I *am* part of the family here. Oldest son. Born and raised in Benidorm. In this bar, to be precise.'

* * *

'One, two, one, two,' says Dan, grinning at me as he hands me the microphone. 'Fancy a duet?'

'I haven't warmed up my vocals. I haven't slept for almost two days, I've done nothing but drink alcohol and eat pizza, but sure, yes, why not?'

Dan picks one of his favourite pop duets and sets up the backing track. Within seconds we are belting out a tune that brings the children hurtling back through the bar to see us performing together. I'm in surprisingly good form considering.

I think the buzz of having just made love to Matteo must be giving my voice an extra edge as I out-sing Jolly Murs at the end, to the extent that he doesn't look quite so Jolly any more.

'I'm so sorry,' I say. 'That was very unprofessional of me. I'm not usually that, erm, loud.'

He is standing open-mouthed. 'No. Don't apologise. That was awesome.'

The children start barking requests.

'They can be little tyrants. You best do at least one,' Dan says good-naturedly.

It feels a bit weird being watched by the family, especially when Lucie comes over to take my hand and refuses to let go. Even Rody comes over to listen. He trades glances with his wife as I sing all sorts of snippets as the kids bellow song titles at me and it becomes a game of how quickly Dan can switch his backing tracks to keep up.

'Okay, kids,' Rody says. 'That's enough. I gather Connie here hasn't slept for two days. I think we should let her get back home so she's in a fit state for tonight.'

How embarrassing.

Before I leave, Martha and Rody take me to one side.

'You have a great voice, Connie. Would you consider a permanent residency here?' asks Rody.

'Residency?' *We're hardly in Vegas.*

'I'm offering you a regular spot. The pay is not bad, better than one-off gigging, and it'll mean you can still do your own thing as long as you show up to do one slot each night. And if you need lodgings, we have plenty of room here above the bar. We can throw that in for free seeing as you saved my baby girl's life.'

'She has a husband, Rody. I'm sure she'd prefer to live with him,' Martha says, chuckling.

Yes, who wouldn't want to live with a man who looks effort-lessly sexy every minute of every day, who is a red-hot lover between the sheets and saves children in his spare time? I have no words. Which is a shame because I really need to clear this misunderstanding up immediately.

'See you tonight, Connie, and thanks again. Please tell your husband the drinks are on us tonight. We're looking forward to thanking him in person.'

'Well, he's not exactly...'

They've gone. They've raced off to see what the banging in the kitchen is. I wander back towards the villa in a daze.

A job offer?

Accommodation included?

A singing career here on The Strip?

And a chance to see what could happen between Matteo and me?

With shaking hands, I video-call Liam and Ged en route to let them know the exciting news. How shocked they will be to find out that while they've had to put up with me being super boring and penis repellent over the years, I've just had the wildest time of my life. I'm filled with joy at seeing their faces on the screen.

'Hey, you two. How's it going?' I'll be polite and not launch straight in with my ginormous news – me, me, me.

I'm met with an almighty huffing and puffing as they exhale noisily in unison. It doesn't take much to excite these two.

'Tell us *everything*! Do *not* pretend something didn't happen. It is clearly written all over your face,' Liam says, peering at me closely.

'Whatever do you mean?'

'You look glorious, glowing, effervescent, darling,' declares Ged, his sharp eyes sparkling. 'You've finally shagged someone. Hip hip, hooray!'

'Well, it was more of a journey of self-discovery and emotional healing,' I say, ignoring their cheers as I peer off into the middle distance. 'I had to lose myself in the chaos in order to find my truth.'

I smile enigmatically, my mind drifting back to the recent, luxurious memories of my and Matteo's union. I'm a spiritual window. I'm an overflowing font of inner peace. I'm so hashtag blessed. We all take a beat as I tell them about Matteo, the festival and the new job offer. Liam's eyes well up, and Ged swishes a hand over his face like he's trying to stop a flood of tears, and they both jump up and down, hugging each other.

'Do it. Have an adventure, Connie. You deserve it,' says Ged once all my news sinks in.

'I *love* him!' squeals Liam in my face. He's googled Matteo already. 'He's so *handsome*! Those eyes! That moody look. I'm all aquiver just thinking about him.'

'Yes,' I agree, staring deliciously into space. I've been terribly distracted all week with that exact same issue. Matteo is *too* handsome. He's distractingly handsome. I nod absent-mindedly.

'Those thighs, Ged, can you see them? And those arms? That chest!'

'That's *enough*, Liam! Bye, darling. Good luck with tonight. Love you.'

I click off the call and float back to the villa. I let myself into the cottage, sink onto the unmade bed, my new favourite place in the whole world, and immediately fall into a deep sleep.

* * *

I wake late afternoon to the sound of voices around the pool. The girls are up. I'm the happiest I've ever been in my entire life. I pull on my robe and make a coffee to take outside. The sun is high in the sky, and it is a beautiful day. I take my notebook and scribble down some lyrics, humming tunes that wouldn't sound out of place in a Disney movie. I'm literally bursting with happiness as I watch musical notes fly from my pen on to the page. A lustful urge shoots through me at the thought of what lies in store for me later.

As I slip my bikini on, I hear shrieks and splashes. Tash and the girls are enjoying themselves by the sound of things. Then I hear a male voice. I listen closely but can't make out what is being said. I hope they haven't invited a load of randy nuns over. I want to announce my romantic newsflash to the Dollz and hear them get all excited for me. I hear the unmistakable screech that belongs to Tash followed by lots of splashing and shouting over whose turn it is to have a go on Enreeky next.

Jesus Christ, not in the pool! Aware of the irony that only hours ago I was defiling the Jacuzzi myself, I wonder why he has popped by.

'Enreeky? Enreeky? What are these photos of Connie doing on your phone? When did she go cliff diving?'

'And there's one here of her and David bloody Guetta! How come we didn't get invited to the VIP section and she did?' I hear lots of tutting and complaining from the girls and smile smugly to myself.

'And that's her dancing with Matteo on the boat, isn't it?' Tash asks. 'Ah, don't they look lovely? What a cute couple.'

I'd kill to see that photo of me dancing with Matteo. I'll be able to send it to Ged and Liam. I could casually ask Nacho to send me the photo. I can't help giggling. For the first time in my life, I feel high and exuberant. Ged and Liam were right. I haven't been living my life at all, I've only been drifting from day to day. And now it's like I have options. I don't have to go home, back to that non-existence, if I don't want to.

Before I can change my mind, I race up the path and pull the gate open to join them from my hidden dwelling. I slip through to the pool area. Tash has her back to me, so she doesn't know I'm standing behind her, but I see some of the girls have clocked me and are wondering where I have magically appeared from. I grin widely back at them. I'm bursting to blurt out my news.

'But why does Matteo have his arm around someone else in this photo?' Tash asks. 'Is that Alex? Christ, Liberty, you were bang on the money there, pet. Look at the date. It was only last week.'

I stop dead in my tracks.

'And Enreeky, what's this photo of you and him together trying wedding suits on in a shop? Whose wedding is it?' There's a pause while the splashing comes to an abrupt halt. 'Enreeky! Are you getting married?' Tash yells across to him.

I hear Nacho yell back, amid loud 'boo's from the girls. 'No. It isn't me getting married. It's my half-brother, Matteo. This weekend. Before he goes to Los Angeles.'

My words become lodged in my throat.

'Matteo is getting married?' booms Big Sue. 'To Alex?'

'He's leaving Benidorm to move to LA?' gasps Liberty. 'But what about Connie?'

'We'll kill him,' roars Cherry at the same time.

25

All the air suddenly leaves my lungs, like I've been jabbed in the solar plexus. I grab the barbeque stand for support while I quickly fathom what Nacho's saying. I'm briefly aware of Tash losing it and yelling at him.

'What the fuck is your brother messing around with Connie for if he's getting married? Does she know?'

Brother? Getting married? Alex is his fiancée? Los Angeles? Not fucking complicated?

For a split second, Nacho's face drops as he realises I'm standing right behind Tash. He can probably see my devastated expression and my 'I've just been shagging your about-to-be-married brother' hair. I don't wait to hear the rest. I let out an accidental cry and stumble quickly back through the gate to the cottage.

I've been played, haven't I?

What a fool I've been. I think quickly back to all those times that Matteo just happened to turn up as if destiny was sending us right into each other's path.

Only it wasn't, was it? He could've just asked his friggin'

brother where I was! Or even easier, he could've checked his brother's Instagram and he would've seen where I was each day. I try to retrace my steps since we arrived as I wrench open the cottage door, slamming it behind me.

My mind is darting around, as though I've suddenly become a pathologist, fitting pieces of a grizzly crime puzzle together. I have a flashback to Nacho telling me in the café that his brother was the good-looking, clever one! No wonder Matteo knew this cottage so well. He owns half of it! He probably does this all the time with whoever just happens to get the cottage. My mind immediately conjures up disturbing images of Matteo and Nacho preying on the many women who come to stay, competing against each other, laughing at how gullible women can be.

Oh fuck, I think I'm going to be sick.

I run to the bathroom and throw up. Then I burst into huge, noisy tears that just won't stop. My bed is still warm from him. My body still sore from him. My whole spirit was lifted from being with him.

He totally had me hook, line, and sinker, didn't he?

I slide down onto the bathroom floor, double over and sob my heart out until I am drowning in self-pity. I cry because I've been a fool, because I should have known the happiness would never last, because I'm still devastated my mother died and I've no other woman to turn to, because I have no idea what I'm doing with my life and I'm afraid I'm just going to waste it doing nothing. I'll be stuck on this misery train forever.

Out it all comes like a white-water rapid.

'She's in here!' I hear someone yell loudly, and the door opens to reveal all the girls peering in at me.

'I'm fine!' I bawl, tears streaming down my face. 'It's nothing. I'm fine.'

They part in perfect formation to let Tash hobble through, ankle still like a couple of ripe beef tomatoes. 'I'm guessing you heard me shouting to Enreeky, did you?'

I sniff loudly and nod my head, which brings a fresh stream of loud tears. Tash hands me a towel.

'Come on, pet, we'll look after you,' says Liberty kindly. 'We've all been there, haven't we, girls? Remember me and Mehmet?'

They all nod their heads, and we listen to Liberty, who wants to get something off her chest. It's the harrowing account of how she could have been Mehmet's fourth wife if only karma had been kinder to her and blessed her with an accidental pregnancy to trap him with. Even I have heard this story three times this week.

Big Sue reaches in and lifts me up like a newborn kitten and carries me through to my lounge. She puts me gently down on the sofa. The girls take a good look around.

'What is this place?' Cherry remarks. 'How did you find it?'

'Is this where you've been staying?' asks Tash. 'It's fucking lush.'

Big Mand picks up the remote, presses a few buttons and they watch open-mouthed as a TV slides out, the air con blows, music plays and the twinkling lights transform the lounge into a magical romantic honeymoon suite. I can't help but remember that first soulful evening with Matteo. I let out a fresh howl of sobs.

'I'll neh... eh... eh... ver be happy eh... eh... ver again,' I wail, remembering the way he set my pulse racing and my bones on fire with just a single touch.

'Men are right users. They're such twats, aren't they?' Cherry says, slinging her arm over Liberty, before suddenly turning to me. 'Connie? Did he make you any sort of verbal contract? You know, like, any commitment that would render him liable? We could hit him where it hurts.'

'Yes, or we could get the nuns to show him the meaning of respect,' says Liberty.

'No need. Big Sue's a sensei in ju-jitsu. She could snap his neck like a twig.' Big Mand demonstrates with her hands.

'Erm, now I think about it,' I say, slightly anxious at how things are escalating, 'things weren't quite that serious between us.'

Cherry elbows her way to me. 'The hell they weren't. We all saw what a fool you were prepared to make out of yourself for him. I know shame when I see it,' she announces to everyone. 'It is totally my thing.'

'No, Cherry. Shame is *my* thing. I'm trained for exactly this sort of shitshow. I'll handle it.' Liberty lifts my chin. 'People forget I'm not your typical blonde airhead doctor.'

'Fuck off, Liberty. You're not even a real doctor, never mind a typical one,' says Cherry.

'I have a PhD.'

'Yes, but what in? Psychology? You've never actually said.'

'Mood Management. It's practically the same thing,' Liberty says.

'It's not practically the same thing at all. Connie has real issues. She's too intense, closed off, damaged.'

'What she needs is to watch Netflix, the *Bridgerton* buttocks scene.' Tash looks around. 'Somebody, quick, get it on your phone. Whose account do we all use? Big—'

'I'll never forget my first love,' says Cherry, cutting her off. 'Very powerful, Connie. Very raw. Very real.' She reaches down to stroke my arm. 'Robert... or Richard. No, it was Gary. That's right. Gary.'

'It wasn't friggin' Gary.' Liberty frowns. 'Unless he was two-timing you with me and his wife and his other wife.'

'Come on, before they kick off,' says Tash softly. 'I've got something that will help.'

'So, what kind of help is better than the *Bridgerton* buttocks scene?' I ask through my tears.

'Cocktails, love. Four for the price of one. At The Knee Trembler, remember?' Tash gives my shoulder a squeeze.

'No. Definitely not,' I say, shaking my head. 'We have a show to put on. A really important show. We can't turn up drunk. We need to be really good.'

The Dollz look at each other.

'She's quite cute really, isn't she?' Liberty says. 'She has no idea how all this works. None at all. Bless.'

Cherry clicks on some upbeat music and they all leap up. Big Sue drags me to my feet. While I'm sniffing up tears and dancing around, I summon up a smile for the girls. They may be nun-obsessed boozehounds at times, but at least they're all here for me now. Tash surprises me by reaching for my hand.

'It's just like me and Mehmet all over again,' Liberty sighs, giving me a supportive shrug. 'Only my two-week relationship lasted a lot longer than yours.'

'Right, that's enough crying over wankers for one day. Let's go,' insists Big Sue.

I am pulled from the room into the harsh light of day, across the pool to the kitchen where Big Mand, with her arm now the width of her leg, sets up tequila shots. After two shots each, we are unanimous that we should get dressed up and head into Benidorm to see Michael Bubble play live at The Knee Trembler before we head to Voices to do our set before we get too drunk to walk.

'That's all that matters,' I say.

The Dollz wait patiently for me to elaborate.

'Friends. It's friends.'

'Friends,' they chorus, and we clink glasses. Suddenly, I need to own my truth. Own it big time. I drape my arm around Big Mand's shoulders while she is showing us how sexy a dance one-armed body-popping on the kitchen table can be. 'I love you, Big Mand. You're my best friend. You're all my best friends.' I feel a gush of gratitude that they are here to share this traumatic experience with me.

'Oh yeah, here's your share of the kitty back,' says Tash, pushing a basket full of money towards me. 'And I think a man-free night will do us all good.'

'Like a detox,' agrees Cherry. 'A cleanse and deflate. Let's deflate ourselves of men.'

'And Connie, we will choose your playlist for tonight. You should sing heartbreak songs and soft-rock ballads to expel the negative energy build-up. You like to take your audience on a journey, don't you, pet?'

'Great idea. She should do some accusatory songs about men being liars and cheats.'

'And some heartbroken ones to show her despair and self-loathing and how it's all his fault she's a steaming mess.'

'Yes, and then some "I'm over you" songs in case he's there watching. Some real "fuck you" type angry woman anthems.'

I stare wide-eyed at them.

'And then finish with something that says, "I don't need you – I've moved on – you're history, you piece of shit – I hope you rot in hell."'

'That's quite the journey,' I say worriedly. I just haven't got the strength to argue or think straight.

As they charge upstairs, Tash yells, 'Hoargghhhay can pick

us up in an hour. Let's get to it. Bring on the Girl Power. Connie, eyebrows! Make them strong tonight, love.'

I dash back to the cottage and throw myself into the shower to wash the smell of Matteo from my body. *I am a bit tipsy so it's perfectly acceptable to completely overreact,* I tell myself. I am going to look stunning tonight and not like some easy fool taken for a ride by the first handsome prince to come along.

Well, he turned out to be quite the frog, didn't he?

No wonder he was so mysterious this whole time, stringing me along so I wouldn't catch him out on social media. I step out of the bathroom in my robe, and with shaking hands video-call Liam and Ged to let them know the sad news.

'Connie! What's wrong?' Liam says, loosening his spiked dog collar with a saddened expression. I'm interrupting their PVC night. Although to be fair, they've started early. The last Friday of every month, while I'm at the gym, they spend the evening in bun-less chaps, spanking each other.

'It's Matteo. It's all... it's all off,' I choke. I see the pair of them have no idea what to do with this new information. I give them a moment to process.

'You literally called us a few hours ago ready to Say Yes to the Dress to him and now you're calling it off?' says Ged. 'But you're both cosmically entwined. You said you were the yin to his yang. Two lost souls—'

'You said you held the key to his lock,' Liam butts in.

I do wish they weren't such good listeners at times.

'He's supposed to be marrying someone else this weekend and conveniently forgot to tell me,' I say, wringing out yet more fresh tears.

They gasp.

'The cave was no magical coincidence. It was cleverly

orchestrated. He must have known Nacho had invited me! They're brothers for eff's sake and he never told me.'

They gasp again.

'And the bar in Benidorm. He knew I was in Zara. All he had to do was hang around outside, easily hidden in the crowd, and then he could follow me to Tiki Beach.'

'It's like an episode of *Vera*, isn't it?' says Ged.

'Yes, but involving a hot Spanish love throuple,' Liam says, waving his multi-pronged leather whip around. 'Surely there's been some mistake. There must have been a reason why he didn't tell you. Has he called?'

I shake my head.

'He will, darling. He will. I'm sure of it.'

'You don't just give someone a new passion for life and what you modestly described as the most soulful and incredible sexual awakening any human has ever experienced, and not follow it up. He'll call, babes. He'll call,' Ged agrees.

But they're both looking at me forlornly.

'How did it all feel so natural and so unplanned? And how come he seemed like my absolute perfect soulmate? How could that be the case when I didn't even know him at all? What kind of idiot would fall for someone so quickly? And the magical lip hover! All fake!' I wail, bashing my palm against my head. 'We obviously weren't meant to be.'

'Have you been daytime drinking, babes?' Ged asks.

* * *

'Here, Connie, here it is! Give me your phone,' yells Cherry as I approach the kitchen. She whips it out of my hands and plugs it into hers. 'It's your journey for tonight. It's got everything on it. You falling in love, you being badly let down, you finding out that Matteo is a liar and a cheat who couldn't handle you, you being completely devastated, you falling out of love, you getting back up on your feet because you are an incredibly strong, sexually empowered and bootylicious woman, and to finish' – Cherry looks around at the group with a huge grin – 'we're all going on stage to sing "I Am What I Am". What do you think?'

Fuck, is what I think.

Matteo is going to think I'm a complete nutter who is obsessed with him. Before I can protest, Big Mand has some advice.

'Yes, hold your head up high, love. Who cares if he thinks you're easy meat?'

'Too right. Connie, there's no need to be ashamed of who you are,' says Liberty.

'I didn't realise I was,' I say apprehensively.

'Women can be a steaming hot slutty mess *and* still be sexy,' says Cherry. 'Am I right?'

I'm not at all sure the Dollz have a proper handle on what exactly is going on inside me right now. I wonder if I've given the wrong impression with all the weeping and wailing.

'But it's more about the deceitful way he's carried on though,' I say gingerly. 'Not telling me about their relationship. Cheating on his fiancée? Not the slut-shaming part.'

'If I was going to marry Alex, I'd definitely cheat on her,' says Liberty, screwing up her nose. 'Just saying.'

'But that doesn't mean Matteo should be cheating on Connie with his own fiancée, does it?' Cherry says. 'I mean, I'm awful to Tony but if I ever caught him cheating...' She makes a scissors motion down below.

'Possibly not, but I think what we're forgetting here is the more important fact that Matteo doesn't find Connie's kind of sexy... well, sexy,' says Big Mand. 'He should be more open-minded. Lots of fellas are into manic-depressive types. Look at whatshisname from *Twilight* and whatsherface. She never cracked a smile and yet he still went with her.'

'I bet he fell for Connie's vulnerability. Men like a project. A fixer-upper,' says Liberty softly. 'That's what draws so many fellas to me.'

'I absolutely don't think it is,' argues Cherry. 'What draws the fellas to you is your distinct inability to keep your—'

'Yeah, show him what he's missing,' says Tash, throwing a hankie at me. 'Wear that. He'll die. I promise you.'

I clasp the scrap of material in my hands. Cherry hands me my phone just as it starts to ring.

'Who's Mr Window Seat?'

My jaw drops.

They all look at me knowingly.

'Decline!' they yell at Cherry. 'Decline!'

She swipes the call away, and it springs to life again. I desperately want to hear Matteo deny it all and tell me there has been some huge mistake. I see her press 'accept'. A feeling of relief floods through me. It's time to woman-up and take control of the situation. It's better to hear the truth from the horse's mouth. I reach out to take it. But Cherry puts it to her lips.

'I don't think so, Mr Window Seat! You are clearly not ready for this jelly! You had your chance and you've blown it!' she yells into my phone before clicking off.

'We've all been here before. Trust us, it's for the best,' says Liberty.

Crap. I'll never get to the truth or hear what he has to say.

26

We arrive at The Knee Trembler to find it in full swing with many, many inebriated people spilling out onto the promenade. We pile in.

'Whose round is it?' booms Big Sue.

'Mine, I'll get them,' I say, nervously ordering a round of Skanky Lady cocktails.

Even though I dread seeing Matteo, it would be much, much worse if I see him and make a total mess of the gig because I'm drunk. I will sip like a lady, pretending it's cough medicine or something, and not throw the cocktail down my neck like I see the Dollz are currently doing, even though I've begged them not to and they have promised me faithfully.

'Connie!' Cherry roars a few seconds later. 'Drink up. It's my round. Same again?'

The Dollz are knocking men out of the way to clear a space for dancing when Tash yells, 'I know what this place needs!'

She takes a huge gulp of her cocktails, one in each hand, before slamming them down on the table. She wipes her mouth with the back of her arm dramatically and then charges unsteadily on her massive heels over to the DJ with a threatening expression on her face. Moments later, the speakers bellow out 'I Will Survive'.

'I walked down the aisle to this tune!' yells Cherry. I try not to look shocked. It's certainly unconventional. 'The aisle at Tesco's!'

We all honk our heads off because Cherry has just told the funniest joke of all time.

Honk, honk, honk.

I'm surprised to find I am having a good time and fully manage not to think about Matteo for at least two more drinks and another round of honks. We get loads of man-attention, but we are simply not interested. We laugh, we drink, we honk... then suddenly I remember that my heart is catastrophically broken, and I yell how much I *hate* all living men and send a bunch of them scattering away from us.

'It's time to go,' barks Big Sue. 'Soundcheck! Hoargghhhay is outside.'

'What soundcheck?' My mind has suddenly gone blank.

'*The* soundcheck,' she booms. 'Come on, Dollz. Let's go.'

Thankfully, the sun is setting, and the air is much cooler. I gather my inner strength. All this drinking isn't helping me. Before we get on the bus, she gathers us in a group hug.

'Once we arrive at Voices, Cherry, you run interference. Big Mand, you're on surveillance ops with me. Liberty, you and Tash do a recce of the place,' she commands, sounding like British special forces. 'Don't worry, that bastard is getting nowhere near you tonight, Connie, pet. Not on our watch.'

I have no idea how to feel about our new tactical manoeuvres, but apparently working as a team is key.

Once we pile out of the minibus, the Voices sign towers over the crowds bustling around. There are couples laughing, couples dancing, couples queuing to get into bars, couples hand in hand, couples kissing in the street.

Couples. Couples. Couples.

I feel overwhelmed with what a fool I've been. Just as I wonder if he would even dare to turn up tonight, Matteo stares right at me from the doorway. His face is unreadable. I can tell he's tense just by the way he's leaning against the door frame. My stomach lurches traitorously as he does that slow running-his-hand-through-his-hair thing.

Any minute now the Dollz will launch their covert whatever it was. He won't know what hit him. In a way, it's comforting to know they have my back.

Any minute now.

Any minute.

They're probably wanting to use the element of surprise.

Matteo continues to study me.

A quick glance behind reveals my crack team of bodyguards are engaged in a mixture of activities: smoking tabs, deep in conversation with Jorge, posing for selfies with random men or jabbing at their phones. Every single one of them is oblivious to my plight.

They will be of no use to me. None whatsoever.

I march over to tell Matteo to his face how disappointed I am in him. He beats me to it and suddenly he is right in front of me. For a moment, his face is full of emotion, and we stand there glaring at each other. My heart is beating wildly enough for him to hear it. But before he can speak, the girls surround us, and Big Sue tells him to back the fuck off and leave me alone.

'She's dead high up in social care. She knows all about useless men,' says Big Mand.

'And I'm a paralegal,' adds Cherry. 'I also know about useless men. Plus, I'm married to one.'

'And I'm a lecturer of sorts,' adds Tash, stepping up close to stare cross-eyed at him. 'I teach useless men every day of the week and then eat them for breakfast.'

'Can we talk?' he says, rolling his eyes. 'Connie, it's not what you think.'

Where to begin with my forensic line of questioning?

I straighten to my full height and lift my chin to look down through my lashes. My huge lashes that Cherry stuck on me just before we left. They are incredibly heavy. Like two pastry brushes.

Must not get distracted. Stick to the facts.

'Are you aware… Did you know that you have a fiancée?' I say accusingly.

The Dollz crowd around us to hear what he has to say.

'I am aware, yes.'

It's like a knife to the heart.

'And are you also aware,' I say, unsure as to where I'm going with this exactly. I fully lay the blame at the door of alcohol. I wouldn't normally be so officious sounding. 'That, uh, you are half-brother to our landlord?'

'It had been brought to my attention, yes.'

Oh.

'And, uh, so if your half-brother is correct in informing us that you are getting married next week then why, might I ask, are you fooling around with me?'

This case for the prosecution would be much easier if I'd stayed sober.

The Dollz crowd in even closer so that we can all hear.

Matteo frowns. 'Firstly, I'm not getting married next week. The wedding was called off. And secondly, I wasn't "fooling around" with you. I thought it was something more meaningful than that.'

We all look at each other, our mouths gaping open. We are flummoxed by this honest and frank revelation.

'So what happened? Why did she call it off? Did you cheat on her?' Big Mand says firmly. 'With her sister? Or was it her best friend? Come to think of it, she probably doesn't have one. Unless it's a crow.'

Bewildering where some people's minds drift to.

I'll be crushed if he confesses that he did cheat. I feel like I've been heartbroken for days. It's simply exhausting. His eyes are full of something dangerous. Mine are swimming with drunken tears. He is clearly uncomfortable having this conversation out in the open surrounded by angry Dollz.

'And do you still... do you still love her?' I say, my voice almost a whisper.

'No to the sister, no to the best friend, hard no to the crow and definitely no to still being in love with her,' he says, exhaling loudly. 'And it was me who called off the wedding, not her. And we are no longer engaged. I broke it off a couple of months ago.'

Oh.

'But I do want to explain,' he says, 'and apologise. I never meant to hurt you or lead you on, Connie. When you first indicated your... interest, I thought this wouldn't be going anywhere, which is why I was... well, quite reluctant at first. It was all a bit too soon for me. But you were very persistent.'

Charming. I might go off him myself at this rate.

'I should have explained my situation more clearly before we became involved, but it all happened so quickly and, to be honest, I wasn't expecting things to go the way they did. So anyway, apologies if you thought for a moment that I wasn't a free man, but I am.'

When he puts it like this, he does actually sound quite reasonable.

'I'm not sure now what all the drama is about,' says Big Mand, confused. 'Connie, do you think you've maybe over-reacted?'

'I think you might've got the wrong end of the stick, like,' says Liberty. 'It doesn't sound to me like Matteo has done anything wrong. He might be a fast mover, but he is a *single* fast mover.'

Oh God, what turncoats.

'Maybe you should have explained before we, erm, you know,' I say weakly, keen to shut them all up and get inside. 'Because that's, like, a very fast turnaround in women.'

'It looks bad, but I can explain. Later, in private.'

I nod. Later in private sounds good. He doesn't need to know I've just spent the best part of three hours weeping over him, all because I've leapt to all sorts of unsubstantiated conclusions. For all he knows, I have been engaged in long-term fiscal planning, composing majestic arias or some other useful pursuit that isn't crying.

'I hope you weren't too upset,' he says gently. 'Nacho mentioned that you overheard him talking about the wedding.'

Where to start?

I shake my head, flicking the Dollz a warning not to contra-dict me.

'No. No, of course not. I knew there would be a perfectly reasonable explanation.'

Big Sue raises an eyebrow at me. Probably remembering how I lay quivering in her arms, soaking her in my tears. 'Okay, you've said your bit, lover boy. We've got some business to take care of,' she barks.

Matteo gives the Dollz one last confused look before walking back inside. We race into Voices behind him to see Alex standing with a scowl at the bar.

'I told you girls not to be late,' she says in a sharp tone. 'I hope you've already done a soundcheck because, Connie, I want you on stage in thirty seconds.' She peers closely at us before sniffing the air. 'Are you all... pissed?' she roars in a terrifying manner. She whips out her phone, jabbing away.

'Who does she think she is?' says Tash loudly. 'Although, if I'd just been dumped a couple of months before my wedding by a sexy, hot Latino, I'd probably be fuming too.'

'She must have run over his dog or something,' Liberty speculates as we scurry to find seats near the front, and I leap onto the stage and take the microphone from the stand nearby. I nod to Cherry to plug in the playlist, which she scampers over to do. I notice Dan going over to help her, giving me a thumbs up as he does. The place is heaving. I snap into professional mode. Or at least I would if I had a clue what songs I'm about to sing. I best offer some context. Cherry beats me to it, grabbing a spare microphone as she joins me on stage.

'One, two. Testing one, two.' She taps loudly on the microphone, causing the audience to stop chattering. We look like a pair of low-rent strippers. 'So, this collection of songs might make more sense if I explain that they are about a man,' she says chirpily to the crowd. 'Who none of you know. He's definitely not here, is he, pet?'

She pantomime-winks at me, while I purposefully don't make eye contact with Matteo hovering at the back.

Oh my God.

'Initially, we thought he was a love cheat which had us all

boiling with rage. We were ready to rip his balls off, cover them in hot Tabasco sauce and stuff them down his throat, as you can imagine. Connie here was in absolute bits, weren't you, love?'

She has certainly captured the attention of every single male in the place. And perhaps not in a good way. She has also forgotten that she is meant to be storytelling.

'But apparently, it turns out he wasn't a love cheat after all. And well, anyway, I hope you enjoy this emotional journey with Connie because it's still very raw, isn't it, love? Even if none of it actually happened.'

Jesus.

I look despairingly around the room at the perplexed faces and straight into the eyes of Matteo. I hear the opening notes and begin to sing. It's simply humiliating. Cherry has chosen a nightmarish playlist which I am going to have to brazen out. I avoid staring right at him as I belt out the lyrics of each tune that highlight the tumultuous, short-lived romance we have shared thus far.

Maybe it's because I'm singing tipsy, but I am on fire and out to impress the fuck out of him to hide my embarrassment at having leapt to conclusions. That'll teach me. The next forty minutes fly by as I catapult the audience through what could have been a very nasty breakup resulting in assault and a likely wrongful arrest. When I am done and the final song about how meaningless life can be reaches its climax, I hit the notes perfectly to a rousing round of applause. Grown men are wiping at their eyes. Women are nodding with understanding at each other. I am stunned. The girls are going absolutely wild and everyone in the place is screaming for more. As soon as I'm off stage and replaced by the Dollz, I'm accosted by lots of children and an excited Martha.

'Connie, that was excellent,' she gushes, turning to Matteo, who has come to stand beside me. 'It really felt like an emotional rollercoaster ride. The passion. The heartbreak. The bitterness. The despair. It felt totally real. You have a gift. What a performance. It felt like you took us on a journey.'

I can barely look Matteo in the eye as he turns to me with a shocked expression, saying nothing as Martha jabbers on.

'That song about men always letting us down. If only I could get on stage and publicly humiliate Rody every time he does something wrong. You two newly-weds had a falling out, did you?'

Why is the ground not swallowing me up? Why?

'Oh, it's you!' Martha shouts, recognising Matteo properly, grabbing his hands and shaking them. 'Thank you so much for saving our Lucie. I can't bear to think of what would've happened if you and your wife hadn't been there to save her. Let me fetch Rody.'

We watch Martha dash off.

'We're married now, are we? I do wish you'd told me sooner.' Matteo sounds amused. I'm all flustered again.

Brazen it out, Connie. Hold steady. I open my mouth to explain how it's a funny story, but we are distracted by a loud shriek from behind us.

'Newly-weds? *Newly-weds?*' We turn to see Alex thumping over. 'Newly-weds? What are you talking about? Matteo, what is going on here?' she shouts above the music blaring out.

'I can explain,' I say, swallowing a lump in my throat.

I absolutely cannot explain.

'Matteo is *my* fiancé,' Alex says to me, her voice full of ownership. 'Not yours. No matter how much you keep singing about it.'

'Alex,' Matteo says quietly, clearly horrified at having this discussion in public.

'For fuck's sake, Matteo. It was a blip. Pre-wedding nerves. No reason to call it off!'

Alex launches into rapid Spanish while I step away from them.

'I think we'd best leave them to it,' says Martha, appearing at my side to take my elbow and steer me away. She has put two and two together. 'So, I'm guessing that you and he aren't married?'

I shake my head. 'Sorry. I was about to tell you. I only just found out that he has an ex-fiancée.'

'No worries.' She winks at me. 'I'd pretend he was my husband too, if I was single.'

'What's she saying?' I ask. Martha glances back briefly at the warring couple.

'Sounds like he caught her cheating on him and he called the wedding off. What must she have been thinking to cheat on someone like that?' Martha tuts. 'Where do you fit in?'

'It's complicated,' I say sadly. 'More complicated than I thought. I guess he's got a lot of unfinished business.'

'I guess he has. Come on, best give them some space. I'll get you a strong coffee and show you the apartment upstairs. I'd like to persuade you to stay here with us' – she grins at me – 'seeing as you two aren't actually married... yet.'

Martha shows me upstairs while the Dollz are belting out hit after hit to a roaring crowd. She points out the air conditioning and patio doors, which flood the room with light. There's lots of chunky wooden furniture and a cosy feel about the place. I like it instantly.

'And there's a roof terrace with magnificent sea views,' Martha says before suddenly spinning me around to face away from the sea. 'And mountain views!' she shrieks. 'Aren't they spectacular?'

I peer over her shoulder down to the street below, curious to see what she is hiding from me.

'Don't look!' she yells, but it's too late.

Matteo and Alex are huddled together on The Strip. She is talking passionately to him, leaning into him, clutching at him, and he has his arms around her, cradling her head with his hand just like he did with me. He is speaking into her ear, and she is nodding her head against him. They look like a couple in love. A couple making up. A couple like all the other couples.

I'm wrestling with my moral compass. The respectful thing to do would be to not sully the waters and get right out of the way. He is obviously going to work things out properly with Alex. I've been nothing but a distraction.

Martha puts a gentle arm round my shoulder, which reminds me of my mother. I smile sadly at her.

'Don't let that set you back, love. If you want to build a life here, it must be because it's what you want. Not because you're doing it for a man. Not even one that gorgeous. That's what I told my Dan when he wanted to move to Ibiza to be with DJ Rizzlestix and live in his yurt.'

When I glance back towards Matteo and Alex, they've disappeared.

27

Back at the villa, I toss and turn all night, unable to get Matteo out of my thoughts. By next morning, I'm unbelievably down about it all, even though Matteo sent me a text to say that he was sorry the evening had turned out the way it had, and he would explain, but he'd need a little time. Time. That's the one thing I might not have. We have our final gig tonight and then decisions have to be made. I wander through to the pool to find some of the girls up.

'So it's all off again, is it, honey?' says Big Sue knowingly. 'Can't be easy finding out your fiancée has cheated on you. Christ, I wonder what sort of hottie would out-hottie him?'

'Must have been Chris Pratt or Thor or the *Bridgerton* buttocks guy,' Liberty is speculating. 'Or all three at the same time. I can't imagine why else you'd even think of doing such a thing. Connie, you are so lucky to get a jump on those bones,' she says dreamily. 'What was it like?'

I sigh dramatically. How could I explain that it was like roaring flames, crashing waves and a thunderbolt to the heart all at the same time? She wouldn't believe me anyway. At the thought, I'm reminded of my second big conundrum. Martha was very convincing last night. I loved the apartment she showed me. It was gorgeous. And right on top of The Strip. I could imagine myself sitting on the roof terrace gazing down to the sea, reading books and writing songs. It was small but perfect in every way with the many bookshelves, the kitsch wallpaper, cute little open-plan kitchen into a sunlit lounge, and it had a lovely Spanish vibe.

I let out a huge groan.

'What do I do? I feel like I'm on the edge of a precipice,' I say. 'I've spent so long doing nothing. Absolutely nothing. What a waste of all that time. And now I finally have the chance to do something, this happens.'

'Firstly,' says Liberty, turning over on the sunbed. 'Those years you think you've wasted simply mean the ones ahead of you have tripled in value. You'll make them count. You'll get everything you can out of every minute.'

The words waft over me like a soothing breeze.

'And secondly, what are you waiting for? No one is going to come along and tap you on the back. We are responsible for our own happiness and success. Don't rely on anyone to make it happen for you. It's too much pressure to put on someone else, isn't it?'

'You're right. That's so true.' It's like a penny dropping. 'I think I have been waiting for someone to give me permission to finally live my life. I guess I'm ready to give myself that permission. To start a new chapter.'

I must speak urgently to my therapists about my monumental shift in mindset. I ring Ged, but his phone is off. Likewise, Liam's.

'Has anyone got any Greek yoghurt? I've burnt my shoulders. And my lips,' croaks Cherry from the patio door. 'It must be from when I fell asleep on the sunbed yesterday.'

'Cherry! What have you done? That was the extra virgin olive oil, wasn't it?' yells Big Sue from the pool.

We all see Cherry stumbling towards us, her hair fried, shoulders blistered, her nose and lips peeling and her face red and swollen. 'And I've got the squits. I've been on the toilet for the last four hours. I've lost six pounds already, which is good, but I really don't feel well.'

'That's nothing,' says Big Mand, coming up behind her, holding her arm. 'I can't feel my arm. It's gone completely numb and it's blue. I think it's going to fall off.'

'Stop panicking!' shouts Tash, hobbling painfully out of the patio door to stand next to them. 'We'll drink through it for tonight. It's the last gig then we can all see a doctor when we get – *Argh!*'

Tash looks down at her foot.

'Christ Almighty. When did that happen?'

Tash's ankle is now the size and colour of a pumpkin. I leap up and race back to the cottage yelling, 'Wait there! I'm calling a doctor.'

I grab the card that Doctor Sanchez left me on the kitchen bench. I fleetingly remember Matteo and how tender he was that evening, his kind eyes as he listened to all my woes. I hurriedly ring the number and return to the pool.

'It's okay,' I say. 'He's coming straight round.'

* * *

Half an hour later, we gather in the kitchen to listen out for the doctor. Liberty and Big Sue look worried. Nancy rang Big Sue in the middle of the panicking as though she was watching us on CCTV. It was a very short call involving screaming at both ends until Cherry fainted with a splash into the pool.

I do feel the universe is trying to tell her something.

'At least we managed to get them back to bed. I doubt they'll be able to perform tonight,' says Big Sue, looking downcast as we plonk onto the stools to wait. 'Nancy is going to kill us. That was our last warning. Alex must have rung her and told her we turned up pissed, even though we were all brilliant.'

'Mine too,' I say. 'This whole trip was my last chance to impress her, or I'm out the door. No more singing jobs. No career to fall back on. No nothing. Maybe I should stay here and sing at Voices. I mean, what have I got to lose? But then, it's such a huge step...'

Just as I'm flapping my hands philosophically about, the doctor rings to say he's at the gate. I race through to find not only Doctor Sanchez, but also Jorge screeching up in his minibus and the doors flinging open to reveal Ged and Liam bounding off the bus towards me.

'We're here now. Don't panic! We'll get through this together!' Ged is yelling dramatically.

'Poor Connie! Poor, poor Connie!' Liam is bawling as he scoops me into a huge hug. Doctor Sanchez, Big Sue and Liberty watch as Ged and Liam fuss over me.

'You've called the doctor?' gasps Ged, spotting Doctor Sanchez. 'Things must be really bad. What do you need? Sedatives? Prozac? Uppers? Downers? Tell us, Connie. *Tell us!*'

It takes me a few moments to understand what's going on as I explain in Spanish that my newly arrived hypochondriacs think I'm heartbroken, but the real patients are upstairs. Doctor Sanchez smiles at me while the Dollz make a huge fuss of our new guests. I take the doctor upstairs and stay with him while he quickly assesses the three patients, writes them prescriptions and gives me instructions on what to do for the sunburn, heatstroke, the arm and the ankle. When I come back down, the remaining two Dollz have Ged and Liam sipping cocktails at the kitchen table, discussing me and my recent failure at bagging a man.

'So, you're saying that Matteo wasn't actually getting married?' Liam asks Liberty in an incredulous tone. 'And there was no big drama after all?'

'But then Connie told everyone she was married to him, when she isn't, which *created* a *new* drama but this time involving Alex?' Ged is repeating what Big Sue is telling him.

'Then she saw Matteo and Alex making out, which then created a *bona fide* drama?' Liam is saying in a mystified voice. 'And the wedding is back on, we think?'

There's a bit of unnecessary tittle-tattle from Liberty. 'I think things began to sour after she kicked him in the face while pole dancing on The Strip.'

'And what's this about David Guetta? A fire? Jet-skiing? The black eye? A sex shop?' Liam says as though seeing me for the first time. He breaks into a huge grin.

When put like that, I guess I am made of sterner stuff than I gave myself credit for. 'I'm fine. I'm sure I'll cope somehow.'

'Who is this glorious goddess and what have you done with Connie? I'm not sure she even needs us any more, Liam, honey. We've had a wasted trip,' Ged fusses, loving being the centre of the Dollz' attention.

* * *

An hour later, we go out to sit by the pool.

'Thanks so much for the cottage. It's a dream,' sighs Liam, sitting down with his latte. 'And this villa is to die for.'

'No problem,' I say. 'Consider it part of your engagement present. It's all thanks to Tash for agreeing to share her room with me.' *And hopefully wearing a muzzle.*

'I'll try not to bite you.' Tash gives me a thumbs up. Her leg is bandaged up to the knee. Big Mand is sitting opposite with her arm bandaged up in a sling, and Cherry is in bed with strict orders not to move. She is dehydrated, severely sunburned and has heatstroke.

'So, what do we do about the show tonight?' Tash asks.

'There's no way the rest of us can go on stage without you girls. We'll have to cancel,' says Big Sue glumly.

'But we don't want to let our fans down, do we?' says Tash. 'The nuns are coming to see us.'

'Where can we get another three singers?' Big Sue says forlornly.

'Ged and Liam can sing,' I say tentatively. 'We all did a music degree together.'

The boys' faces light up. 'We'd die to go on stage with you. Dream come true.'

'And Connie, you can take lead vocal,' says Tash.

'Oh no,' I say, panicking. 'I'd never be able to learn the dance routines. I've got two wooden legs. I'd look so out of place.'

'We'll change the routines. Easy ones for you three while we do more complex ones around you,' says Liberty firmly.

There follows some excited discussion as Tash chatters away to me about song choices while the Dollz commandeer Ged and Liam to discuss dance routines and outrageous costume ideas. On Tash's insistence we must captivate our audience early doors before they get too drunk to remember to like us on social media.

I try to put Matteo out of my mind. I'm not expecting him to get in touch with me. He's got a lot on his plate without me adding to it. My whole heart feels heavy as we spend the next two hours locked away in the living room practising dance routines and songs. Luckily, we can put the lyrics up on the big TV screen at Voices to sing karaoke style to and the audience can join in. When we finally break for refreshments, talk turns to the festival.

'Connie,' Ged says. 'Play us your song. The one you did at the festival.'

I blush instantly. 'What if you don't like it though?'

'So what? Will it mean you'll crumble?' he sings. 'Will you lay down and die?'

'No,' I say, giggling.

'That's the spirit. Now let's hear it.'

* * *

After I've finished singing at the piano, Ged and Liam look at me with weird expressions. 'It needs production,' I say nervously when they don't speak. 'But it's a start, don't you think?'

They continue to look at me as though it's my first day at school, and they're waving me off.

It's not the reaction I was hoping for.

'It's excellent,' says Ged. 'Just excellent. Connie, you are thriving out here.'

I suddenly realise why there's a melancholy to their voices. 'What are you saying? I should stay here?'

'Only you can decide that, darling.'

'But it's such a huge decision,' I say, feeling the weight of it. 'What about Dad? What about you two? I'll miss you all so much.'

'What about the adventure you could have here, though?' Ged says. 'With or without Matteo.'

'It seems like you could really achieve something new here. You'd have a job, somewhere to live, a chance to be creative, write songs, meet other singers, learn your craft from the ground up and what it means to entertain people with your gift,' rattles off Liam as though he's been waiting years to deliver that speech.

They're right. There aren't any real arguments not to go for it. Only that it is so far out of my comfort zone, and it has been years since I made a big decision. Years. And even that may have been choosing which of the two universities in my home town to go to.

'You're right. I've got nothing to lose. Even if Matteo isn't on the scene, there's still reason enough to stay. And it's only two and a half hours to fly back to Newcastle, right?'

'Honey, we'll be over every weekend. Benidorm is the gay capital of Spain.'

* * *

'We don't want to be late,' Liam yells from the kitchen. I run the straighteners through my hair one last time. The woman staring back at me from the mirror no longer has that insecure, haunted look about her. I smile at my reflection and feel at peace with myself. I've spent months and months gripped by the madness of grief. All those tears that should have been shed a couple of years ago are finally out of my system this week thanks to this bizarre rollercoaster of high drama. I exhale slowly. Grief has had a stranglehold on me for years and it's time to let it go.

We all pile into the minibus and Jorge helps us carry 'the

injured' on board. Even though Doctor Sanchez told them to stay in bed, the Dollz were insistent. We're leaving early for the gig because there is so much to sort out beforehand. Having Ged and Liam with me has jogged my memory as to how professional and meticulously organised I usually am. Once we arrive, I explain the situation to Martha who, thankfully, is grateful that we are going to rescue the event.

'Dan will do his Jolly Murs after the Dollz to give you a rest between sets, Connie. Really appreciate it.'

'It's the least we can do.'

She raises her eyebrows. 'I know you have a lot on at the moment but have you thought any more about our offer?'

'I have.'

* * *

My stomach is churning as I wonder whether Matteo will show up. The music festival is still ongoing so he will be super busy over there managing the bands, and arranging his upcoming nuptials if Alex gets her way.

'Amaze,' says Ged, eyeing me up and down.

'Ditto.'

He and Liam are dressed in black fishnet T-shirts and tight-fitting pleather shorts. The rest of us are wearing the Dollz' signature strappy corset, stockings and rubber costumes. There's a lot of thigh on show, and big hair and lashes. Tash is very pleased with her make-up job on us.

'You are both extraordinarily comfortable in bondage gear,' she remarks, touching up Ged's powder. He mouths *PVC nights* to me behind his hand.

I still can't believe I'm about to perform as one of the Dollz. It's so far from what I imagined I'd be capable of doing, only last week. So much has happened. I feel a rise of nerves and grab Liam's hand.

He gives it a squeeze. 'This is the most exciting thing I've done in years,' he tells me. 'I'm so glad you took this job. We're going to book the Dollz for our wedding.'

'Showtime, people,' booms Big Mand from the front row table, laden with drinks for her, Tash and Cherry, who is refusing point-blank to follow any of the doctor's orders. The nuns swarm round them before taking seats to cheer us on. I notice Sister Kevin sitting next to Tash ready to do her bidding. She seems delighted at the attention.

Rody announces us on to the stage, and the lights go down. We are ready. It's the most thrilling feeling. A high nervous energy is pumping through my veins, making me feel light-headed and exuberant. I feel like I'm part of a family. It's the opposite of how I usually feel. The dread of going into battle with the audience, expecting them not to like me, forcing them to listen patiently to my woeful songs. It was all about me, whereas this is all about *them*. All about giving the audience what they want and me wanting to entertain them, share in the joy of it all. It's a world apart.

Ged, Liam and I take our places while Big Sue and Liberty stand in between us. The opening notes blast out from the speakers and the next hour whizzes by in a blaze of theatrics. We are beaming at one another as we wiggle our hips in time. Big Sue and Liberty perform a handstand into upside-down splits as we jazz hands and toe shuffle around them. Thumping beats and Cherry directing help us keep in formation as we sing a string of pop classics. Ged and Liam lift me and Liberty into the air, our arms sweeping majestically as Big Sue cart-wheels across stage in time to the music. Finally, Ged and Liam perform 'Islands in the Stream', which is on their bucket list and one of their go-to karaoke songs, while we sing backup, clicking and swaying. Before we end on a Girls Aloud classic, Big Sue thanks the audience and blows Tash, Cherry and Big Mand a kiss. 'We'll end on "Love Machine" because Chezza is a Geordie lass like us, and we girls will always have each other's backs.'

When we leave the stage to thunderous applause, we are all on a huge high. Jolly Murs comes bounding over.

'You guys were amazing,' he says. 'And Mam told me you're going to stay on as resident singer with me, Connie? I'm dead pleased. We can do duets. Plan sets together. It's going to be great.' Beaming, he gushes at Ged and Liam. 'Great costumes, lads. Hey, did you know that Connie and Matteo saved my baby sister from drowning? They rescued her by jet ski. It was crazy. Just like a movie.'

Everyone's jaws drop as they gaze at me with I-can't-believe-you-haven't-fucking-mentioned-this-yet eyes.

'Are any of the Jezebel Music people here tonight?' I ask as casually as possible, not trusting myself to say Matteo's name out loud.

'No, I don't think so,' Dan says. 'The music festival is still on, so they'll all be over there. Do you guys want to go afterwards? I have free passes. All residents get in for free.'

Ged yells, 'Yes, we'll all go!'

'Face the fear,' Liam is telling me. 'We need to see him in the flesh, Connie. It's very important. We've seen him on social media and, frankly, he sounds too good to be true, so we *need* to see him up close.'

'You don't *need* to see him,' I hiss.

'We do *need* to see him. *Urgently*. For *closure*.'

Dan puts on his Jolly Murs face and takes the stage. I'm in bits all the way through his set worrying about seeing Matteo at the festival. Surely there's a way to avoid him. I mean, it's a big festival, thousands of people. I hurry to get changed in the toilets and instead of concentrating on my own upcoming performance, I find my mind constantly wandering to Matteo and all the crazy moments we have shared.

'You seem to be blossoming here,' Ged says admiringly as I sit back down, taking in my pale gold shiny dress, the huge split at the front, my towering sandals, my swept-up hair and jewelled hairpiece and my mother's pearl drop earrings. 'Your father would cry buckets if he could see you. You are shining so brightly.'

He's right. I look just like my mother. A realisation hits me. She will always be with me as I move on through my next chapter. Instead of breaking down like I would usually do, I find the thought comforting. It soothes my soul.

'Whatever I decide to do won't bring her back, will it?' I say resignedly. 'Nothing will bring her back, but she will always be with me. Part of me, just like I'm part of her.'

My voice catches in my throat as a swell of grief washes over me, but instead of the usual crumbling feeling, I remain steady. I cope with it. I let it flow through me until it passes. Ged and Liam wait for me. Like they always have done since my whole life was upended by cancer and its cruelty spread throughout every fibre of our lives.

'If this week has taught me anything,' I say, finally finding my voice, 'it's not to judge others or compare success. And it's time to stop labelling myself a failure for not having had the life I wanted for myself and didn't get.'

I seem to be making a lot of sense.

Before I know it, I'm being welcomed back on stage. I close my eyes and think of my mother and off I go, singing the best I've ever sung in my entire life. It's as though she's with me, willing me on, helping me find my voice. With its dramatic beat and heavy lyrics, my opening song suits my vocal range perfectly. I throw everything I have into it. My expression, my arms, the way I move around; you'd think I'd written the bloody song myself. At the end of the song there is a split second of complete silence before the whole place erupts like an *X Factor* final.

Then I spot Matteo. He's standing at the bar with Rody. I am transfixed by him as my breathing calms. I thank the crowd and introduce the next song. I feel his eyes on me the entire time, fuelling me, giving me the passion needed to belt the song out with the right mix of fury and fever. I allow myself one opportunity to sing the lyrics straight to Matteo. He is staring at me as I finish on a great line about him having a deadly kiss.

People in the audience are turning around, wondering who I'm looking at. A quick flick down reveals Ged and Liam grinning away, twisting in their seats, their eyes pinging from Matteo to me and back again. They are doing ridiculous swooning mimes as though they've forgotten that I am heartbroken over him getting back with Alex. Their faces are beaming at me full of love, full of pride. Just like there's no mistaking their feelings for each other. They seem destined to dance through life together. They've been my family since the moment we all met. My heart swells with love for them. I will end with their favourite song.

'This final song is for Ged and Liam. They say you should always marry your best friend. And unfortunately for me, that's exactly what they're doing. They are the great loves of each other's lives, and I wish them every happiness in their new life together.'

The rest of the set goes in a bit of a blur, as one moment Matteo is watching me, and the next, he has disappeared. I leave the stage feeling like I need to put some distance between me and Matteo and pull myself together. Maybe this isn't healthy for me after all. He makes me feel reckless and impulsive, and out of control. Not in the slightest bit safe or in my comfort zone. How can I stay here knowing I'll bump into him and never be able to be with him because he'll be married to someone else? By the time I reach the others in the front row, I am more capable of seeing how my out-of-control lust for him is clouding my judgement.

'That was the best I've ever seen you!' yells Liam.

'Oh. My. God,' says Ged. 'Connie, you were electric up there. You *owned* that stage.'

The Dollz are fussing around me, shouting compliments and instructions on how to improve my fancy footwork for next time.

'I can't believe he was here,' Liam is squealing. 'He was here!'

I nod sadly.

'Just play it cool, though,' he adds. 'Just play it cool. Let him come to you.'

He still thinks we can salvage this situation, bless him.

'He won't be coming to me. He's getting married,' I remind him. 'To someone else.'

I see a few missed calls from my dad, so I step outside into the warm evening air and ring him straight back. After we exchange pleasantries and briefly speak about how his trip to the Lakes went, his voice goes quiet. I press a hand to my other ear to block out the noise and hurry over to a bench to sit down.

'Connie, love, there's a letter. It's from the Royal Northern Sinfonia. It came here by mistake.'

'Open it.'

Fate can decide for me.

If it's another rejection, then I'll stay here. Nothing to lose.

If it's an acceptance, then I'll leave. Nothing to stay for.

I hear my father wrestle with the envelope, paper tearing while he gabbles on. It seems to go on forever. 'Dear Constance, we are delighted to inform you that we are in a position to offer you a permanent place in our choir...' I hear my father choke and clear his voice. 'Connie, love. You're in. You're finally in. This is what you've always dreamed of. Congratulations, darling. Your mother would be so, so proud of you.'

I take a beat to let his words sink in. The warm air around me begins to feel stifling. I'm suddenly woozy, and I put my hand out to steady myself while I rub my temple.

'Dad,' I say, gasping for air and clutching the phone to my chest for a moment. 'I'll call you back.'

Fate, it seems, has made its decision.

28

We leave Voices and pile into Jorge's minibus to set off for the short, entirely walkable distance across town to the music festival.

'I knew there'd be a new drama. I knew it,' Cherry is saying as though trumpeting out a shopping list. 'I called it. Didn't I call it? I said it'll be Alex trying to knife her or Nancy firing her, or she'll have thrush from wearing that catsuit. Which is it?'

'I detach,' I say calmly. 'I detach from it. There's no drama. It's very simple. I have two job offers. One at home with the Sinfonia, the position I've been trying to get for the last five years, singing classical music.' I shrug at them. 'Or this bizarre one here on The Strip. The last place I'd ever imagined I'd end up. I could make my own music, discover my own voice. I'd sing my own songs.'

It barely sounds real.

* * *

Two hours later and we are all tipsy at the music festival. Ged and Liam are disembarking from our camel rides.

'They're like buses, aren't they?' Ged is saying in disbelief as he leaps nimbly from the camel. 'You have no job one minute and life's as dull as a buffering phone, then all of a sudden two come along at once and before you know it, you've said yes to both of them.'

I've been in a trance, overwhelmed with how inept my decision-making has been. I have no idea what to do and my thoughts are still straying to Matteo every chance they get.

'Connie,' yells Liam, rushing over to help me disembark. My camel does not want to kneel down to let me off, so I am sliding unattractively down its belly sideways, while clinging to its neck for dear life. 'It's him! He's over there! Remember, just play it cool. Let him come to you.'

'Play it cool? In this position?' I say, panicking. I'm almost upside down as the camel tries to shake me off. Liam scoops me into his arms, only to suddenly let go as though he's just realised he's carrying the wrong bride over the threshold. I flump down to the ground in a heap.

'Hi,' I hear him say skittishly. 'I'm Liam. Connie's best friend.'

'Charming,' I say, dusting myself off as I unfold to stand back up. Liam is shaking hands with Nacho vigorously and beaming adoringly at him as though he's meeting his favourite A-list celebrity. 'It's a pleasure to finally meet you. Although,' he says, catching himself, 'we're obviously furious at you for breaking Connie's heart like that. She's been a hot mess ever since.'

I stare at him aghast. *In what way is this playing it cool?*

'Liam, that's not—'

'She's the kindest person we know. And you're a fool if you think you can do better. Your loss is our gain.'

Nacho looks at him, his face amused. 'Yes. Very nice to meet you. I am Nacho. Matteo's half-brother.'

Liam's eyes are out on stalks.

'Christ Almighty. What do they feed you over here? Are you all this handsome? Ged, we're moving to Spain! *Ged!*'

Nacho laughs. He speaks to me in Spanish, telling me that he is very sorry for the way that he spoke yesterday and that some of it got lost in translation.

'I want you to know that my brother does not play games. He would not want to hurt you. He likes you very much.'

My stomach flips at the thought of me being wrong about everything. I've never wanted to be so wrong in my life. I give him a half-smile. He gives me one back before he kisses me on both cheeks and walks away.

'Well, for a first awkward meeting with a family member, I think that went well,' Liam says, turning to me. 'That hair. Those eyes. Are there any more of them?'

I shake my head.

'What should I do?' I say for the millionth time. 'Stay or go? I'm not sure I can handle all the drama that comes with this Benidorm life.'

'Oh, darling,' Ged says, linking my arm. 'Drama just means you are alive. *Alive.* Living a life!'

Liam puts an arm across Ged's shoulders before Ged can fully commit to getting overly emotional. I sense there may be tears. 'It's all we've ever wanted for you,' he says, giving me an adoring look. They know I owe them my life. They are my ship as I sail through these choppy waters.

We walk over to see Dan, the Dollz and the nuns who are all at the main stage. It is in full swing. I do some quick introductions, and Dan asks Ged how he and Liam met but instead of saying we all did the same degree course at university, Ged thinks it is refreshing to try and impress because he is speaking to someone of youth and innocence.

'You met at a privacy night? I've not heard of those,' Dan says. 'But they sound very peaceful. A sort of retreat?'

'Please try not to corrupt my new friends,' I say to Ged, grabbing Dan's elbow to steer him away through the crowd. He doesn't need to know what goes on at Ged and Liam's PVC nights.

'I love this band,' Dan yells. 'I saw them last year in Madrid at the Mad Cool festival. Honestly, Connie, you're going to love living here. There's so much going on. The music scene is one of the best in the world. And as a singer you'll get in free almost everywhere.'

He sounds like he's selling me life insurance, but his enthusiasm is rubbing off. I do love this weather and the culture, and the whole outdoors vibe.

'Where are we going?' I yell as we pass by the stage and the throngs of people jumping up and down.

'I have a backstage pass!' he yells back. 'Come on! We'll watch from up there then we'll meet them afterwards! The drummer is an old school friend of mine. Isn't that awesome?'

The nuns have lifted Ged, Liam and the Dollz onto their shoulders and are barging their way to the front to see The Striped Lions. I turn my attention back to Dan, who is all but dragging me along. My thoughts fly back to the last time I was on stage with Matteo. My stomach gives an involuntary lurch at the thought of him. As we glide through security, Dan flashing his pass like a police ID, we make our way through the hospitality tent at the back of the stage.

We get up to the side of the stage in time to hear the crowd roaring for more. My friends are dancing away on top of the nuns' shoulders. They are having a great time, and I am awash with feelings of happiness for them. I feel at peace. I feel like I truly belong here in this vibrant, colourful, chaotic place. I close my eyes and luxuriate in the feeling while the band whip the crowd into a frenzy with their loud thumping drum and guitar beats. I imagine myself on stage doing the same. I imagine my life as a singer-songwriter. I imagine myself happy.

My mind is made up.

A prickling sensation runs up my spine. I cast my gaze over to the other side of the stage and straight into the eyes of Matteo. He's studying me with interest. I smile sadly back.

I love him.

I simply can't help it.

I've missed him. I tried not to, but I have thought about him every second of every day since I sat next to him on the plane and now that he's here in front of me, I just want to throw myself into his arms. Something in his eyes tells me that he has not had an easy time of it either. He seems weary and drained. He indicates that he'll come over to me. I really shouldn't be encouraging him, so I shake my head reluctantly and lower my gaze so he can't see my sad face and my eyes that want nothing more than for him to sweep me into his muscular arms and kiss me into oblivion. When I look back up, he's gone.

I've done the right thing. He's got unfinished business. It's way too soon for anything to happen between us, even if things don't work out between him and Alex. No wonder he has been conflicted. Our timing is way off.

Moments later, I'm taken by surprise. Matteo is at my side, his gaze flicking to Dan's arm slung casually over my shoulder.

'It's not what it looks like,' I say, flinging his arm off me.

'Matteo! Great job with this year's festival. It's awesome,'

Dan gushes before putting on a stern face as he remembers we are mad at him. I roll my eyes. None of these men are any good at playing it cool.

'Can we talk?' Matteo says with a gentle expression. I can barely hear him. Dan is giving me a not-so-discreet thumbs up.

I follow Matteo down from the stage and into the hospitality tent, relieved to see that Alex isn't around. When we walk in, the place is bathed in soft light. The tent roof is covered in twinkling stars. Romantic, chilled-out music is playing and lots of people are swaying along or lounging on bales of hay.

'Is your cheating ex-fiancée here?' I say, not loving the jealous tinge.

'Emphasis on the ex. And, now, my ex-business partner too,' he says with a relieved sigh. 'That's where I've been all day. Making sure we never have to see each other ever again. She made it as difficult as possible but I'm finally free of her. She's moving back to Valencia. To start over.'

'But I saw you together last night, on The Strip. I saw you hugging. I saw you getting back together.' The words are like glass in my throat.

'You saw me ending things with her. It got a bit messy. We've been together a long time. She made a huge mistake but, to be honest, so did I. I never wanted to marry her. I kind of let myself get railroaded into it because we've spent fifteen years building that company.'

'It must have been tough.'

'I haven't known what to do for the first time in my entire life,' he says into my ear. 'I feel like from the moment you and I met, everything turned upside down. Like for years I was just going through the motions, waiting for that day to arrive.'

I sense him blushing in the darkness.

'That sounds stupid,' he says. 'But I don't know how else to describe it. You have literally turned my world upside down.'

'But what now? How do we be together? I've just been offered two jobs in two different countries.'

'Of course you have,' he says, his eyes creasing. 'Of course you have. Why would you make this easy for me?'

This makes me chuckle.

'Was one of them for the audition you thought you failed?' he asks.

'Yeah, the Sinfonia. I can't believe it. After all this time. And the other one is here at Voices.'

'Congratulations. You deserve it,' he says, pulling me towards a dark corner of the tent where a girl is plucking away on her guitar and another girl is standing next to her with a violin. 'Dance with me?'

Matteo takes me in his arms. We swirl easily around the dance floor as though we are floating through a night sky bursting with stars. I stare into his eyes, lost in the moment. This feels right. This feels like home. All that hollow emptiness I have felt, the longing but not knowing what I long for, the uncertainty, the self-doubt, the constant feeling of failing at life while everyone else is winning – it all drains out of me. The grief for my mother will never leave me but, without all the other baggage, I know I'll be able to live with it and not let it rule me.

I rest my head against his impressive chest and feel his heartbeat.

'Do both,' he says as the music slowly comes to an end.

'How?'

'Be your own boss.'

He's making it sound so easy.

'Be your own boss,' he says again as though it's obvious.

'Stay here to work at Voices. Let them know you'll do tours with the Dollz for Nancy a couple of times a year and speak to the Sinfonia about their tour dates and book them in too. You can commute back and forth like I do. Martha and Rody seem like nice people, and they'll want to keep you on. And of course, you should make your own music too. I have a recording studio in the basement of my office.'

It's starting to sound easy. Maybe it is. I've been in the mindset that I have to put all my eggs in only one basket when, actually, I can design my own career and be the master of my own fate. I sound just like Ged and Liam rolled into one.

I take in his kind, moody eyes and his worn-out expression, which thankfully is saving him from being too handsome and too sexy. It just goes to show if you stop struggling to work everything out, stop planning your life down to the smallest detail and just 'live in the moment', then solutions appear and truths to be owned emerge.

'And you know,' he's saying shyly, 'if you think it's too soon for us to get together then...'

I put a finger to his lips to stop him. Now he's going too far. The sexual tension crackles between us. I want it all. I want the love, the career, the new friends and the crazy life that comes with it. I lift my eyes to meet his. He is trapped in the same thought. I am dying to kiss him, but I know that he will be embarrassed in front of his staff. We lock eyes until a sudden thought breaks the spell.

'Did you say that you're off to America? Wait, was that supposed to be your honeymoon?'

'No, I'm going for work. I'll be in LA for a few months,' he says, grinning. 'I'm going to pursue my own dream of producing music. Want to come visit?'

OMFG, how cool would that be? I can barely hide my excitement. This is my life now!

'LA?' Tash says, swivelling her head around at the same time there's a break in the music. 'Yes, we'll come.'

Christ Almighty. Where did she come from?

'Connie, pet, you did promise, like,' says Cherry, appearing from absolutely fucking nowhere to fluff her mane of glorious red hair at us. With a cocktail in each hand, she is no longer looking so dehydrated. 'We'll rent another villa with a pool but all with en suites this time to save squabbling.'

Where was this kind of swift decision-making when we needed it earlier this week?

'I've heard LA is chocka full of fit men who really know how to treat a woman. I'm *in in*,' Liberty says forcefully, sashaying over. 'I remember that promise. Verbal contract, legally binding, isn't it, Cherry?'

'Yeah, and I'll leave the kids at home. No point ruining a perfectly good vacay,' she says, leaning across as though we are already packed to go.

'We'll come too.' Big Mand and Big Sue emerge into the tent from the darkness outside. Tash elbows me discreetly to look down. I notice they are holding hands.

'Count us in. We can do our pre-moon there.' Ged and Liam wander over to join in the fuss.

Shitting hell.

Matteo arches a stern eyebrow at me. It's enormously sexy.

'Can you get us in the cool clubs? VIP tickets this time though, babes?' Tash says to him, making it sound like more of a telling-off than a question. The girls crowd round. They'll never forgive him for not letting them in the VIP section on the yacht. Never in a million years. I think he knows it too. 'And free bar, yeah? And an extra ticket. I'm thinking of inviting Sister

Kevin because I forgot to propose to him, and LA feels like a better fit for that anyway.'

Unruffled by this intimidation, Matteo throws his head back and laughs. 'Maybe. I'll see what I can do.' He's certainly not going out of his way to win them over, that's for sure.

He'll just have to learn the hard way.

He takes my hand, leans in and murmurs in my ear, 'I could be your Mr Window Seat.'

Oh my. This is really happening. Any thoughts of taking things slowly fly too easily from my mind, which is currently filled with lust and candy love hearts and a hot tub with our name on it. In LA it'll be his fear of flying and my expertise with the sick bag he's after, I remind myself.

'I do,' I gush without thinking. 'I do.'

His eyes balloon at the powerful and inappropriate matrimonial vibe I'm accidentally giving off.

'I mean yes. Yes, I will.'

Still sounds like I'm responding to a non-existent proposal.

'Sorry. I meant... What was the question? Well, whatever you asked, it's a yes. I'll do... anything.'

Anything? And why has my voice gone all husky?

'Cenicienta,' he says, his eyes sparkling with amusement and promise as he twirls me around.

All this sexy talk has created a stirring within. I'm suddenly and uncontrollably over-aroused. I will take a beat to compose myself. I'd hate to scare him off at such a delicate point in our journey. On the other hand, I feel like this should be a kissing moment. When there is a break in the music, I reach up on my toes. He obviously feels it is too, as he instinctively sweeps me closer to him. As we lock lips, I hear a clicking sound behind me.

Liam is busily snapping away. 'What? You said you wanted

some mugs and pillowcases made up of you kissing Matteo, and some wall art for your new place. And this pic would make a seriously lovely screen saver.'

Matteo looks from Liam back to me.

'Apart from you being mildly obsessed with me, is there anything else I should know about you before we take things any further?' he asks.

So much for playing it cool.

'No. I promise I'll totally behave from now on.'

'Shame,' Matteo says. 'I'm rather hoping you don't.'

Oh my.

ACKNOWLEDGEMENTS

So many writer and reader friends helped me get this book to publication. Huge thanks to all of them. I started writing this novel to cheer my mam and sisters up after we lost my dad to cancer very unexpectedly. I never in a million years thought that it would get to be published around the globe so enormous thanks to my wonderfully talented editor Francesca Best for her brilliant support and the entire Boldwood team for welcoming me into the family. Special thanks to Amanda Ridout (#bosslady) for the super-fun title and to copy editor Jennifer Kay Davies and Ross Dickinson for helping get it in shape and the clever Alex Allden for making it look fabulous.

I'd like to thank all the lovely women at Comedy Women in Print, especially Helen Lederer and my fellow long/shortlisters who have been excellent cheerleaders. All at Curtis Brown Creative for their support and encouragement during the many, many writing courses that I have become addicted to. When I started out, I had no idea about how to save a cat. Now I know things like every character needs an arc and a book will never be finished, only ever abandoned. Constant tinkering is not an option.

Last but not least, my awesome and talented writing tribe and beta readers who help fix all the terrible first drafts: Jayne, Jess, Julia, Farrah, Cristal, Amanda (my writing tribe aka The Coven), Nichelle, Kim, Keith, Claire, Cara, Joanna, John (my Curtis Brown 6-monther writing tribe). And a special thanks to all my fabulous friends who cheerlead me on: Alice, Nicky, Linds, Wendy, Helen, Deb, Genize, Shauna, Mrs B, Mags, Paula, Maria, Shelley, Janine, Anna, Kate and my sister Philippa who is always first to see everything and my lovely aunties who encourage me to keep going. And the Lyons boys who always have my back and never moan that I now live in a crazy fantasy world, talk about my novels incessantly and have completely forgotten how to do housework or cook meals. I am living the dream!

I could not do any of this without them. I have enormous respect for anyone who sets out to write a book and gets to the end without wanting to hurl themselves off the nearest cliff. Be nice to writers – we are ALL in varying states of emotional collapse.

ABOUT THE AUTHOR

Jo Lyons is the bestselling author of uplifting, laugh-out-loud, warm-hearted romantic comedies, and was shortlisted for the prestigious Comedy Women in Print Awards in 2021. She spent years working abroad in sunny destinations like Turkey, Spain and the south of France at a vineyard (trying her best not to drink them out of business).

Sign up to Jo Lyons' mailing list for news, competitions and updates on future books.

Visit Jo's website: www.jolyonsauthor.com

Follow Jo on social media here:

facebook.com/Jo-Lyons-Author

x.com/JoLyons

instagram.com/hinnywhowrites

bookbub.com/authors/jolyons

goodreads.com/jolyons

tiktok.com/@jo_lyons_author

bsky.app/profile/jolyons.bsky.social

Boldw⊕⊕d

Boldwood Books is an award-winning fiction publishing company seeking out the best stories from around the world.

Find out more at www.boldwoodbooks.com

Join our reader community for brilliant books, competitions and offers!

Follow us
@BoldwoodBooks
@TheBoldBookClub

Sign up to our weekly deals newsletter

https://bit.ly/BoldwoodBNewsletter